A SECONDHAND MURDER

A SECONDHAND MURDER

LESLEY A. DIEHL

A Secondhand Murder

W RLDWIDE®

TORONTO • NEW YORK • LONDON
AMSTERDAM • PARIS • SYDNEY • HAMBURG
STOCKHOLM • ATHENS • TOKYO • MILAN
MADRID • WARSAW • BUDAPEST • AUCKLAND

Recycling programs
for this product may
not exist in your area.

A Secondhand Murder

A Worldwide Mystery/April 2018

First published by Camel Press, an imprint of Coffeetown
Enterprises, Inc.

ISBN-13: 978-1-335-50652-8

Acknowledgments

An abundance of research went into this book. I was aided and abetted in shopping secondhand by my cowboy, Glenn. I am fortunate to have someone at my side as dedicated as he is to finding a bargain.

I grew up respecting thrift. My paternal grandmother, a tiny woman who barely reached five feet, reused dishwater and sewed ties made of grosgrain ribbons onto her daughter's size 10 shoes to make them stay on her size 6 feet. Granny wore petite 6, my aunt tall 14, but Grandma took her six-foot-tall daughter's clothes in and up with stitches, paper clips and staples to make them fit her elfin form. My love of bargains and secondhand items came through my family DNA.

Thanks to the many consignment shops who have allowed me the opportunity to satisfy my love for inexpensive shopping. Especially helpful to me in answering questions about the consignment business was Cindy Staffin, owner of Transitions Boutique in Oneonta, New York. There are hundreds, perhaps thousands more consignment owners who helped me in my research by selling me bargain clothes, shoes, household goods, jewelry and—back in the seventies when it wasn't considered a no-no—a fur coat.

And I must mention all those Saturday yard sales without which my cottage would be empty and Glenn wouldn't have his set of brass Ping golf clubs.

I especially want to thank all those nameless people who consigned their possessions or set them out on tables for yard and garage sales. I'd be naked without you.

To my paternal grandmother,
Minnie Appel Diehl,
a woman dedicated to recycling
before it was popular.

ONE

I JERKED THE dressing room curtains closed, swallowed, then swallowed again. The lump in my throat wouldn't go away. I opened my mouth to speak, but I was at a loss for one of my usual, Eve Appel, sassy gal retorts—the ones I generally have on hand to fend off difficult situations. What's the protocol for a dead body showing up on the opening day of business? I took a deep breath and punched 9-1-1 into my cell and managed to tell the dispatcher about the emergency. Not bad. The lump was gone. I made my voice as cool as the breeze wafting from the window air conditioner. I didn't want to alarm our customers. "Madeleine, could you help me a minute? I think we've got a problem with Mrs. Sanders." I might be able to fool others with my calmness, but Madeleine, my business partner and lifelong friend, would know better.

She poked her head of bouncy red curls around the hallway corner. "I told you the damn dress would be too tight. I was right, wasn't I?" she whispered.

"C'mere." I signaled her. "You don't have to whisper. Mrs. Sanders can't hear you." I shoved the curtain to one side and pointed, my red nail polish making a bloody colored blur as my finger shook. I stuffed my hand into my pocket.

Madeleine's ivory skin turned an even whiter shade of pale. "Gads."

Mrs. Sanders lay face up on the dressing room floor, a knife protruding from her chest.

"The dress is way too tight," Madeleine said with a nervous giggle, a sure sign she was in anxiety overload.

"Madeleine, get a hold of yourself." I grabbed her hand and leaned in to get a better look at the body. "The knife... I think it's from that cutlery consignment we took in on Monday."

"She was looking at them earlier before she spied the cocktail dress." Madeleine said as she turned her head away from the body.

"I just called the police." I held up my cell.

"Thank goodness. You know I fall apart in crises." She pulled the curtain closed and leaned against the wall, her tiny freckled hand over her heart.

"Buck up, girl. You just make certain no one comes back here."

"Did I hear something about the police?" A woman appeared at the end of the hallway.

Oh, no. It was Mavis Worthington. She was the writer for *About Town*, a new monthly magazine that offers in-depth coverage on people, charity events and business enterprises in the area. She wrote the "What'Sup in Town" column. If she couldn't find anything 'sup, she made it 'sup. On any other day, she wouldn't have even been in the store, but today was the grand opening of our consignment shop, Second to None. Madeleine and I had sent her a personal invitation and a Ten Percent Off coupon to entice her to cover the event.

"No, no." I steered her out of the hallway, back into the main part of the store, which was filled with customers. "Did you see the lovely selection of Capris we got in, some in more statuesque sizes?" Enormous sizes was what I meant. Mavis was an abundantly proportioned woman, whose ample body seemed to quiver when she walked.

She nabbed several pairs off the rack.

"I'll need to use a dressing room." She nodded her head toward the cubicles.

"Uhm. No."

"No? You can't expect me to buy these without trying them on first."

I wrung my hands and twisted my body in the direction of the dressing rooms, then back to confront Mavis. I must have looked like Gumby. Dressing room? Definitely off limits, especially to the town's professional gossip.

"We've had a bit of an accident. You can't use the dressing rooms."

"What kind of accident?"

"Ah, well, you see..." I was stumbling around like a teenager whose mother had found her birth control pills. I couldn't tell her the truth—that we were keeping a dead woman in the dressing room next to the one she wanted to use.

"Well?" She held up the teal and coral pants and shook the hanger at me.

"We've had a leak, and the only unoccupied dressing room has a wet floor." I smiled. Close enough to the truth.

"Too bad, but I'm certainly not going to buy these without trying them on." She made an impatient gesture toward the sign displayed behind the cash register that said: "All sales are final."

"For you, Mavis, this sale is not only twenty, rather than ten percent off, but it's not final. You can bring them back if you don't like them, or if they don't fit right."

"Great. Then I'll grab a few more things while I'm at it." She headed toward the dress rack near the front windows. I hadn't intended to offer her the entire store at a reduced rate, but I had more important things to do than worry about how much merchandise Mavis hauled out the door. Getting her to peruse more clothes would keep her around until the cops showed up while also steering her away from "What'Sup" in the rear of the store.

Madeleine stuck her head around the corner of the dressing room hallway. "Where are the cops?"

I rushed up to her. "They should be on their way." I motioned toward Mavis, who was loading yet another dress onto the growing pile in her arms.

"Maybe we should close the store and tell the customers to come back tomorrow," Madeleine said.

"No! The police will want to interview everyone."

"People have been going in and out, and Mrs. Gaulfield looks like she's ready to leave."

Mrs. Gaulfield didn't look like a killer, but I wasn't going to pass judgment. I rushed past Mavis and threw myself in front of the door. "You don't want to leave."

"Why not?" The tall, thin woman shifted her purse to her other arm. "You're charging mighty stiff prices for secondhand stuff."

"Classy, designer quality, secondhand stuff, gently worn by women of excellent taste," said Madeleine, barely keeping her temper in check.

"Go back to the hallway," I hissed in her ear.

She smiled at Mrs. Gaulfield and nodded. "The most discerning women of impeccable taste." She fled to the back of the store where I hoped she was retaking her post in the dressing room hallway.

I placed a gentle restraining hand on Mrs. Gaulfield's arm and whispered in her ear, "We're having an unannounced thirty percent-off sale in several minutes. Stick around and you can get that silk blouse for fifteen dollars."

Her eyes lit up, and she spun on her heel, making tracks to the blouse round where she pulled a filmy turquoise item off the rack. Hugging the material to her, she said, "I'll look for a skirt to match."

"Thirty percent off," I heard her crow as she zigzagged her way back to the skirts. If I didn't get control of my nerves, I'd sell off the entire store before we'd even developed a following.

I was about to turn and check on Madeleine when a white Cadillac parked in front of the store caught my eye. I was certain it was the one Valerie Sanders usually drove when shopping or delivering things to the store. The car's paint had always attracted my attention—pearlescent white. A scruffy-looking man, about thirty-something, a weeks' worth of beard on his narrow face, leaned against the front fender. A relative? Chauffeur? Possible thief waiting to break into the car? I shook my head. Maybe it wasn't the deceased's car. There must be a hundred or more Cadillacs in Florida with the same paint.

Was this what I left Connecticut for? Scrub palmetto, cattle, alligators and dead bodies? And just when I thought I was getting adjusted to the place. Madeleine had moved here a year ago after an aunt died, leaving her a house. She invited me to help her redecorate and, when the store came up for sale, we bought it together. I thought I liked the untamed nature of this place, but now I wondered if I should rethink that. Maybe Eve, city girl, did not belong here.

TEN MINUTES LATER, two uniformed officers corralled our customers near the racks of purses and shoes while Madeleine hovered at the end of the dressing room hall, waiting for crime scene techs and a detective from the police department to finish examining the body. She had directed the detective into the dressing room while I tried to appear calm and unconcerned, although everyone knows cops in a consignment shop can't be good.

Mrs. Gaulfield was still clinging tightly to the turquoise blouse, and I saw Mavis paying more attention to a pair of sandals than to the officer interrogating her. "What's happening back there? Eve told me it was a leak, but that's a police uniform, not a plumber's. Was there a robbery? Or worse?"

Ignoring her questions, the officer asked for her driver's license.

"Hold these." Mavis unloaded her clothes into my arms and rummaged through her purse. "Oops, wrong purse." She giggled, handing me the purse with the price tag attached and taking hers back from me.

"Someone's back there in the dressing room. Who?" She shifted from one foot to another trying to get a better look behind me. The officer examined her license and handed it back to her.

I shook my head, tossed her items on the nearby counter and joined Madeleine in the hallway.

"Guess who's in there?" Madeleine pointed at the dressing room.

"Mrs. Sanders. Some crime scene techs and a cop."

"No. I mean, yes, but guess who the police detective is? It's someone we know."

I knew only one person with the police department, but she was a uniformed officer. "It can't be Frida, can it? You must be mistaken."

A woman, nearly as tall as I, long brown hair curling over her shoulders, emerged from behind the dressing room curtain. Our friend Frida. She adjusted the shoulder holster beneath her jacket.

"Damn thing doesn't fit right under here. It needs tailoring." She pinned us with a very cop-like gaze. "My first case as a detective and it has to concern you two." The expression on her face said she was unhappy with us and certain we were to blame for the incident.

"It's not our fault," I said.

"We didn't do it." Madeleine shook her head.

"Maybe, but where the two of you are, there's bound to be trouble."

She was, of course, referring to the incident at the spring rodeo. Somehow, Madeleine's curiosity about the bulls had led us to the pens where someone—I'd bet my share of the store on it being Madeleine—fell onto a lever or something. The gate swung open and about ten bulls stampeded through the rodeo arena and the fairgrounds, knocking over concession stands, leaping onto the merry-go-round and running off into the scrub until the cowboys were able to round them up.

For a tiny person—only five two—Madeleine was very clumsy, except on the dance floor where she moved like a ballerina. Off the dance floor she moved like a tiny elephant on speed. Although my appearance was unusual for these parts—six feet without my strappy stilettos and spiky blonde hair, or maybe it was just unusual in general—I wasn't clumsy or accident prone. I was Madeleine's friend and so Frida lumped the two of us together.

"Mrs. Sanders was just shopping. That's all." I felt I should defend Madeleine's reputation.

"That was awfully courageous of her." Frida's voice snapped with sarcasm.

"Now that's mean," said Madeleine.

"Sorry, gals. Cop humor, but this is no laughing matter."

Madeleine and I nodded our heads in solemn unison.

"The back door near the dressing room, is it always locked?" Frida gestured toward the doorway.

"Locked from the outside, but anyone inside can turn the deadbolt and get out," I said.

Frida's gaze travelled the shop. "Snazzy duds." Her eyes rested briefly on the cluster of customers. "Snazzy customers."

Sure they were. They had once been West Palm's wealthiest. Until they invested their money with Bernie Madoff and lost it. These days, society matrons were able to hide their newfound poverty and make a little money by consigning their clothes with us.

"Take a look around. Is anyone who was in the shop earlier now missing?"

Madeleine and I surveyed our customers.

"There were so many women in the store today, it's

difficult to say who's left already. We're cash only, so there's no record of who bought what."

"Well, the two of you better put your heads together and think back. I want a list of everyone you can remember being in here."

Madeleine grimaced. "We don't know everyone by name."

"Work on it. You do know the name of the victim, right?"

Madeleine gave a weak smile. "Oh, sure. She is, I mean, she was Mrs. Valerie Sanders, probably the most respected socialite from West Palm. She brought in a lot of nice things."

"But the knife…" I wanted to cooperate, but, when I pictured the body, the lump in my throat returned and I had to swallow it to talk. "It was taken from there." I nodded my head toward the display counter where the knife holder still sat.

"Knife?" Mavis had maneuvered herself away from the other customers and was standing near the dressing room hallway. "Someone was stabbed?" Her voice echoed throughout the store, occasioning looks of horror and murmurs of concern. One woman sighed and fainted into the arms of a police officer. Another pushed several customers out of her way and ran for the door.

"This is not good," Frida said, as she waded into the fray to reestablish order.

"Poor Mrs. Sanders." Madeleine reached into her pocket and extracted a tissue.

"Poor us. We're done for." I shook my head.

"Eve!" Madeleine might be a klutz, but she had manners and enough emotional sensitivity not to be crass. Graceful as a Lipizzaner but socially a stumble-bum, I handled my horror at finding the body by envisioning the going-out-of-business sale we'd have to run after losing our clientele to murder.

TWO

I WAS WRONG ABOUT the sensibilities of the women shopping in our store. The next morning a line of ten or so stood in front of the place waiting for us to open. Once they got inside, they fought each other for the dressing room where "it" had happened. When Frida arrived to ask us more questions, everyone got on their cells to tell their friends about the newest "in" place in town.

By the end of the day, our inventory was down. Even those items tagged as our most recent acquisitions sold well. Our policy was to reduce the prices of anything left on the racks for over a month by ten or fifteen percent.

"If this keeps up," said Madeleine, "we won't have anything to sell by the end of the week."

Word of what happened here might not have reached the coast yet," I said. "When it does, if today is any indication, we'll soon have the West Palm society ladies in here drowning us in their worn tennis whites, golf togs and cocktail dresses." I leaned back against the counter for a breather. I hadn't taken a break since the doors opened and the crowd poured in.

"Is this one of *her* dresses by any chance?" came a voice from behind me.

"Her?" Madeleine looked puzzled.

"You know, the woman who…yesterday?" The customer nodded her head toward the dressing rooms.

At a loss for words, Madeleine looked to me for help.

"We keep our donors' names and the items they give us private."

"Oh, you can tell me. I won't say a thing." The woman, wearing a pants suit printed with fuchsia flamingos running through emerald green ponds, leaned over the counter as if she expected me to reveal the secret of the dress' former owner only to her.

Madeleine pulled on my sleeve and whispered, "Tell her the dress belonged to Mrs. Sanders. What can it hurt?"

"Madeleine Boudreau, shame on you. A deal is a deal, and we vowed to keep our donors' identities secret." I turned back to the woman, who appeared to be on the verge of salivating on the dress in her eagerness to know its provenance. "I can't tell you."

"Well, I never." She flung the dress on the counter and strode toward the front door.

"Lost that sale, didn't you?" A man's voice. A man! In a women's consignment boutique? I grabbed the counter for support and looked up into a pair of azure eyes. Up. Get it? He was taller than me. That wasn't his only virtue. He had brown hair, sun-streaked and worn long. It curled over his shirt collar. I tried to catch a whiff of his aftershave. None. Just the clean smell of Dial soap coupled with a strong whiff of sexiness.

I leaned forward farther and would have fallen onto the floor, but a bronze arm handed me a business card. I took it.

"You're a private dick?" I asked, feeling my cheeks heat up at the word. "Um, PI," I amended. Alex Montgomery, the card read. Investigations.

As he extended his hand to shake mine, the polo

rider on his turquoise knit shirt galloped ahead several paces, propelled by well-developed pecs.

"You are the proprietor of this establishment. Right?"

"Along with my partner here." I motioned to Madeleine, who moved closer to the counter to stand next to him.

She looked up into his eyes, blinked once and sighed. "Madeleine Boudreau." She stuck out her hand and hit the earring display rack on the counter, knocking it to the floor. As she bent to pick up the jewelry, PI Montgomery stooped to help her, and I could see trouble coming. I rushed around the counter and tried to push him out of the way. I was right to do so, for Madeleine's rear end hit our display mannequin, which wobbled precariously on its one plastic leg (we'd picked up the model at a rummage sale for a buck—the other leg had been lost somewhere). As it plunged toward the floor, the long necklace Ms. Plastic was wearing flew over the PI's head, the mannequin flipped around and Mr. Hottie found himself pinned to its silk-clad chest by a rope of ersatz pearls.

"Don't move or you'll strangle yourself. Madeleine, get up off that floor and ring up Mrs. Nile's sale. I'll take care of Mr. Montgomery." *Oh, how I want to take care of Mr. Montgomery.*

Mrs. Nile must have had the same thought. She appeared to have lost interest in the shorts set she had brought to the counter and was eyeing Mr. Montgomery (or Alex, as I wanted to think of him now) with the hunger of an alligator in a drought looking for a new breeding hole.

I prevailed, probably because of my height. Also

because I can be very commanding if I want to, and I wanted to at this moment. I pushed Mrs. Nile—I tried to push gently—toward Madeleine. "She'll ring you up." I turned back to my PI guy.

"Alex, uh, I mean, PI Montgomery, please remain calm. I'll get you free in a moment." Actually he looked both calm and amused. A sense of humor. Good. I like that in my men.

I extracted him from the pearls while he righted the mannequin. I envied her the momentary closeness with my private eye. For once I wished I could emulate Madeleine's awkwardness. I yearned to stumble straight into those strong arms.

"I think you were about to introduce yourself." He cocked one eyebrow.

"Not really. You're the investigator, so I assume you already know my name. Right?"

He laughed. "Eve Appel, right? Like in Genesis." So that flash of humor hadn't been a momentary fluke.

"What can I do for you? You're not here to buy your wife, girlfriend, life partner, date or significant other of either sex a gift, are you?" I covered all the bases.

"No. Actually I'd like to talk to both of you about what happened here yesterday."

"How is that your concern?"

Madeleine shoved me to one side. "Someone hired you to investigate the murder?" Eagerness to cooperate in any way possible was written all over her face, as was the desire to cook him dinner, ply him with wine and undress him in front of her fireplace. I shot her a look that said, "I saw him first, and I didn't try to strangle him."

"No. Actually, I was investigating Mrs. Sanders.

Maybe the two of you can shed some light on her situation. She brought her clothes here for consignment. Isn't that odd for a woman who had millions?"

I shoved Madeleine to one side and pushed her behind me. "Are you suggesting this place isn't a business the elite would frequent? Why not?" I placed my hands on my hips.

"Well, you do sell secondhand merchandise."

"Classy, previously owned, high-end items." Madeleine offered her usual sales pitch and poked her head around me.

PI Montgomery took a step backward. "Okay, okay, I get it. I'm not passing judgment on the quality of your inventory. Just wondering why someone who could afford everything new and haute couture would drive sixty miles through rural Florida to buy her dinner dance gowns when she could have her chauffeur take her to City Place."

"We don't ask our customers why they shop here," I said. "We're just happy they do."

"Pleased they bring their clothes here for us to sell, too," Madeleine added, breaking into one of her high wattage smiles.

"The current economic downtown has been a leveling factor for the wealthy. We took advantage of that to open this place. I can't see how interrogating us about Mrs. Sanders' reasons for doing business here helps your client, whoever he or she is." I wasn't sure why I wanted this guy to understand our business philosophy, but I did.

As much as I didn't want to chase this hunk off, I wasn't too happy with his questions about our customers. Some of them were eavesdropping and, apparently dismayed at the direction the conversation was taking, had hung their items back on the racks and were sidling toward the door. I knew that several of them had driven over from West Palm and didn't want it revealed that they did their shopping in a cowboy town in rural Florida.

"Yeah, but why come here when there are dozens of high-end consignment shops on the coast?"

I knew the reason why, but I'd be hung by my acrylic nails from the nearest Sabal palm before I blabbed these matrons' rationale in the middle of my shop.

I grabbed the PI by the arm and steered him toward the office. Madeleine followed so close in his tracks she seemed to be Velcroed to his leg. I turned on her.

"Get back out there and smooth some ruffled feathers. You're better at that than I am."

"But I want to—"

"No, you don't. You want to sell dresses, shirts, pants and jewelry. You fall into things. I get in trouble because of my mouth. That's the way it is, and we might as well play to our strengths." I dragged Mr. Montgomery into the office and slammed the door behind us. He was smiling.

"You're really something." His smile went from friendly to seductive. "How about we have dinner tonight?"

"Yes. I mean, no. At least not until you get something straight. Women shop here because they don't want their friends knowing their income has taken a plunge and that they can no longer afford the finer stores. They don't want to chance running into their society friends in a consignment store on the coast because they know their friends are in the same boat." I paused to catch my breath.

"But—"

"I know what you're going to say, that eventually they'll run into someone they know here, but they find it easier to make up a good excuse for being here than in a thrift shop in West Palm."

"Like what?" The smile was gone from his face. He seemed interested.

"Like, they're slumming, or looking for the real Florida, trying to find Florida as it used to be or they're into cowboys."

"Interesting." He paused. "Are you into cowboys?"

Was I? I thought about it. I'd been here for only three months. I liked going to the local cowboy bars with Madeleine and dancing up a storm with a lean, tanned guy in jeans and a Stetson. I looked at my private eye. No cowboy there. Chinos and a knit golf shirt. What could be less Western?

"I don't know a lot of cowboys. Obviously not many come in here."

"So where does one meet them?"

I couldn't see where he was going with this.

"Uh, in a bar maybe?"

"So, take me to a bar tonight after dinner. I'll see if I can keep up with the competition."

COULD HE! TWO STEP, salsa, jitterbug, slow bump and grind. I was blown away. Everyone watching us seemed to be as well. The cowboys who were sometimes my partners when Madeleine and I hit the Gator and You Bar or the Tasty Frog Grill were high-fiving the two of us on the dance floor. By the time we left—after food service stopped and everyone had lit up a cigarette (a quaint tradition in Florida)—I was exhausted. It was a good thing PI Montgomery didn't have anything more athletic on his mind than a good night kiss.

"I'll call you." His gaze held mine for a moment longer than necessary.

As soon as I closed the door, I threw my purse on the dining room table, stripped off my three-inch heels, grabbed my phone and sprawled out on the couch.

"Madeleine, I think I'm in heat."

"What do you think your hubby will think of that?"

I THOUGHT ABOUT Madeleine's question. Jerry wouldn't really care if I found someone, permanent or temporary, that jangled my hormones. It'd probably be easier for him to get out of the marriage if I had something on the side, as he wanted me to believe *he* did. He was wrong about one thing. I had no intention of making anything easy for Jerry, not after he had humiliated me in front of all my friends at my thirty-fifth birthday party by arriving two hours late with a blonde in tow. Everyone thought I should forgive him for his little peccadilloes. I would have, if that was the problem. But I knew Jerry. He wasn't drunk, and the blonde was rented. *That* was the real humiliation. He manipulated our relationship the same way he manipulated his business associates. The man didn't have an honest emotional bone in his body. Maybe I wasn't any better. The only real friend I had was Madeleine. The rest were just acquaintances I occasionally hung out with—playing tennis, having lunch, attending parties with the "right" people, shopping. I've always liked shopping. That's why running a consignment shop with Madeleine had seemed a natural step for me. Well, perhaps I'd miscalculated just how natural it was here. Swerving to avoid an alligator in my lane or a feral hog dashing across the road was not exactly what I had in mind when I moved. Until Mrs. Sanders' murder, I had believed that the endless pastures opened something inside me. Maybe it was all the heat and humidity melting my cold Yankee heart like a popsicle under the summer sun. Or maybe it was just heat stroke.

As for my PI, I didn't really care at this point if the kiss was genuine or not. That had been one hot kiss, and I was eager for another. I plunged into sleep with the thought of his full, firm lips on mine.

The ringing of my bedside phone disrupted my dreamy desires. I looked at the caller ID. Jerry. Wouldn't you know it? He just had to insert himself into my life down here, didn't he? I took the phone out of its cradle and, without answering, punched the off key. I turned toward the window. The moon was rising and its light danced across my bedroom floor, finding its way finally onto my bed. I touched the silver with my fingertips, listened for a moment to the whisper of the palm fronds outside my window and fell asleep. I dreamed of azure eyes.

THREE

By the following morning, reality struck down my nighttime fantasies and made me wonder if the kiss had been real.

Madeleine sat on the end of my bed waiting for me to finish toweling off in the bathroom. "I tried your cell and got no answer. Same with your landline. Why do you bother having these devices if you turn them off all the time?" Since she had a key to my place, I wasn't surprised to find her in my bedroom when I awoke. I was, however, surprised at the early hour and shocked when she told me the reason for her visit.

"Frida our cop friend called. There were no prints on the knife, but since it came from our store, we're persons of interest in the case."

"Mmmmm." I sipped the cup of coffee she had brought and stared through the bedroom window.

"That's all you can say? 'Mmmm?' We're *suspects*."

I glanced at her, then took a longer look. Silly of me not to notice immediately. The early hour, coffee from the newly opened, fancy coffee bar. All signs she was overwrought. My usually neat-as-a-professional, organized friend had popped out of bed at Frida's call and failed to shower, put on makeup or do something with her hair. It looked like mine, but my style was on-purpose punk, not bed head tangle. She was upset and assumed I'd be the same.

"Well, let's see," I began in that cool tone of voice I couldn't help adopt in a crisis even though I know it annoyed the hell out of Madeleine.

She humphed at me and rolled her eyes. "I don't want to go to jail."

"You're not going to go to jail," I insisted.

"I don't want to be a suspect."

"That's not going to happen, either." I hoped.

"She didn't commit suicide, you know." Her voice began an upward spiral.

"Kind of hard to stab oneself to death, although I bet it could be done." I stirred another packet of sweetener into my cup.

"Why are you being so, so, so—"

"I'm being so-so-so about this thing because I know I didn't do it and you didn't do it…well, not intentionally, at least. You didn't fall into her while carrying that knife display, did you? And not tell me?"

"Arghh." She tossed her cup in the waste can and stormed out my bedroom door.

I followed her. "I'm kidding, honey."

"I know you're kidding, but someone has to open the store. Clearly, you're not ready." She stood in the hallway and stared back at me, a look of disgust on her face.

"I'm not?"

"You need to comb your hair."

I stuck my head back into the bedroom and glanced quickly in the mirror. How the hell did she think I got that punk look? If I combed it, all the pizzazz would be gone.

"I'm fine, but have *you* looked in a mirror?"

She turned toward the hallway mirror and squeaked

like a mouse. "I look like I fought with the cat all night."

"I'll open. You go home, take your time and get presentable. I'll call Frida back."

I didn't believe we could possibly be suspects. No one intending to commit murder would grab a knife and plunge it into the victim in their own business. Unless that person was really, really dumb or didn't own a television and hadn't watched all the recent crime shows. On occasion, I found my new friends in Florida to be somewhat naive, but I couldn't think of anyone who qualified as a stupid or TV-challenged killer. No one in Sabal Bay possessed those dubious qualifications. All I had to do now was share my reasoning with Frida. Should be a snap.

"So, NO PRINTS on the knife?" I'd convinced Frida to meet me at the local Tic Toc Restaurant for coffee. She didn't want to appear to be socializing with a suspect, so I ran in for the coffee. We sat in her police cruiser and talked. If you were willing to bend the rules a little, you might see the cop car as an extension of an interview room at the station.

"You can't really believe we had anything to do with Mrs. Sanders' death." Madeleine might not like my logical side, but Frida, being a cop, had to respect it.

"It was your shop. You were right there. Opportunity. I have to run with it."

"No you don't. Who says?" Anger and just a droplet of anxiety were watering down my desire to be reasonable.

"Captain Tony says, that's who. He's my boss."

She crumpled up her cup and turned to me. "Besides, there's more. Do you have something you'd like to tell me about you and Valerie Sanders?"

The question caught me by surprise. I couldn't imagine what Frida might have on me. "I have no idea what you're talking about."

Frida stared at me for a moment. "Okay, if that's the way you want to play it. You could cooperate by coming down to the station this afternoon and answering some questions."

"I'll answer them now."

"Now, I'm doing you a favor as your friend. Later, you'll be doing me a favor by coming to the station to save my butt with Tony."

"What about Madeleine?" I asked.

"No one could possibly believe tiny little Madeleine could stab a woman the height and size of Mrs. Sanders."

What she wasn't saying was that I was the most likely suspect once you gave up the suicide theory.

"You assume I'm smart enough not to spread my prints all over the murder weapon like butter on toast but dumb enough to kill her in my own shop." I leaned back against the car door and crossed my arms over my chest. "So, what's my motive?"

"Who knows? Maybe you didn't like the clothes she brought to your store for consignment."

"You're kidding, right? I wouldn't care if she brought in a nun's habit as long as I thought someone would buy it. I don't have to like the stuff people bring to the store. I just have to believe someone else will pay money for the item."

She shook her head. "Forget it. Captain Tony says we talk, so we talk. How about three?"

I opened the door and got out, then turned and stuck my head back into the car. "Should I bring a lawyer?"

"You can if you want, but you're not being charged with anything…yet." Frida offered a rueful smile, as if to excuse her role in the upcoming interview, waved at me and sped out of the lot.

It was still early so I strode back into the restaurant, indicated to the hostess I wanted a booth and ordered the breakfast buffet. Anger paired with disbelief gave me a hearty appetite. Returning to my booth after loading my plate with eggs, bacon, pancakes, pastries and a slice of toast, I noticed someone had joined me for breakfast. He was seated with his back to me as I approached the booth but I recognized the sun-streaked hair curling over his collar. My favorite PI. I almost dropped my plate.

"Hi." I tried for nonchalant but sounded more like a hormone-addled teenager.

"Saw you come in. I guess you had an early morning chitchat with the local gendarmes."

"To be continued this afternoon at the station."

"Fingerprints?" He stirred a packet of sugar into his coffee.

"Nope." The tingle in my tummy was more than simple hunger for food. I tried to satisfy it by stuffing a large forkful of pancake into my mouth. I nodded and swallowed. "Like anyone would be dumb enough to leave their prints."

"Certainly, we know you're smart."

"I had no reason to kill Mrs. Sanders. That would be like killing the golden goose."

"You didn't like her very much, did you?"

I dropped my fork on the plate. "What do you mean? I hardly knew the woman."

"So you say, but my sources indicate that's not the whole story." He stared at me. Last night I thought those azure eyes looked inviting. Now they looked more like ice. He smiled.

"You said you were investigating Mrs. Sanders. Sounds like you're trying to nose into my affairs. Why?"

"Don't get mad. I'm not accusing you of murder, you know." He took a sip of coffee.

"I'm not mad." I was a little miffed, peeved even, but not really mad. Okay, I was mad.

"Oh yes you are, and when you get angry, you stick your chin out and turn your head ever so slightly to the right. Your cheek twitches, probably from clenching your teeth. Did you know that?"

I had lost my appetite. I grabbed my purse and slid out of the booth. "I don't recall inviting you to join me for breakfast. I just remembered I have an important appointment."

"That would be…?" He also stood.

"That would be none of your business."

I stalked out of the restaurant, then remembered as I approached my car that I had forgotten to pay my bill. Damn. Now I'd have to go back in there and face him again. I gritted my teeth, stuck out my chin and slammed through the door. He turned from the counter, credit card in hand.

"Don't worry about it. I got it. Your treat next time."

"There won't be a next time." I spun around and

pushed open the door. By the time he reached his car, I was already starting my engine, wondering what the man knew about Mrs. Sanders and me.

FOUR

I opened the store right at ten. This morning there were no customers waiting for me to unlock the doors. Maybe word had spread that Madeleine and I were suspects. Grab a bargain and lose your life. The mad consignment shop entrepreneurs.

Madeleine showed up several minutes after I did, looking like her usual, put-together self. That is, if you didn't look too closely at the worry lines around her mouth and brow.

"Don't do that," I said.

"Do what?"

"Wrinkle your forehead like that. The lines will become permanent."

She looked, at first, as if she didn't believe me, but then rushed to one of our mirrors and almost pressed her face against the surface. "I think you may be right. Even when I stretch the skin upward," she pulled at her forehead, "I can still see a fine line across the middle." She turned back to me. "You know, I never used to worry. But ever since we decided to go into business together, it's been one thing after another. I guess I could consider Botox, but it's so expensive."

"So you're saying it's my fault you need a face lift?"

"Not a face lift, silly. A little procedure. With a needle."

I don't consider needles of any kind in my face a

"little procedure." More like an invasion of pain. A kind of cosmetic house of horrors, where the syringe is loaded with poison.

"You're overreacting to the recent stress but that's certain to go away soon," I said. Or so I hoped. "Besides," I added, "remember what happened to that doctor and his wife when they got a hold of some nonmedical grade Botox several years ago? With your propensity for accidents, you'd find someone who'd inject you with sheep urine or something."

She turned back to examine her face in the mirror.

"C'mere." I took her head in my hands and scrutinized her brow, cheeks and chin. "It's a hair."

"What?"

"It's not a line. There's a fine hair embedded in the makeup on your brow. There. I removed it. Take a look."

She did. "You're right. The line is gone."

Well, of course, I had lied. There was no hair, but I was the one who told her that the lines would become permanent if she continued to worry, so I did my best to undo what I had done. I'm a good friend.

It's funny, but the Botox scandal had started me thinking about the odd things that had happened since I moved down from Connecticut. In the Northeast, the news always revolved around politics, banks, and the stock market. There was some of that here, but Floridians had their own spin on scandal. The Botox mix-up was one of many newsworthy items for the aging and overly tanned denizens of this place.

Another big story focused on the death of a string of polo ponies due to contaminated vitamin supplements. Last month several more horses died from food laced with poison. Something to do with a Chinese company that had also been selling lethal baby food. Last I heard, the investigation was ongoing. They were trying to determine whether the bad horse feed was intentionally tampered with or if it had been a manufacturing accident.

The story had dropped from front-page news and I hadn't had time to read the paper all the way through since Madeleine and I opened shop, so I didn't know what was happening with the ponies. Why should I care? This train of thought triggered a memory from Connecticut. Then there was the comment Valerie Sanders made just last week...

I could have used the library for information, but I decided on another source. I could kill two birds with one stone. Oops, not a good choice of words. But I did owe him a phone call.

"Could you take over the floor? I'll go through the items dropped off yesterday," I said over my shoulder to Madeline.

"Sure. We're not very busy today, anyway. I wonder why?"

"Today's Thursday. Everyone goes to the coast on Thursdays. You know that."

"I do?"

I smiled and headed for the office. Another tiny lie for my partner, but I didn't want her to be concerned about the murder jeopardizing our business. I worked my way behind the racks of clothes waiting to be tagged, slid to the floor, and flipped open my phone. I had to be careful about how I approached him with my questions and be prepared for only half-truths—the story of our marriage.

I punched in the number and waited. "Hi, Jerry."

"Evie, baby. I tried to call you last night, but you didn't answer. Hot date?"

I remembered PI Montgomery's lips on mine and wanted to say yes, but the more recent memory of his breakfast interrogation overshadowed the romance and kept me from answering the question.

"This is not a social call. I need some information."

"I'm disappointed. When are you coming home? I'm trying to honor your request for space, but you need to stay in touch."

I couldn't help myself. "How's Bobbi or Billie or Bonnie?" The girl at the party. The drunken date.

"Who? Oh, you mean Monica."

I didn't think that was her name, but Jerry was so fast on his feet, and off them, that he could have already rented another bimbo. I'd been gone for over three months.

"Yeah. That one."

"Well, funny you should ask. That's why I called last night. I've got a little problem here."

"Later. Right now I have a question I need you to answer. Several years ago you visited someone in Stonington who was interested in using you for a financial consultant. Wasn't the name Sanders?"

There was a moment of silence. "Yeah. Leon. Poor fellow. And I do mean poor."

"Poor?"

"In more ways than one. Had a real lummox of a wife, Vera or Vivian or—"

"Valerie?" I suggested.

"Could be. Anyway, her family had money. He was only the manager, and she never let him forget his role.

But I heard recently that his money vanished. Bad market or bad investments. I couldn't say. He thought my advice was too far out there, but… Go figure. He took the conservative road and lost it all anyway."

"Right. What I want to know is, was he interested in polo ponies?"

Again Jerry hesitated, as if trying hard to remember what he knew or figuring out how to edit the information—a more likely possibility. "Leon? God, no. His son-in-law, well, that's another matter. Guy's from South America. I heard he's into the ponies. What's this got to do with us?"

"Nothing at all. Thanks for the information. I'll be in touch."

I flipped my phone shut and wondered where the investigation into the ponies' deaths stood now. Intentional poisoning? There had to be insurance money involved. The owners would want to collect on that as soon as possible. What had Valerie told me when she and I talked at the shop? "This downturn won't be for long, my dear. I'll be back shopping on the coast soon, so take advantage of my temporary poverty. I may find that my investment scheme got some horse manure on my boots, but never mind about that. So what?" She had tapped my shoulder with a brilliantly lacquered nail. "So what?"

I had listened with half an ear because I assumed Valerie, like the other women in her social class, exaggerated both their poverty and their schemes for getting rich again. I tuned most of the whining out, as I had with this conversation, but I *had* noticed Cory Burnside listening in with more interest than you might expect. Afterwards, she pulled Valerie to one side and the two of them engaged in an intense discussion that did not seem to be about charity events, Manolo Blahniks, or the theater. Now I wished I'd listened to Valerie more closely and done some eavesdropping of my own.

Dead polo ponies and Valerie's so-called "horse manure" investment scheme. At the time I thought she was using the phrase metaphorically. Maybe she meant real horses. How was any of this related to Valerie's death? Should I share my information with Frida?

I LIED YET AGAIN to Madeleine and told her I was getting a pedicure at three. She seemed a bit put out by my leaving the shop, but I calmed her down by calling attention to the absence of customers.

She acquiesced. "I think we need more merchandise," she said. "This stuff is so picked over, our racks are almost bare. Everyone's seen what we have."

I didn't want to share my concerns, but I was beginning to worry that being murder suspects wouldn't be good for business.

"So why don't you call some of our clients in Stuart and West Palm? We'll take a run over there tonight and pick up any items they want to offer." We'd begun to offer this service to protect women who didn't want to take the chance of being seen too often in the unfashionable part of Florida, namely, anywhere off-coast. I could almost hear them mouth the words "cowboy country" as if they'd eaten a sour pickle. Since we didn't advertise on our van, no one in the classy coastal neighborhoods we visited questioned our presence.

"Call Cory Burnside," I said.

"She's south of West Palm. That's a long way to drive tonight. We won't be back until after ten."

"You got a hot date or something?"

"No. Obviously, you don't either. I thought you were pretty taken with that PI guy."

"I slept on it and realized he wasn't such a good dancer after all."

CAPTAIN TONY WAS called away on other business, so Frida and her partner, Trevor Timble, interviewed me. The only furniture in the room was a wooden table with a teetering leg, three metal chairs and a window air conditioner that made the room only marginally cooler than it was outside. About what you'd expect from a small-town police department.

Frida was one of only three detectives on the force. Timble was due to retire soon and the third detective, Fred Walling, was out on medical leave. According to the local paper, he had suffered extensive injuries when his cruiser hit a bridge abutment. Timble looked as if he was already gone. He had less meat on his body than a gnawed dog's bone. He sat with his chin on his sunken-in chest, gaze fixed on his notebook. He said nothing when Frida introduced us. I remembered him at the shop on the day of the murder, making a mess of the skirt rack as he looked around the crime-scene. I lowered my head and sneaked a peek at this face. His eyes were closed. This was the lead detective on the case? It was a good thing Frida had over twenty years in as a uniformed officer.

Frida sat down in one of the chairs and looked at Timble. He held his pose of alleged notebook inspection. Captain Tony probably assigned Timble to show

Frida the ropes. That wouldn't happen today or anytime between now and his retirement.

"Detective Timble has a few questions for you."
Frida turned toward Timble and waited.

"Trevor," she urged him on.

He cleared his throat and his head jerked up. "All
yours." He uncrossed his legs, recrossed them and
shifted in his chair. His head slowly bent to its former position. I looked over at Frida and felt sorry that
she was saddled with Timble for a partner. I shouldn't
have wasted my sympathy.

I liked Frida. She, Madeleine, a woman from a
nearby apartment complex named Frances Ogilvey,
and I met once a month for dinner. Four gals, without
men, chatting and enjoying a night out. Nothing much,
but over the months, we'd shared our stories. Frida was
a single mom with two kids to raise, I had my phi-
landering husband and Madeleine, well, she probably
had the best track record with men. They were drawn
to her like bears to honeycomb. Frances was thrice
divorced and desperate to try matrimony again. We
drank a little, laughed a lot, and went home reasonably
sober. We had to behave, Frida being a cop and all.

Last month Frida told us that she'd passed the detective's exam and was first on the list for promotion.
Apparently, with Timble's impending retirement—
God, was that a snore?—Captain Tony had decided
that her time had come. I was happy for her and certain she'd do her job—not play favorites, of course,
but take under consideration important factors such
as friendships.

She sighed and laid her notebook on the table. I

looked at the open page and read her writing upside down. I was in trouble.

She bent forward and leveled her gaze at me, tapping her pen on the edge of the table. Tap, tap.

"I'm disappointed in you, Eve." Tap, tap. She paused as if to give me the opportunity to confess how disappointed I was in myself. I tried to appear both innocent and naive. That's not a look I wear well. I can do confused, nonchalant, sarcastic, and—if you let me use my mouth—ignorant and cool. The gentler expressions are not in my repertoire.

"You had the opportunity this morning to come clean. You didn't." Tap, tap and another pause.

Enough of our playing cop and suspect. I slammed the palm of my hand down on the desk. "Fine, then. You win."

The sound woke Timble. "You got a confession?" He stuck his pencil in his mouth, wet the tip, and prepared to write.

"Valerie Sanders and I didn't like each other much."

Frida nodded. "Go on."

"We had a bit of a disagreement."

"This was when?" She grabbed her notebook off the desk and jotted something in it.

"Last week."

"It was a disagreement, you said?"

"Right."

Timble continued to look awake, but I could tell he wasn't excited about the direction I was taking the conversation. His eyelids again drooped over his eyes. I didn't feel guilty for putting him back to sleep.

"Want to tell us about it?" Frida locked eyes with me.

"Not really. It was private business."

"A woman is dead, murdered. I don't think you need to be concerned about keeping your business arrangement a secret anymore."

I'd never seen this side of Frida before. She was like a snapping turtle—she wasn't going to let go, not with my finger in her jaws.

"Okay. Fine. It was more than a disagreement. I punched her in the chops."

FIVE

I read what Frida wrote in her notebook, the one she so cleverly placed on the desk in front of me, so I would know I had to 'fess up. Frida's pupils didn't even dilate with surprise when I announced that I had I hit the woman. No wonder she got the promotion to detective. She was one smart lady. She got the truth out of me. And someone else. Now I had to do some swift maneuvering of my own.

"The reason you assaulted her?" Frida's pencil was poised over her notebook, ready to get the goods on me. Timble came to life, scribbling nonstop in his little black book.

"You assume the assault was unwarranted? She came at me first. I only hit her to protect myself."

"Still. The reason for the two of you getting physical?"

I didn't realize I was holding my breath until I let out a sharp sigh. "Can't you guess? Valerie Sanders was cheap. She may have been rich, but she was tight with her money. Maybe that's how she got so rich. She wanted me to take a smaller percentage for the consignment of her castoffs. I told her no. She went crazy. Came at me as if I had accused her of buying her clothes at Sears." Privately, I was pretty certain she did buy some of her stuff at Sears, but then sewed on designer labels. That's how damn cheap she was.

"And then?"

"Once I gave her a good bop on the puss, she seemed to come to her senses. Grabbed her purse and left. The next time I saw her was the day of our grand opening, the day she—"

"How did she act toward you that day?"

"As she usually did. Like I was lowlier than the help she hired to clean her toilets, but a necessary evil." I glanced at my watch. I'd been here for over a half hour. Madeleine would be frantic if I wasn't back soon.

Frida and Timble exchanged looks and nodded at each other.

"Okay. You can go, but we may have additional questions."

"Well, I have one of my own. Who told you Valerie and I had a run-in?"

"Madeleine. This morning on the phone. I asked her if she knew of anybody who didn't like Valerie. She volunteered your name."

I could feel the blood rush to my face. That little rat! Here I'd been trying to protect her by lying about my whereabouts this afternoon. Once I got back to the store, I intended to up her stress level. Her wrinkles be damned! But before I did that, I needed to find out what she'd overheard between Valerie and me.

Had she heard the real reason for Valerie's attack? If so, had she told Frida? If Frida knew I hadn't been honest about the reason for our confrontation, she'd be examining my background, which wouldn't stand up to that kind of scrutiny and could lead to too much interest in Jerry's dealings with the Sanders family. Oh yeah, as usual, Jerry had lied to me. I knew him well enough to detect the dissembling in his voice when we talked. He was up to his armpits in the Sanders' investments. Not that he could be involved in the murder. No way. Nuh-uh.

I KEPT MY mouth shut about the fact that Madeleine had been shooting off hers to Frida until we were already headed for the coast.

"They've been burning the sugar cane fields south of here all day," I said. "You can still smell that acrid scent in the air." It was not an odor I savored. I rolled up the window and turned on the air conditioner.

Madeleine said, "Should we go to Cory's first, since it's all the way on the other side of West Palm?" She lowered the vanity mirror on the visor and examined her face.

That did it. "I told you this morning," I said. "There's no wrinkle. I lied to you. Your forehead is as smooth as the inside of a cream puff."

"Why are you yelling at me? You've been acting funny ever since you picked me up at the store. If you're going to treat me like that, let me out here."

I almost did just that, but we were driving the 714 East after the commuter rush hour had already passed, and I doubted anyone would be on the road. She'd get eaten by an alligator crossing to hunt overnight in the swamp on the other side. She'd surely blame me for that. I could just see her shaking her tiny freckled fist at me as a gator swallowed her whole.

I slammed my fist on the steering wheel. "Why the hell did you rat on me?" I said. "I thought we were best friends and then you blab to the cops."

"What do you mean?"

"You told Frida that Valerie and I had a fight."

"You did."

"It was private."

"Half the county heard you."

"Did you tell Frida why we fought?"

"The shop's take, right?"

I looked over at her face, but in the dim light I couldn't tell if she knew more than she was saying. "Whatever. You owe me one."

"Do not."

"Do so. And here's how you can make it up to me." I told her about my concern for our business, and that I was worried the shop would suffer if Mrs. Sanders' murderer wasn't identified sooner rather than later. I told her my brilliant plan. She must have felt some guilt about talking to Frida because, to my surprise, she agreed to help me out.

It wasn't much of a plot. Mostly just the old good-cop-bad-cop routine put to good use by the good-consignment-shop-owner and the bad. I don't have to tell you what part I was playing, do I?

Getting Cory Burnside to confess to us what she and Valerie had been scheming about on the day of the fight would only be possible if her husband wasn't home tonight. Rumor had it that Randolph Burnside spent as little time at home as possible. He was too involved in making money, something he seemed to do very well. I figured he needed all the cash he could get just to pay for the extensive "procedures" his wife underwent. Cory lived by that old dictum, you can't be too rich or too thin, and its addendum—too wrinkle- or sag-free. Her face had undergone surgery so often that it was painful to look at her. She appeared to be in a state of perpetual surprise. One more lift and her eyebrows would join her hairline.

We pulled up in front of Cory's large house just as the sun was going down. The stucco dwelling sat back from the road, sheltered amid a variety of palms and oaks. A manicured lawn seemed to invite visitors to take off their shoes and walk across the green carpet, but a sign indicating the property was protected by a security system suggested the grassy invitation was not serious. I rang the bell and expected a servant to answer. Cory showed up instead.

She kept us waiting at the door while she grabbed a load of garments from a hallway chair and loaded them into my arms. "Could we come in for a moment?" I asked.

She looked surprised at my request. That reaction wasn't what piqued my curiosity. It was the alarm I saw in her eyes.

"It's about poor, dear Valerie." Madeleine looked appropriately sad.

"This really isn't such a good time." She tried to close us out, but I'd already placed one of my size-ten feet in the door and I now stood in the foyer, looming over her. Madeleine ducked past me and went to stand next to her.

"Well, fine," she said, "if you don't stay long. I'm expecting someone."

"We'll stay for a quick drink. That's all." I walked straight ahead, across the marble entryway and into a dimly lit room beyond. The space was overcrowded with potted plants, heavy teak furniture and lots of leather—couches, chairs, even the lampshades were made of animal skins. That East Indian look that is so popular in south Florida.

The back of the room was fashioned out of glass, and through it we could see a beautifully landscaped garden filled with royal palms, bougainvillea and a plethora of tropical flowers. Standing guard over the garden was a huge oak that dwarfed even the largest of royals. In the center of all of this beauty stood a pool into which a waterfall cascaded. I dropped the clothes on a leather sofa and walked through the open doorway into the warm night.

"Too bad we didn't bring suits," I said. "A dip after the day I've had would feel great."

Cory muttered with irritation, Madeleine apologized for my manners, and I threw myself onto a chaise lounge.

Cory stood at my side looking down at me as if she wanted to drown me in the clear, blue water but was worried the pool service would never be able to clean up the mess.

I reached up and took her bony hand. "Madeleine's right. Please forgive my manners, but this had been quite a day. Here we are, all of us, so…so, well…so aggrieved at Valerie's death. Horrified, too. Then to have the cops act as if I was at fault! Have they been to see you, dear?"

The triple whammy of my apology, the news about my run-in with the cops and my inquiry into her own dealings with the law seemed to have the desired effect. I had intended to confuse her and, although her face appeared as startled as ever, her eyes, the true barometer of her emotional state, jumped around in their sockets, signaling fear or concern. Or was it terror?

I pressed my advantage. "Oh, they'll be here soon enough. Or they'll summon you to headquarters. Let me tell you, that place is a dump."

She plopped down on the end of the lounge. "You mean they might insist that I drive there and be interrogated in some backwater police station? If my friends find out about this, I'll just die." She put her head in her hands and began to sob.

"What did you expect? You were close to Valerie. Of course they'll want to talk to you." I reached out. Madeleine rummaged in her purse, found a tissue and handed it to me. Cory held out her hand for it. I blew my nose and tossed the wad back to Madeleine. "You'd better have a good story for them when they arrive."

"Story? Why do I need a story? Besides, Valerie and I weren't even that close. Once she and her husband lost all their money, well, we weren't running in the same circles anymore." She sounded angry, not scared.

"What about your recent, uh, troubles?" There was sympathy in Madeleine's voice. Madeleine gave me a sly look, indicating she was taking a shot in the dark.

For a moment, I thought Cory might deny the fact that she and Randolph were having "troubles," but she chuckled instead. "Isn't that the funniest thing? Valerie recently mentioned a project she and her husband had gotten involved in. She promised a good return on our investment, but I told her Randolph wasn't interested. Randolph does his own investing, doesn't follow his friends' lead. That's what gets so many people in trouble, you know, following along. I didn't even ask her for details."

"She and her husband had enough money to invest?"

"Yes."

"You sure you don't know what kind of project?" Usually I can tell when someone is lying—I have had plenty of practice being married to Jerry—but Cory's face gave away nothing.

"Don't be coy," she said. "I assume the investment involved you and your estranged husband, as usual." Her tone was clipped and accusing.

A figure emerged from behind one of the silver palms. "Now that's something I didn't know. I'll bet the cops don't either." Lean, casual, hands in his pockets—my investigator playing eavesdropper in the garden.

Dumbfounded, I turned to Cory. "Is *this* the person you were expecting?" I couldn't have been more surprised and less amused. Alex and Cory, a new take on *The Odd Couple*? "Since when do you let PIs wander around in your azaleas?"

"I told him to come in through the back. I didn't want to explain the presence of a strange man at my door to any neighbors who might be watching."

"Isn't this cozy?" Alex wandered over to the bar cart. At first I thought he was going to reach out and make himself a drink. Instead, he twisted one of the bottles around and read the label. "Johnnie Walker Green. Rich stuff." He looked at Cory with a question in his eyes.

"So? My son likes Green label. He brought it over." Cory sounded defensive.

Alex was dancing around something. What? Why not simply ask? So I did.

"Excuse me, but I'm missing something here. Is

Cory the person who hired you to track down information on Valerie?"

Alex didn't reply, only flashed an infuriatingly enigmatic smile.

I turned my attention to Cory. "Why would you need a PI to investigate your friend?"

Cory jumped to her feet and pointed an accusing finger. "Get out of here, you two. I don't want you in my house ever again."

Madeleine grabbed my hand and pulled me off the lounge.

"Fine, fine. We'll leave." We walked out of the pool area and entered the house, grabbing the consignment clothes off the couch on our way through the library, or great room, or whatever the current lingo is in ostentatious living.

I didn't make it far. "Leave those right there. I've changed my mind about consigning with you." Cory followed us to the door and slammed it behind us.

"Nice work," Madeleine said. "We found out nothing, and we no longer have her clothes to sell. Did you see that suit and those pants?" She continued muttering indistinctly as she headed toward the van.

"If I'd known she had Johnnie Green, I would have insisted on that drink. I love Green," I said, turning left at the end of the sidewalk and strolling up the blue-stone pathway toward the back of the house.

Madeleine was still heading toward our vehicle. When she realized I was no longer behind her, she turned around and ran after me. "What do you think you're doing?"

"I want to hear what they're saying. You go back to

the van and drive off. That way they'll think we left.
I'll meet you at the corner as soon as I get what I need."

"What do you need?"

"To find out who Alex is working for and how my
husband is involved in all of this."

"You're going to spy on them?"

"Get going or they'll know we're still here." I made
a dismissive gesture and proceeded up the walkway.
In front of me was the gate to the garden area. The
lighting on the grounds was just bright enough to give
the plantings a romantic ambience, but dim enough to
allow me some cover. I reached out and pushed open
the gate.

Once inside the garden, I was able to hear the voices
ahead of me, but I couldn't make out what they were
saying. I'd have to get closer. Sneaking from behind
one tree to another near the pool, I was able to hide
myself in the shadows and plants.

"The investment project?" she was saying.

Valerie's project? I had to know what was involved
and how Jerry figured in all this. Alex lowered his
voice, making it impossible for me to discern what he
was saying. I spied a bougainvillea whose branches
and flowers spread over the lawn and flowed toward
the deep end of the pool. Beneath its shadowy cover
loomed low-growing lantana, and unless I tried to
crawl on my stomach across that area, I'd be out in
the open. I needed cover.

If Jerry was involved in Valerie's scheme to get rich
again, he might be implicated in her death. I didn't love
the jerk any longer, but I still had a soft spot for him.
Slinking around like this was typical of the things I'd

had to do to rescue Jerry from himself. The story of our relationship: he got into trouble. I got him out.

I sighed in resignation, got down on my stomach and made like Rambo, crawling along the ground, using my elbows to pull me forward. Hard work. The lantana was woody, but if I tried to avoid the sharp branches by getting up on my knees, the thorns from the bougainvillea would grab my shirt. I had gone only a few feet when a voice from overhead asked, "May I help you?"

SIX

I LOOKED UP into a chiseled face—a jaw like Dudley Do Right and a head of sweeping hair like Donald Trump. He was dressed in white trousers and a blue blazer, an apricot ascot tied at his neck. I could hardly believe my eyes. He was a snapshot taken at the races, and I don't mean the Indy 500.

I twisted myself around to face him and offered my hand. "You must be Randolph Burnside. I'm Eve Appel, one of your wife's, er…friends."

He grabbed my hand and pulled me up. On my stomach, I hadn't been able to gauge his height. Once standing, however, I saw that I towered over him. The man had never seen five feet. I could have stomped on him like a pesky cockroach, but this was his property, and I was a trespasser, so I had to make nice.

He seemed unworried about the differences in our heights and unmoved by the presence of a giant woman crawling through his lawn. If anything, he appeared amused and curious.

"Cory usually has better manners than this. I'm surprised she left a friend to crawl around in the hibiscus and creeping myrtle. Please, come on in for a drink."

He started up the path toward the pool and beckoned me to follow. When I didn't, he turned and smiled. "I wouldn't want to believe that you're actually a burglar or a stalker."

Okay, so he wasn't quite as oblivious to my creeping around as I had first assumed. What the hell. I had little choice. I worked on my excuse as we entered the pool area.

To my relief, Cory and Alex were gone. Perhaps they'd moved inside to continue their talk elsewhere, but the poolside room was also empty. Their meeting had to be business. Although I wasn't certain that I liked Alex as much as I originally wanted to, I also didn't want to believe that he and Cory were having a more intimate liaison. He didn't seem like the type who was into processed women.

Randolph gestured toward the lounge I'd sat in before. I slid back into it.

"Your pleasure?" He gestured at the bar cart.

"Hmm?" I had been thinking of my PI, not listening.

"What would you like to drink?"

"Johnnie Green, double, rocks."

He stopped abruptly, spun on his heel and walked back toward me.

Oops, I'd goofed. Green wasn't something many people stocked in their bars. So how could I have been so certain that he had it?

"Now I know you. You were my son's date at our luau last spring."

At this moment, Cory appeared at the library door, the expression on her face hard, unpleasant. "I don't think so, dear. You're confusing Eve with Serena. They're both tall and willowy."

Gosh. I'd never been called "willowy" before. "Thin," "angular," maybe, but the tree reference hadn't been used to describe me. If I had to use a plant descriptor, saguaro cactus sprang to mind.

"I found your friend in the garden." Randolph took her hand and placed a kiss on one of her smooth cheeks. I was surprised his lips didn't slide off the Botoxed surface.

"Well, you see, I'm from the Northeast originally, and I was admiring your landscaping. I'm not familiar with all these plants." I swept my hand outward to indicate the area.

"She was on her hands and knees." Randolph's eyes danced, perhaps an indication that he found that position preferable to my standing over him.

"I fell. I think I tripped over the roots of that big tree. What is that, anyway?"

"A banyan," said Cory.

"From the Northeast, you say? We used to have a place there. Where do you live now?"

"West of here." I made it sound like it was blocks, maybe a few miles, not several counties away.

"She has a small place near Sabal Bay." Cory might just as well have said "the city dump."

"Never been that far west," Randolph said. "Just to the polo matches in Port Mayaca. Ever been there? It's about as far west as I like to go. Saw some gators on the lake there that must have reached over fifteen feet." He filled a heavy crystal glass with liquor, dropped in an ice cube and handed me the tumbler.

The doorbell sounded. Randolph gave Cory a confused look. "Is Marcia here?"

"No. I gave her the night off. I'll get it." Cory hustled from the pool area toward the front of the house.

Randolph continued standing at the end of the

lounge, rocking back and forth on his heels and toes, looking me up and down.

"How tall are you, anyway?"

"How tall are you?" I shot back.

He tossed his head back, the wave of abundant hair barely moving, and guffawed. "That's a good one." Was it sprayed in place to cover a bald spot? He removed the handkerchief from his breast pocket and wiped his eyes. "A good one."

I could hear voices issuing from inside the house. Familiar voices. One was Madeleine's. The others belonged to Alex, Frida, and Timble.

"Oh, boy. Now that everyone's here, we can have a party." I raised my glass in a salute to the newcomers and looked over the rim of it at Cory. "I told you the cops would be coming around soon."

Frida gave me a look of disgust. "I found this one," she pointed to Madeleine, "at the corner, and this one," Alex smiled, "was leaving by a door at the back of the house. You're wrong, Eve. This is no party. I have a few questions I need answered."

So did I. I settled back into the lounge with my drink and tried to hide my look of gleeful curiosity.

Frida walked over to the lounge, reached down and took the glass from my hand. "The two of you can leave." She nodded her head at Madeleine and me. "Let's see," she consulted her notebook. "PI Montgomery, I'll be in touch. Soon."

"Don't you want to tell him not to leave town?" I reluctantly rose from the chaise and shot PI Alex a sharp look. Madeleine grabbed my arm and tried to hurry me out. I was waiting for Alex.

"He knows the script." Frida gave him one of her

best police smiles—lips slightly curved upwards, no teeth, no amusement in her eyes.

"Let me walk you out." Randolph placed his hand in the small of my back and guided me toward the door. I moved away from Randolph's presumptuous gesture and stepped ahead of him.

"Don't leave me here with these, these police people," said Cory, but Randolph was already walking toward the front entrance.

Alex pulled the door open and gestured to Madeleine and me. "Ladies."

Impulsively, I grabbed Alex's arm and smiled into his face. If I couldn't be in on Frida's investigation of the Burnsides, I could at least grill Alex about his surprising appearance at the house. I wasn't about to let him get away once we hit the street.

"You've got quite a grip," Alex whispered in my ear. "We weren't on such good terms when you left the restaurant this morning. Change of heart?"

I tightened my hand around his arm—his yummy, muscular, warm, sexy arm—and felt his hand on my rear. I jumped away from him, about to slap that smug, sexy, yummy—never mind. He looked surprised at my movement, and I realized the hand on my ass wasn't his. It was Randolph's. The gremlin was coming on to me!

"Please come back. Soon. Anytime." Randolph gave me a wink. "Bring your tiny friend, too." He gave Madeleine a look of dwarfish lust.

A threesome? As if reading my mind, Randolph shrugged his shoulders and pursed his lips. I didn't want to imagine what he had in mind, but I couldn't help it. An unpleasant vision of Cory interrupting a naked Randolph as he pursued Madeleine and me around the pool almost caused me to lose my Johnnie Green into a bed of azaleas.

"You don't look very well." Madeleine reached out and put her hand on my arm. "Are you okay?"

"You need to sit down?" Alex took my other arm.

"I could use a stiff drink."

"You just had one. Back there." Madeleine gestured with her head toward the house.

"I didn't get to finish it. You up for a drink, PI Montgomery?" I gave him my best flirty look. I even batted my eyelashes.

"You got something in your eye?" Madeleine was just being mean.

I rode in Alex's car, afraid that if I let him take off by himself, he'd bolt. He had to have known that I was up to something. He wasn't a total idiot. Madeleine was driving behind us and I kept sneaking glances of her in the rearview mirror. She looked as if she was having an argument with herself. I hoped her better side—the one telling her to drive home and leave me to flirt—wouldn't win.

Once we were all safely in the bar, I grabbed his hand again. He had questions to answer.

"You can let go now," said Alex. The three of us had selected a booth at the rear of the bar. "I think the circulation in my arm has been cut off for so long that it'll have to be amputated."

"I'll give your arm back if you answer my question."

"I can't promise anything, but for you, I'll try." He mimicked my eyelash batting and gave me a sarcastic smile.

"Fine. Point taken. Let's get down to business." Thank goodness. Another eyelash bat and my lids would fall off.

The bartender came out from behind the bar. "We got no table service here. You'll have to order at the bar."

"Can't *you* take our order?" Madeleine produced her most winning smile.

"If I take your order, I'll have to take everyone's order."

We looked around. There was no one else in the place.

"Rules is rules." He returned to his station.

Madeleine's smile slipped. "Oh, I'll go. I think the two of you have some things to work out."

"There's nothing to work out. I just need to know what the hell Alex was doing at Cory's house."

"I'll have a Bud." He pointed at me. "She'll have a scotch."

"I'll have one, too." Madeleine licked her lips.

Alex shook his head. "You'll have a coke. You're driving home." I chuckled at Madeleine's look of irritation before she headed for the bartender. Now she could finally appreciate how annoying this man could be.

Alex turned his attention to me. "As for your question, it's none of your business. Why were *you* there?"

"Consignment shop business." I smirked at him. We were at a stalemate.

He ran his hands through his windblown hair. I'd love to have done that for him and messed up his coif a bit more.

"Have you considered this, Eve? Maybe the killer

made a mistake and wasn't after Valerie Sanders, but someone else."

What an interesting speculation. I wondered what had provoked it. Had his chat with Cory uncovered a new lead? My heart raced with excitement and eager curiosity. "Oh yeah? Like, who?"

"You."

I laughed.

Madeleine returned with our drinks. "You think Eve was the target?" She slid into the booth beside me. "Yeah, I could see that."

A small sliver of fear crept up the back of my neck. I ignored the feeling and took the offensive. "You can? Why is that? Because people find me irritating, overbearing, and unpleasant?"

"Well that, of course, but mostly your looks." Madeleine took a sip of her coke.

"My looks make people want to murder me?"

"No. I mean you look a lot alike."

"You can't mean Valerie and me." My very best friend was insulting me, and, what's worse, she was doing it in front of a man I found…interesting.

"She's right. You and Valerie are similar in appearance. I mean, were similar." Alex looked quite satisfied about getting Madeleine to side with him.

How could the two of them compare my racy, unique, spot-on style to Valerie's south Florida society matron guise? "How? How were we alike?"

"Don't get your thong in a twist. What I think we mean," Madeleine glanced at Alex for confirmation, "is that you were both unusually tall women with blonde hair. Of course, yours has black roots."

"That's intentional. It's a look, not a mistake!" I was yelling now.

"You both hung around the consignment shop. If someone had hired a killer and given him or her a description, the killer could have mistaken Valerie for you." Alex began peeling the label off his beer bottle with his thumb.

I took a slug of my scotch. With the next swallow, I hit the bottom of my glass and started to chew my ice cubes. "That's silly. Why would anyone—I mean serious now—*anyone* want me dead?"

Madeleine rolled her eyes but kept quiet.

Alex continued to build a pile of soggy label pieces on the table in front of him. "There's your reluctance to give your husband a divorce." He refused to meet my eyes.

"How would you know anything about that?"

He concentrated on his thumb, then raised his eyes to mine. "It's my business to know. That's all I can tell you." He stood and threw several bills on the table. "Drinks are on me. I gotta go."

As we watched him walk out, I caught my reflection in the mirror behind the bar. My mouth had fallen open so far a Humvee could have driven in. Madeleine looked the same.

I grabbed my purse and ran after him. Madeleine was right behind me, but by the time we reached the parking lot, he was already pulling out, fast.

"That was so sweet of him," said Madeleine.

"What was sweet? Paying for our drinks?"

"No. I think he was warning you to be careful. I think he likes you. A lot."

"He was fingering Jerry, and that's stupid. He can't

know anything about Jerry if he thinks Jerry would hire somebody to kill me, just to get me to finalize the divorce. Jerry's a bit impulsive and impatient, but he's no fool. Who would the authorities look for first if I died under unusual circumstances? Him, of course."

"I'm sure you're right."

I considered the possibility that Jerry had hired someone to kill me and rejected it. He was far too cheap to pay anyone to do that. A hit like that had to cost a lot of money, unless, of course, you hired some idiot who couldn't tell a society matron from a flashy, sexy, displaced Connecticut know-it-all broad. I reconsidered. Now *that* sounded like something Jerry would do. The more I thought about it, the more I realized that Jerry had never done any work that he could have gotten someone else to do for him, especially if the price was right. I wondered how much the bastard thought I was worth dead.

SEVEN

"WE DIDN'T KNOW Valerie all that well." Madeleine's tone of voice told me she was having second thoughts about being here. She squirmed around in a folding chair in the back of the room. The funeral director had set up several additional rows of chairs for Valerie's service because the space had been filled beyond capacity.

"It's the professional thing to do. Will you sit still?" I wanted to put my hand on her head to stop her from wiggling.

"My seat is uncomfortable. You'd think a place with this much class would have better seating."

"We're not going to be here for very long. Stop thinking about your butt."

Our presence at Valerie's funeral was more than good business. I had insisted that we attend for another reason. I had to get a better look at Valerie. Was Alex right? Were she and I alike? I should have had a better picture of the woman in my mind. I'd seen her in the store at least three or four times. We'd had a confrontation. I'd even discovered her dead in my shop. Why couldn't I call up her image to make the comparison? Maybe the trauma of the murder had wiped out some important neural connections.

From where we sat in the back, I couldn't see into the casket, and I knew the lid would be closed before the service began. Once that happened, my chance to make comparisons would be gone forever.

"I'm going up front to pay my respects to the family."

"You don't know the family. We never met them."

"C'mon. You said your fanny was killing you." I yanked her out of her chair.

"I don't want to get too close."

"For God's sake, she's dead, and it's not like she had a contagious disease." I grabbed her arm and walked her to the casket. I spotted many of our West Palm customers among the mourners as we passed, but no one gave us a nod of recognition. Just to be contrary, when I passed near Cory Burnside and hubby, Randolph, I waved and mouthed a hello. She sniffed and turned away, but randy Randolph gave me a smile and puckered his lips as if to blow me a kiss.

I stood in front of the casket, looking down at Valerie Sanders. She was at least five years older than I, but they were well-preserved years. Her lips were full, her nose was long and she had high cheekbones and blonde hair—short, but not cut in the same punky style as mine. I couldn't see any resemblance beyond the general impression of tall, cool, blonde. Besides, she was heavier than me. I shook my head. Only an idiot would…

"Your sister?" asked a woman who came up behind me. "I didn't know Valerie had a sister."

I turned to deny the relationship, but another voice interrupted.

"Now do you see what I mean?" I felt Alex's breath on my neck. He stood close. Too close. His shoulder rubbed mine, sending little shivers down my side.

I ignored him, grabbed a hold of Madeleine once more and steered her toward the family. I offered my hand to a man I assumed to be Valerie's husband. He was short, balding, his eyes red-rimmed, either from crying or too much alcohol.

"My condolences."

Beside him stood a young woman whose face reminded me of Valerie's, but this woman was thinner, younger. A daughter. She gave me one of those you-can't-be-anybody-important looks, then leaned into the man at her side and whispered in his ear. From his dark good looks, I guessed him to be the South American husband. He glanced over at me, put his arm around her shoulder and pulled her close. Ah. Constance and her rich polo–pony-riding husband—Eduardo, or Emilio, or Edmond.

The woman standing at Eduardo's other side moved closer to him, her hand coming to rest on his coat sleeve. Her face was exquisite—angular, but not masculine. A family member? She had Eduardo's café au lait skin and chiseled features. Perhaps his sister. She gave me a dismissive up and down look as if my presence was a fashion faux pas.

I turned my attention back to Valerie's husband, who shook my hand, a look of puzzlement on his face. "You are?"

"Eve. From Sabal Bay."

His puzzled expression remained. "I don't remember Valerie mentioning your name. She had friends over there? I'm surprised."

"We were both fascinated by old Florida. I just met her several months ago, but I'm so distressed to hear of her death in…that shop."

He nodded at my words, as if he too found her place of demise as unpleasant as the death itself. "Valerie was quite a gal. She loved to go to unusual places." He spoke as if trying to explain her presence somewhere other than on Worth Avenue. His pleasant remembrance of Valerie, which had animated his face for a moment, faded. He grabbed a handkerchief out of his pocket and wiped his eyes. "Her wandering got her killed, didn't it?"

"She's not one of Mom's friends." The voice came from a younger man standing slightly behind Valerie's husband. I watched as the interruption turned Mr. Sanders' remorse into concern, then irritation.

"'Mom?" I was puzzled. He didn't look like Valerie.

"Valerie was Dwight's, my son's, stepmother." Mr. Sanders spoke through puckered lips, as if he had sucked on a lime.

Dwight looked familiar and out of place here among the well-groomed and fashionably dressed icons of the Palm Coast. His clothes hung loosely on him and he was unshaven. What did I know about the fashion trends of the younger generation? Perhaps he was going for the European look, with several days' growth of beard and his baggy, unpressed suit.

"This woman and her friend here," the son nodded his head toward Madeleine, "own the shop where Mom was killed. They weren't friends. The cops told me they think she might have done it."

"What are you doing here?" Mr. Sanders' face had that still, cold look of anger on it. His lips pressed together in a hard line.

"Probably gloating that she got away with it." Dwight's voice was reedy and whiny.

That did it. This little twit was annoying. I wanted to grab his rumpled lapels and shake him, but Alex, reading my mind, placed a restraining hand on my arm. "Let's go. I'm sure Dwight didn't mean anything by his remarks. We'll leave Leon, uh, Mr. Sanders, to his grief." Alex nodded to the family and steered me away from them.

"But…"

"He's right." Madeleine shoved me from behind, and the two of them guided me toward the door. On the way out, I saw a smirk on Cory's face. The tip of Randolph's tongue darted out of his mouth to lick his lips as I passed. Mourners who frequented our shop cast their eyes down toward their programs and feigned ignorance of my identity. As if guessing that I might use this opportunity to launch into one of my diatribes about hypocrisy, Madeleine quickened her pace and the sea of faces became a blur as she and Alex wrangled me out of the funeral parlor.

MAYBE ALEX AND Madeleine thought they had rescued me, but they were wrong. Once outside, I bumped into Detective Frida and her mentor/sidekick, Timble.

"It's not what you think. I'm not attending the funeral of my victim to get my jollies," I said.

"Well, since you're here and Madeleine's here and… well, well, it's PI Montgomery again. The two of you should find better places to meet."

"You're as perceptive as Eve said you were." Alex gave Frida a one-hundred-watt smile.

Had I said something to Alex about Frida? I didn't recall that, but there had been a lot of wine and dancing and…that kiss. I couldn't remember everything I had said on our date.

Frida smiled back at Alex, the wattage on her teeth equally blinding. "I've been looking for a chance to speak with you, especially since you and Eve seem to be such good friends. You turn up everywhere together. Now is good for me. What about you?"

"Now? Uh…" This time his voice carried a note of concern. "As for Eve and me, well, we've had a few dates, but…"

"A few? I only know about one. There were more and you didn't tell me?" Madeleine looked at me with accusing eyes.

"One date only."

"Two, if you count breakfast." He held up two fingers.

"One." I thrust out my chin in defiance. "Why would I go out on another date with you when the first was so disappointing?"

Frida stepped between the two of us. "Okay, let's take this back to the office. Trevor will be staying here to cover the funeral. Why don't we rendezvous back in Sabal Bay in, say, an hour?"

IT TOOK ME two hours to negotiate the drive from the coast to the Sabal Bay Police Station.

"Why are you driving so slowly?" Madeleine squirmed around in her seat impatiently. "Are you trying to make us late? Frida won't be happy."

"I'm just enjoying the scenery."

"You've driven this road a hundred times."

The 714 is one of the most memorable stretches of road in rural Florida. It passes between rows of palms and large oaks draped with Spanish moss. Like old-fashioned ballroom dancers, the trees reach out over the roadway as if to link hands with their leafy partners on the other side. Residents of the area refer to it as "the canopy." The government is always threatening to cut down the trees in order to expand the road into a four-lane, but those against destroying the natural beauty of the route always prevail with petitions to leave it unchanged. I never tired of driving through the cool, shadowy tunnel, but this afternoon, I was focused less on the scenery and more on the thoughts in my head.

"The woman at Mr. Sanders' side? That was Valerie's daughter. Same height and build, but Valerie was a blonde and her daughter's a brunette."

Madeleine tossed me a glance. "Most blondes are."

I ignored the implication of her words.

"And her husband…"

"Eduardo. Handsome, isn't he?" Madeleine rolled her eyes and grinned.

"His face is too controlled, too angular for him to be one of the good guys. There was that female clone next to him, the one who looked as if she caught a whiff of swamp gas."

"That's a rash judgment, isn't that? We were at a funeral. What did you expect? She'd be cracking jokes? Besides, Alex's face is angular, too."

"Yeah, but his eyes are azure, not reptilian."

"Reptilian is not a color."

"It is in my book." I turned into the police parking lot. Frida's cruiser was already there, as was Alex's car. He was leaning against the door, legs crossed at the ankles, the epitome of cool confidence.

When we got out of the car, Alex gave me a slow smile. "I took you for a better driver. I thought you might at least go the speed limit," he said.

"I had some things on my mind. Do you know who that woman was? The one standing next to Mr. Sanders?"

"Valerie's daughter, Constance, and her husband, Eduardo Pacheco?"

"No, the other woman next to Eduardo." I don't know why I asked him. How would he know? Yet he answered me quickly enough.

"Marie Artois. Valerie's social secretary. I think she's also a friend of Eduardo's."

My, he knew a lot about that family.

He opened the door to the building and ushered us in with a sweep of his hand.

Frida met us in the hallway "There you are. I was beginning to think you skipped out on me."

I scrutinized her face for sarcasm but Frida wasn't easy to read. It was no wonder she had made detective so quickly.

She led all three of us into the same interview room, the same one I had been questioned in just days before. A navy blue jacket lay on the table. Frida picked it up and held it out to Madeleine and me. "Recognize this jacket?"

Madeleine and I nodded. It was a loose fitting, unstructured jacket, no lining, boxy, fashionable several years back.

"Good. You seem to be on top of your inventory."

I took the jacket and noted the tag hanging off the label in the back. From our shop. "It's ours, but what's the stain on the sleeve and front?"

"Blood. Valerie's blood. Whoever killed her wore this jacket over his or her clothes while stabbing our victim, ran out your side door near the dressing rooms, then tossed the item in the dumpster down the street."

"It had to have been a woman, someone from the crowd of customers that had been swarming the place on opening day. I'd have noticed if a man had come in." I shifted my eyes to Alex and—I couldn't help myself—smiled.

"Eve's right," said Madeleine. "A man would have stood out. I can't remember any that day. Not that we don't welcome them in to shop for the women in their lives." Madeleine smiled at Alex.

"And these?" Frida pulled a pair of leather gloves out of the jacket's pockets.

"Also tagged. Also ours." I reached out for them.

Frida moved them beyond my grasp. "Evidence. There's Valerie's blood on the gloves and we're examining them for epithelials."

"It could be a man," said Alex.

"Weren't you listening?" I asked. "We just covered that."

"Not entirely. Someone could have come through the side door, grabbed some items from the return rack just outside the dressing rooms, put them on, stabbed her, then left through the same door."

"That door is always locked from the inside." At least, it's supposed to be.

"Maybe Valerie let someone in," said Alex.

"How could that person get the knife from house goods in the main part of the store without either Madeleine or me seeing him? Hims, remember, are noticeable."

"Maybe Valerie had the knife on her. Perhaps she had picked one out of the display and taken it with her to the dressing rooms." He certainly was quick with the theories.

Frida shook her head. "Why would she do that?"

"She *was* looking at the knives. I noticed that," said Madeleine.

"She took the knife for protection." Yet another bold speculation on his part.

"From whom?" I gave a snort of disbelief. He was spinning a wild tale here. Something I suspected he liked to do to get everyone riled up. He had done the same with me at the restaurant when he suggested I was the intended victim.

"From the person she opened the door for, the person she arranged to meet at your shop." He leaned back in his chair and grinned. Smug.

Frida leaned forward toward Alex, her usually soft brown eyes now hard as black ice. "You seem to have a keen interest in this case, Mr. Montgomery. Ms. Appel told me you came into her store the day after the murder, saying you'd been hired to get information about Mrs. Sanders. Care to tell us what that's about and who hired you?"

"Can't. Private between me and my client."

"Your client could be a killer. Have you thought of that?"

"I have and if I thought there was anything illegal going on, I'd drop the client and tell you first thing." He had the look of an innocent schoolboy.

I didn't buy that angelic façade for a minute. I caught Frida rolling her eyes and knew that she didn't either.

Frida stood and walked around the table until she stood inches behind Alex. "You need watching, Mr. Montgomery."

Oh, boy, did he, but not in the manner she had in mind.

He smirked, unperturbed by the threat. "Want me to try on that jacket to see if it's a fit, Detective?"

"I know you didn't kill her, but I hope you're right about your client's innocence. Meantime, I'm going to keep an eye on you." Frida bent over him, close enough that she could have blown in his ear. She didn't, of course, but I envied her position. Alex turned his head and their faces almost touched. Frida didn't retreat a millimeter. Neither did Alex. They simply eyed each other without blinking until Frida reached out and picked a piece of something off his shoulder. She stood up to examine it in the overhead light. "A blonde hair, I believe." She winked at me.

"That could be anyone's hair." I could feel a flush work its way up my neck and onto my cheeks.

Alex grinned. "Oh, I'm pretty sure it's yours. This is the same coat I was wearing when we went dancing."

I gritted my teeth so hard I thought they'd crumble into dust. The man was so annoying. And so sexy.

EIGHT

THE ANSWERING MACHINE LIGHT was blinking "5" when I got home. I hit the play button and scanned my almost empty refrigerator.

"It's Jerry, baby. Call me."

"Jerry here. It's important that you call me."

"Jerry. Call. Soon."

"It's me. I need to talk to you."

"I'm in trouble and need your help."

I picked up the phone and called Madeleine. "There's nothing in my fridge. How do you feel about some Mexican food? I need to get out of the house, anyway."

"What do you mean? You've been out all day. We could order a pizza or Chinese."

"No, no, no." A beep. Call waiting. "Look, if you don't want to eat with me, just say so. I'm starved."

"If we had stayed at the funeral, I'm sure we would have been invited back to the house. I'll bet the food was to die for. Oops, bad choice of words. You know what I mean. But instead…"

"Yeah, yeah, I get it. We spent the afternoon in a much more exotic setting, the interrogation room of our local police station. Look, are we on for dinner or what?" Why were we arguing over food?

"Okay. Give me at least an hour to get ready—"

"Now! I mean, I want to go now. I'll meet you at the

Mexican restaurant in the plaza." I hung up, grabbed my purse and hurried out the door. My cell rang. I checked caller ID. It was Jerry, so I shut it off. In my book, hunger trumped a call from my husband. No *emergency* of his had ever warranted instant action on my part. When he said he was in some kind of pickle, it usually meant with a woman or he needed money or he was in jail for running a red light under the influence. If this case was the exception, then too bad. He had cried wolf one time too many.

I should have known better than to expect Madeleine to be on time. She went nowhere in public unless she was perfectly turned out. So I waited. I was on my second Margarita and second bowl of chips and salsa when she finally appeared, breathless. She wore a colorful, multi-tiered ankle-length skirt and white peasant blouse. On her tiny, French-pedicured feet were slave sandals, the strap around the ankle emphasizing the shapeliness of her slender feet.

The handsome, dark-haired waiter looked at her with admiration and perhaps a hint of Latin passion. She tilted her head and pursed her Cupid's-bow lips. "I'll have one of those." She pointed at my glass with the ring finger of her left hand. An awkward movement, but the gesture showed she wasn't wearing a diamond or a wedding band.

Before I could even take a breath, her drink appeared in front of her with another, much larger bowl of chips and salsa.

"You're late." My tone was snappish.

Madeleine opened her mouth to explain her tardiness, but I raised my hand to halt her words. "Not only did I miss your company earlier, but now that you're here, the service has improved about a thousand percent. When I arrived, the waiter took fifteen minutes to even make it over here and another fifteen to get my drink."

"How many of these have you had?" She took a demure sip of her Margarita and licked her lips.

"Never mind that. I've got a crisis on my hands."

Madeleine looked skeptical.

The waiter scurried over and asked if "madam's drink was to her liking."

Madam dropped her glance and fluttered her eyelashes. "Perhaps a little too sour." He grabbed the glass with a waiter-like flourish and swept the offending drink away to the bar, returning in less than a nanosecond with another. He hovered at the table while she took a small taste. He cocked one dark eyebrow.

Madeleine looked him right in the eyes. "Perfect." I couldn't tell if she meant the drink or him.

He flashed his Latin smile and departed.

"Why didn't you just ask him to join us? Or better yet, you could accidentally drop your phone number onto his serving tray."

"About this crisis." She settled back into the booth and threw her arm across the back of the seat, hitting the head of the man seated behind us.

"You saw what happened today. PI Montgomery is way too nosy about my life. And when I got home, I had 5 messages from Jerry demanding that I call him. I've got two men I want to avoid. Then there's the murder thing."

"I thought you told me not to worry about the murder thing."

I skewered her with what I wanted to believe was

a scathing look, but the tequila had already taken the edge off my usually razor-sharp regard. "What I haven't told you is Valerie Sanders and I go way back."

"Yeah, I know that."

"What! You know what?"

She caught the waiter's eye, a feat difficult to accomplish now that more patrons had entered for dinner, and pointed to her glass.

"Valerie and I only chatted briefly at the shop, but she told me a bit about the two of you. She said she knew you from Connecticut and that she wouldn't have brought her clothes to us if she had known you were one of the owners. I guess using your maiden name fooled her. Good thing for us, too. She really didn't like you, did she?"

"Well, no, but—"

"Does Frida know?"

The waiter placed another drink in front of her and asked if we wanted to order.

I pointed my finger at the kitchen. "Go away."

He did.

"See, now that's probably why Valerie didn't like you. You're so rude."

"What did she say about me?"

I never did find out because just then an explosion rocked the restaurant, blowing out several plate glass windows in the front. People screamed and ducked under their tables. Others ran for the back. Waiters dropped their trays and rushed toward the back of the room. Cooks streamed from the kitchen into the dining room. People just entering hit the floor, covering their heads. Some of them crawled away from the noise toward the bar area, which was on the left and to the back. Shouts, cries, and moans filled the room. The manager rushed into the main part of the restaurant, trying to assure patrons that everything was fine. Luckily, the window seats had all been empty, so the flying glass only cut a few people.

"Everyone be calm," the manager said. "It looks like one of the cars in the parking lot caught fire and exploded. That's what blew out the windows. I called nine-one-one."

It was all over in a few seconds. I too had dropped to the floor and crawled under our booth, where all I could see was people's feet running back and forth. I had to know what was happening. I peeked from under the tablecloth and raised my head a little so that I could look out the windows. Sure enough, something was burning out there. What was once a car was now only a mass of twisted and seared metal, flames shooting from the wreckage. Despite its mangled state, something about the former vehicle looked familiar to me.

I heard sirens and saw the blue lights of emergency vehicles on the road. I stood up and glanced across the table to where Madeleine had been, but she was gone. I looked under the table. Not there. I peered around the room and found her hanging onto the waiter at the end of the bar.

How did she get over there?

I watched her plant a kiss on his cheek then walk back to our table.

"He rescued me. He was standing at the end of our row of booths, and he could have run the other way, but he tore over here, picked me up and carried me toward the bar, farther away from the windows. Now that's what I call service."

I stood up and glared across the room at our waiter. "What about my safety?" I yelled. "What about me?" I pounded my chest, stuck out my chin in a belligerent manner and then slumped back down onto the bench. It was good to get that off my chest even though he probably couldn't hear me.

"You told him to go away. Remember?"

EMTs arrived and checked over the patrons who had been hit by flying glass. Luckily, they had all been seated far enough from the windows that their wounds were superficial. A few people were still hysterical from the shock, so emergency personnel examined and calmed them as well. Meanwhile, fire trucks surrounded the vehicle and were extinguishing the flames.

"Some excitement, huh?" said Madeleine's waiter, who was refreshing the drink she had spilled thanks to his Tarzan act.

I clasped my empty glass with a grip almost tight enough to break the little green-glass cactus stem as I watched the fire fighters spray fire retardant on the smoking vehicle. To be precise, they were spraying the hood of *my* car. My sexy red Miata convertible. The only one I'd seen in these parts. The one that always got me attention when I drove into a parking lot. The one that was paid for. The car I just had washed and waxed for $150 at SudsUp, where the guy applying the coat of wax told me he lusted after my car. My car. Not me. Gone. What happened? An accident? Or…

By the time Frida arrived at our booth, I'd propped my chin on the edge of my Margarita glass for added support. "Your car is a total loss," she said.

"Right." I raised my head. Frida's blurry face came

into view. I licked a bit of salt off the edge of my glass. "Maybe another drink?"

Madeline chimed in on this one. "You've had enough. I told Paco not to serve you any more Margaritas."

Frida looked puzzled. "Who's Paco?"

"My, I mean, *our* waiter," Madeleine said.

"She's right. I've had enough and he's her waiter, not mine. I could hardly get a tortilla chip out of the guy."

"She seems to be taking the car thing awfully well," said Frida, turning to Madeline. "Well, if you overlook the drinking."

"Tell me. Tell me…" I grabbed Frida's arm.

"Tell you what?"

"I forget." I propped my head on my elbows and looked across the table at her. "Oh, yeah, tell me how that happened to my car."

"We don't know yet, but we think somebody put an incendiary device under your hood."

"They killed my car on purpose? The perp committed car murder?"

"What's an 'incendiary whatever'?" Madeleine asked, while sending a flirtatious finger wave over to Paco, who was standing near the kitchen door. He smiled and waggled his fingers in reply.

"A bomb. Someone put a bomb under my sweet little car and Boom! Well, you heard it. Blammy. In a million charcoaled pieces."

"Lucky you weren't in it." Frida's words poured over me like cold water. I was suddenly sober.

"I want to go home." I rose on shaky legs. I could

have been crisped in that explosion. "Wait. First I have to go to the bathroom and throw up."

FRIDA DROVE ME home in her cruiser. We left Madeleine sitting at the bar, waiting for Paco to get off work.

"That's twice now. Someone's trying to kill me."

"There was something before the car?" Frida turned her head toward me, a look of concern on her face.

I relayed Alex's comment about how Valerie and I looked alike.

"Your PI thinks you were the target?" Frida seemed to take his idea seriously. "I never thought about that possibility. When were you going to share this with me?"

She turned the corner and started to pull over to the curb in front of my house.

"No, no. Go! Go!" I tried to jerk the wheel out of her hands and turn the car back into the middle of the lane.

"Let go of the wheel. What are you doing?"

I would have stayed at the restaurant and watched Madeleine and Paco feed each other chips and salsa if I'd known Jerry would be sitting on my front steps. There it was, the answer to my demolished car and the nagging doubt about the killer missing his intended target.

I jumped out of the car, grabbed him by the shirt-front, jerked him to his feet and began to shake him. "You creep. You sent a cheap hit man to do me in and when he bungled the job, you hired someone to blow me up in my car. Well, he got the car, but I'm still alive." I balled my hand up into a fist and prepared to hit him.

Frida grabbed my arm. "Whoa. Who is this?"

"My husband and the guy who tried to kill me. Twice! Arrest him."

NINE

OKAY. MAYBE I was wrong about Jerry. Maybe he didn't hire anyone to do me in. Maybe he did the work himself, but I had my doubts. Jerry might have been inspired to simplify his life by getting me out of it, but he didn't have the cojones to get his hands dirty.

I could tell that Frida was reluctant to arrest him. She didn't draw her gun and her handcuffs remained on her belt.

"So this is Jerry, your husband who lives in Connecticut, right? And you suspect him of long-distance attempted murder?"

I looked down into Jerry's cola-colored eyes. We were the same height when barefoot, but, you know me, I like my stilettos. From my birds-eye perspective, Jerry's expensive haircut didn't hide a growing bald spot. I still held onto his shirt. He struggled against my hands, trying to pry them off his lapels.

"Look, Evie, I have no idea what you're talking about, but if someone's been trying to kill you, I need to know what's going on. I'm worried. I tried to reach you several times today to let you know I'd be in the area."

I stuck my face closer to his and narrowed my eyes. His eyes did a little dance around their sockets, a sure sign he was keeping something from me.

"See. He admits it. He was here. If he didn't plant

the bomb himself, he had someone else do it." I grabbed more firmly onto the fabric.

"Evie, honey, this is a four hundred dollar shirt. Could you back off a little?"

"The car bomb was vintage Jerry, you idiot. You hired a real boob to do your work for you."

"Calm down. Why would I want to kill you?"

"Because I won't sign the divorce papers?" That couldn't be the reason. Jerry wasn't the type to worry about such legal status designations as married, separated, or divorced.

Frida stood listening to our exchange, her hip cocked to one side, her right hand on the butt of her gun.

"I don't get it," Frida said. "Why won't you just divorce him? From what I've heard at our get-togethers, you certainly don't love him and you moved all the way down here to get away from him. He cheats on you almost daily, gambles away huge chunks of money at the horse races and associates with known felons. I think the magic's gone. Why not just sign on the dotted line?"

Jerry looked shocked. "She said all that about me?"

"And more, but I've got to get back to the office to file my report on the bombing and fire." Frida continued to look at me with curiosity while I twisted Jerry's shirt tighter in my hand.

"Once I get on my feet financially, I'll cut the jerk loose. Until then, I owe him money. He fronted me for the consignment shop."

"I'd forgive the loan, but…" Now he attempted to wriggle free of my hold by grabbing my hand in his and prying at my fingers.

I held tight. "We signed a legal agreement for the

money. I owe you the original amount with interest, and I intend to pay."

"I've got to run," said Frida, "but here's a thought. You don't have to be married to pay back the money. You're not making sense, Eve."

By now, Jerry and I were engaged in a tug of war with his shirt. I let go suddenly and he stumbled backwards, catching himself only a second before his butt hit my steps.

"Fine. Here's the thing," I said. "I'm on his health insurance policy. I can't afford to pay for my own insurance until I make a go of the store. I need you, Jerry."

"That's the nicest thing you've said to me in months." He smoothed his shirt, pulled the front down and tucked the bottom into his pants.

"I'm not trying to be nice. It's just the way things are. I don't want to need you, but I do."

Frida flapped her arms against her sides. "Well, there you are. That makes sense. When it appears the business is definitely a go, you get your divorce. What could be easier?" She turned to leave.

"Yeah, but I need the papers signed *now*. My girlfriend's pregnant. That's why I was trying to reach you. I need to marry her."

"Oh, don't be a drama queen. Lots of people wait until after the baby's born to tie the knot. In a couple of months the shop should be in the black. You can wait until then." I paused. I didn't really believe that Jerry was behind the car bombing or Valerie's death. In all fairness, I was the drama queen, but right now I saw both fear and desperation on his face.

"What's up? This can't have anything to do with uh—"

"Monica."

"Monica's pregnancy. I don't see you as the kind of man who could be pushed into a shotgun marriage. You're just trying to get my sympathy."

Frida had turned toward her car, but she hesitated. "So you *do* have reason to want Eve out of your life?"

"Yes, but not one good enough to kill her."

"What would be enough to kill for?" Certainly not the arrival of a stork. I suspected something else was going on with Jerry. He kept looking up and down the street, his feet restless on the sidewalk, as if he might need to put them to work suddenly and sprint out of there. He shook his head.

"Jerry. Tell me."

"My girlfriend's pregnant and she says it's mine, but—"

"So," Frida broke in, "wait until the kid is born and have a DNA test." Frida looked at Jerry as if he was the dumbest man she had ever met. Which, in my opinion, certainly could have been true.

"Okay, there's a baby on the way, and she told you it was yours. What else?" I knew there was something bigger than pregnancy bothering him.

"Her last name is Napolitani." He wouldn't look at me.

Now I got it. "Her father is Nappi Napolitani, right?"

Jerry nodded his head.

"He wants you to marry his daughter regardless of the paternity issue."

Jerry nodded his head again.

"I'm the only thing standing in the way of a nice, big Italian wedding."

Jerry nodded his head.

I stood there in the warm Florida night and stared off into the scrub palmetto fields beyond my house.

"Give me the papers." I held out my hand, and Jerry fished them out of his jacket pocket along with a pen. I signed and handed him the pen and the papers. "Frida, would you mind giving me a ride over to the Burnt Biscuit Bar?"

Frida hesitated. "Don't you think you've had enough to drink?"

"I'm stone cold sober. By the way, Jerry, do you think Nappi keeps the work in the family or does he farm out his hits to independent operators? I mean, just so I know what to look for, in case you don't get word to him in time."

"I don't know. We're not that close. I mean, aside from his daughter, all my dealings with him have been business."

"So there's a contract out on you?" Frida asked as we made our way back to the cruiser. "Knowing that might make it easier for me to find out who planted that device in your car."

"Oh goody for you." I opened the passenger door.

"I really can't drive you to a bar. I'll drop you at headquarters. It's down the street from the Burnt Biscuit."

"Wait, Evie!" yelled Jerry.

I got into the car, slamming the door and locking it. Now I was out of his life, I longed for him to be out of mine. He banged on the window. I hit the button and let the glass descend an inch.

"What?"

"I thought you might put me up for the night."

"Your thinking is wildly delusionary. There are hotels, you know."

"Fine. I thought we could be friends, but you're making yourself rather difficult to like."

"Boo hoo. What a loss for me."

"One last thing before you go get drunk."

"I'm not planning on getting drunk. I'm planning on rounding up as many cowboys as I can find to protect me from your bed-partner's relatives. You've made my life very difficult and possibly very short."

"That money you owe me? Even if I call off Nappi with these divorce papers, he's not gonna like an outstanding loan once I'm family."

Oh, crap! That hadn't crossed my mind. "I'll pay you. Just tell him that."

"Are we done here?" Frida tapped her fingers on the steering wheel. "I wasn't kidding. I've got paperwork to do."

"Punch it, sister." She did, and I watched in the side view mirror as Jerry faded into the sweltering central Florida night. I hoped an errant alligator would invite Jerry along for an underwater swim.

Frida drove for several blocks without a word. Then she slowed and turned to me.

"You believe him? That some Mafioso is responsible for your destroyed car?"

"Maybe."

"Despite the bungled job?"

"It could have just been a warning."

She drove on in silence for a few blocks. "I'm gonna

drop you here and go back to have a few words with your ex."

"Take him down to the station, feed him lots of coffee and deny him the bathroom. But I'll bet he doesn't know anything more than what he told us tonight. Feel free to make him uncomfortable for the sake of information." I paused. "Nah, just do it...for me."

NOTHING BRINGS OUT a cowboy's chivalry like a gal in danger, unless, maybe, there's a calf that's wandered off from its mama. In my case, letting all my dance partners at the Burnt Biscuit Bar know that my life was being threatened by the mob was like driving a chuck wagon into the midst of a cattle drive. I was three deep in Stetson protection. I only wanted one or two of them to provide backup for the evening—I assumed Jerry would deal with Papa Napolitani soon, thus ending the threat—but somehow, every one of them got involved in arranging my protection. They promised twenty-four-hour surveillance of my house, my store and my person. I assured them protection was only necessary for the night. They assured me I could have what I wanted, for as long as I needed it. Cowboys are real gentlemen that way.

Rob Cassidy, owner of one of the largest cattle ranches in the area, insisted I borrow his extra pickup truck when he heard that my car now resembled a burned meat patty. A call on his cell, and several minutes later, one of his hands showed up with the keys to an old Ford Ranger. Upon inspection, I discovered that this generously loaned green truck had over a hundred thousand miles on her and the pungent smell of cow manure embedded in the fabric of the seats.

"I know this isn't your style," Rob said, closing the driver-side door for me, "but it's all I've got right now. My Escalade is in the shop. That old one-horned Brahma bull took offense when I drove it into the pasture. Protecting his ladies, I guess. He punched out the side panel. I'm driving the other one right now, but as soon as I get the first one back, it's yours."

"Oh, don't worry. This is fine for tonight. I've got rental on my insurance policy, so I'm sure I'll have something to drive by tomorrow night."

I pulled out of the parking lot and drove off toward home. In my rearview mirror, I spotted my babysitter for the night, Cody Frenchot, in his Ford pickup. Another car followed behind him, too far back for me to identify either make, model, or driver. Another protector? Or the hit man?

I chided myself for getting so worked up about Jerry's future father-in-law. Daddy probably called off the hounds when Jerry phoned him, divorce papers in hand. Surely I'd seen the last of his handiwork in my charred car, and I was finally safe again. Unless he wanted to encourage me, using some equally unpleasant technique, to pay back the loan sooner than I had planned.

My cell played "Cheap Sunglasses."

"Hello."

"We need to talk," said PI Alex.

"So talk."

"In person."

"You know where I live and you must know I'm heading there now. We can have this conversation on the front steps."

"What, no nightcap?"

It was a tempting offer, but I'd had a long day. "I need sleep after the evening I've had. I'd rather not be bothered by some PI who thinks a couple of dances and a goodnight kiss make me an easy target."

"Ooh, we are testy tonight."

I flipped my phone shut and turned into my drive. Cody pulled over to the curb in front of the house, and our mysterious tail did the same. Not a hit man at all, Alex stepped out of the car. Before he could approach me, beefy Cody jumped out of his truck and positioned himself between Alex and me.

"Looking for someone, buddy?"

The two stood toe to toe, each well over six feet, Cody outweighing Alex by a good twenty steer-roping pounds.

"It's okay, Cody. He's something like a friend."

"Well, you said some fella from up north was after you, and this guy sure don't look like he belongs here." In the light of the rising moon, Cody took in the polo shirt and khaki pants that were Alex's signature wear.

"He won't be here for long. He's harmless." That was a lie. No one as yummy looking as Alex could be completely harmless.

Cody continued to stand there and, for a moment, I thought he intended to plant himself permanently in that spot on my lawn. Finally, having made his point, he settled back on his boots and turned toward his truck.

"I'll be right here if you need me," he said.

"Make this quick," I told Alex. "I've had a tough day."

"I thought you might like to know," he said. "My client objects to my association with you, so I'm out of a job."

_____

TEN

"OUT OF WORK, are you? And I'm supposed to do what?" I stood facing him, eye to eye, my hands on my hips. "Hire you?" Maybe that wasn't such a bad idea. I wondered what the going rate was for a private investigator. I was even more curious about why he had sought me out to unload his troubles.

"Could we go in and get comfortable?" He was pleading.

Get comfortable. Could that be a euphemism for something else, something I shouldn't be thinking about? I couldn't help myself. A picture of his naked body in my bedroom appeared in high-def in my mind. I was only guessing, but it looked fine. My imagination was in overdrive after all the time spent alone.

"Uh, sure." I waved to my guardian angel Cody and unlocked the door.

"Coffee?" I tossed my purse on the couch. He hesitated as though about to refuse, then nodded. I headed toward the kitchen.

"Are you okay?" he asked, starting to follow me.

I turned to face him. Big mistake. His damn azure eyes explored my face, then traveled down my body. "Sorry for the inspection, but I heard about your car."

"I'm fine, really."

He walked toward me.

"Sit." I pointed at the couch. He sat.

"I guess you must be a little nervous after tonight's events."

He had no idea. I had sweated so much from anger and fear that my clothes felt wet as the Serengeti plains during rainy season.

If I could just keep myself busy while he sat sprawled on my couch, I figured he had a fighting chance of not being jumped by a damp broad emanating tequila and estrogen. I fled into the kitchen to make coffee, but the task of activating my simple Mr. Coffee machine wouldn't keep my hands off Alex for long. Why couldn't I have a complicated device like an espresso maker? Those gadgets took too much time and concentration to allow for seduction.

"Talk to me." I was lurking, er, working, behind the kitchen island. "You can begin by telling me what happened with your client."

Out of the corner of my eye, I saw him start to rise from the couch. I yelled at him to sit again. He ignored me. "Don't come in here. I can't make coffee when somebody's in my kitchen."

"Forget the coffee, then. Come here."

"In a minute." I punched the brew button and looked at him. Damn, but my hormones were unruly tonight. He walked over to me and took my hand, leading me to the couch. He was doomed.

"My client let me go because he said my relationship with you created problems. I find that odd, don't you?"

"Maybe. I could say more if I knew who your client was, but I can guess."

He was holding my hand, turning it around in his and massaging the fingers.

"That's still confidential information. You know I can't reveal a client's identity."

Then the truth hit me. He wasn't here out of concern for me. He was simply on a fishing expedition, and not the kind where you end up with a crispy trout in a pan.

"Oh, don't be so coy. If your client let you go today, it's because he, not she, saw us together at the funeral. When he, not she, asked you about it, you admitted that we had gone out on a dinner date."

Alex pulled back, surprise on his face. "Wow, great powers of deduction."

"Mr. Sanders hired you and now he's expressed some concern about your relationship with me, and you want to know what set him off. Am I right? Oh, and, of course, you're just worried sick about me."

"Evie..."

I pulled my hand out of his. "Don't call me Evie. Only one person calls me Evie, and that's—"

"Me." Jerry walked out of my bedroom, a towel wrapped around his middle, his hair mussed as if he'd stepped out of the shower and dried off just moments before.

"You should have told me you had company." Alex spoke through clenched teeth.

"If only I'd known," I said. "Jerry, what the hell are you doing in my house? I thought I told you to get a hotel room."

"Yeah, well, I tried, but there's a Western Days Festival in town. They're all full. I should have known. There were no car rentals available at the airport when I flew in. I had no choice."

I walked over to him and jerked the towel off. Underneath, he had his shorts on. As I had suspected.

I was fuming with frustration. And maybe just a little bit of fear. "The last thing I need right now is for your future bride or daddy-in-law to find that you spent the night here."

I spun on my heel and looked at Alex, whose expression had changed from irritation to amusement.

"You need to wipe that grin off your face. Both of you get out of my house." I raised my voice loud enough that my cowboy babysitter could hear, and, right on cue, he banged through the door.

"Shouldn't you be holding a pistol? What is that anyway?" I pointed to the very ugly weapon that Cody was holding in his hand.

"It's a cattle prod."

"That sounds lethal," I said.

"And electric. You heard the lady." Cody waved the prod. "Out."

"But my clothes…and a ride. I've been taking taxis all over." Jerry eyed the weapon warily. By now both he and Alex were out the door and standing on my porch.

"Wait a minute." I marched into the bedroom and returned with Jerry's clothes. He reached for them, but I whipped them out of his reach. "Did you call Daddy Napolitani and tell him I signed the papers?"

"Of course. I'd be in as much trouble with him as you if I hadn't been successful."

"And the loan?"

"We didn't talk about that."

There was enough commotion on the porch to alert the neighbors. Lights came on in houses on both sides of the street and people poked their heads out the front doors. A black SUV cruised by, slowed, then sped up.

"This isn't a block party," I called out to the curiosity seekers.

"What papers?" asked Alex.

I snapped at him. "None of your business."

"Let's go, boys." Cowboy Cody gave a wave of his hand as if herding two harmless little dogies.

"What papers?" I heard Alex ask Jerry. Jerry stopped on the sidewalk to pull on his pants and shirt, the latter still wrinkled from its earlier run-in with my fist. He hopped from leg to leg, putting on his shoes. He stuffed his socks into his pants pocket. At the curb, the two of them conferred for a moment. I couldn't hear what they were saying, but moments later Alex drove off with Jerry in the passenger seat. *Damn!* Now I'd given the two of them an opportunity to bond. That couldn't work out well for me.

WHEN I HAD the opportunity to talk with my insurance agent the next morning, he asked if Madeleine had been with me when the car blew.

"We were together, but this time, she wasn't responsible for the destruction."

Matt, my agent, and Cody, my bodyguard, sat at my kitchen table, where we were all having coffee. When Matt had arrived earlier, he'd evinced no surprise at seeing Cody outside my place. News traveled fast around here, probably because it was so flat. There was nothing to get in the way of gossip as stories blew from one side of town to the other.

"I sure do like that little gal." Matt smiled, then shook his head. "We dated a few times, but she's real accident prone. I always worried that something would happen while we were on our date and she'll end up in the emergency room or in jail. I just couldn't handle the anxiety."

Cody nodded in agreement. He was the one who had been with her when she accidentally let the rodeo bulls out of the pen.

"I'm sorry, that little beauty is a total loss."

At first I thought that Matt was still talking about Madeleine. "Maybe therapy will help," I said. "She went to see a counselor just last week."

Matt looked puzzled. "You took your car to a shrink?"

"No, Madeleine went to a shrink." Both Matt and Cody perked up. "But I'd wait awhile before asking her out again. Better wait to see if the therapy takes."

Matt nodded and slid several papers across the table to me.

"So, here are the papers for your rental. The check for the car should be in your hands within a few days. It's not like there's any question of repairing her."

I RETURNED THE truck to Rob Cassidy, thanked him profusely and agreed to dinner at some point. Why not? The man was good-looking, rich, and single. I was grateful, poor, and recently divorced—very recently divorced. I tried not to make comparisons between him and PI Alex. My head told me to leave Alex alone, but every other cell in my body shouted "Go for it." My body won in a landslide. Why fight the popular vote?

I pushed into the back door of the shop only five minutes before we were to open. Madeleine stood in the middle of the store tapping her tiny, boot-clad foot and looking around.

"We're no better off today than we were two days ago. What we have here is boring."

The expression on her face told me that the euphoria she'd experienced in the restaurant last night with Paco had failed to spill over into the rest of the evening.

"So what happened?"

"I just told you. We got nothing."

"No, I mean with Paco."

"Who?"

"Your chips and salsa, perfect Margarita guy."

"Married."

"How'd you find that out?"

"His wife told me. You know, she's really nice."

I said nothing and waited.

"She heard about the blast at the restaurant, so she grabbed the kids and went to see if he was okay. She and I sat at a booth and talked. The kids're great, too. A five-year-old boy and a girl, two years. I told her to come into the shop, and we'd give her a ten percent discount."

"You're taking this very well."

"Don't believe it. I'm furious at him, that Mexican Lothario. It's not her fault. What do you think about asking her to join us for cards night with the gals?"

"I don't even want to give her the ten percent off. Are you out of your mind? You're just trying to get rid of the guilt you feel for flirting with a married man. Let it go, sweetie. You didn't do anything wrong."

"Okay, but I think she'll expect the ten percent."

"Fine. Look, why don't I take over the store today? You go back to the coast and visit our customers. See what you can bring back. Now that Valerie's funeral is over, I'm sure you'll find the women eager to go through their closets and weed out their clothes. It'll be relaxing for you."

"I'll go if I don't have to visit Cory."

"You don't have to visit Cory."

She produced a tiny smile then sighed. Her shoulders drooped. "What about you? You had one hell of a night."

"I want things to get back to normal as soon as possible. That means running this store. So shoo. Go find merchandise."

After Madeleine left, I looked around our little shop. She was right. We were down on goods by fifty percent. The publicity associated with the murder had worked to our financial advantage, at least for a while. Now I worried we'd be looked at as no different from the other consignment shops in town, even though we did feature high-end clothing. That also meant we charged higher prices than the others. I didn't know how long we could cash in on the bad luck of wealthy women to realize a little additional spending money. Of course, recent news suggested that there were other Bernie Madoffs out there ripping off their friends, families and wealthy investors, so maybe we still had a long run ahead of us.

In the meantime, I decided that it was time to clean up the mess in the back room. We had bags and boxes piled in the corner, many of which had been there since before Valerie's unfortunate demise. If I didn't cart that stuff to the dumpster out back, we'd have no room for new merchandise—assuming Madeleine was successful in getting some. She would be. The woman had enough charm to talk the West Palm society matrons out of their Rolls Royces if she wanted to, but we didn't carry them.

I pulled handfuls of crumpled newspaper out of the cardboard boxes and stuffed them into a trash bag. I worked steadily for several hours. No customers came into the store. It was as I suspected. The novelty of the murder had worn off and the horror of it had set in. Our business was sure to suffer. I broke down the boxes, tying them with twine and piling them at the back door to be loaded into the recycling bin. Wiping sweat from my face, I looked at what I'd accomplished. Only one corner of the room remained a mess of boxes and packing material. As I crumpled up a wad of packing material, something sharp bit into my hand.

"What the hell?"

I dropped the paper and looked at my thumb. A thin line of red erupted along its base and ran in a small rivulet onto my wrist. I looked down at the papers I'd thrown on the floor. Among the crumples lay a knife. It looked like the one used to kill Valerie, the one we thought came from the cutlery holder in the front of the shop. Obviously, either Madeleine or I had been careless when we unpacked the merchandise and left one of the knives in the box. This one.

Blood dripped onto the floor.

The shop bell rang, announcing a customer.

"Have a look around and use the dressing rooms if you like. I'll be with you in a second," I said.

As I ran from the back room, I caught sight of a woman looking through the front racks. Her back was turned to me.

"I had a little accident." I rounded the corner to the

hallway that led to our bathroom, where I grabbed some toilet paper to stem the flow.

I sat on the closed toilet lid nursing my wound. The knife in the body wasn't from our cutlery set. Someone else's then. Whose? We thought Valerie grabbed a knife out of the set and took it into the dressing room to protect herself and that it was *that* knife the killer used on her. But we had inadvertently failed to unpack one of the knives to the set and didn't notice it was missing when we put out the display. The murder weapon couldn't have been our display knife. Supposing she brought a knife from home to accomplish the same purpose? Or the killer had?

"Can I help?" asked a voice from the open doorway. "Or am I interrupting something private, as usual?" I jumped up from my seat. My intruder's glance traveled to the floor, where the bloody tissues I'd tossed toward the wastebasket lay. His eyes came to rest on my hand.

"Oh, it's you."

"That cut looks pretty bad." Alex pulled the toilet paper off my thumb and examined it. "You could use a stitch or two."

I glanced down at my hand. With the toilet paper and pressure off the wound, the cut began to bleed again. I certainly couldn't drive.

"Okay, fine," I said, "but I need to stop by the police station and drop something off with Frida first."

He helped me off the throne and followed me into the back room.

The knife was gone.

I turned on him.

"Did you take it?"

"Take what?" That azure innocence again.

"Was there anyone else here when you came in?"

"Someone was just leaving as I entered. A woman."

"Yeah, she came in as I was running to the bathroom. I only caught sight of her back. What did she look like?"

"Maybe you should sit down for a minute and tell me what's going on."

Instead of taking his suggestion, I dropped to my knees and began to shuffle through the newspapers lying on the floor. "Maybe she came in here and accidentally kicked it out of sight."

"Kicked what out of sight?"

"Never mind."

I couldn't find the knife. Suddenly my vision clouded, my stomach did a cartwheel and everything appeared in an ugly shade of blackish yellow. "That's a really bad color for you," I said to Alex, who appeared discolored along with the rest of my world.

Next thing I knew I was lying on my storeroom floor with my legs propped up on a chair and my head cradled in Alex's arms. He was sitting on the floor with me.

I stared up into his eyes. "You'll wrinkle your khakis."

"I'll take that chance."

Admit it, girl, this feels good, well, as good as anything can feel after you've fainted. I snuggled closer to him. He didn't back off.

"Okay. When you're feeling up to it, we're off to the emergency room."

"But Frida—"

"Frida can wait."

"Okay. I think I want to stay here for a while." Why waste a good cuddle with a sexy man?

"You have to go to the hospital. Let's get you up." He held out his hand and helped me to my feet.

The dizziness seemed to have subsided.

"Hey, wait a minute. If someone came in here and then left as you entered, why did I only hear the shop bell ring once?"

With Alex's help, I walked on my Jell-O legs out of the back room and into the shop. The door opened as we made our way past the counter and toward the front racks.

Madeleine entered, her arms filled with clothes. She took one look at me, then shifted her gaze to Alex and tossed the clothes over a rack.

"Eve, what did he do to you?"

I shook my head to indicate Alex wasn't at fault. Madeleine stopped midstride. She turned toward the door and looked at the push bar.

"What happened to the bell?" The bell, which had been tied on a ribbon so that it would jangle when the door was opened, lay on the floor. It was crushed flat, as if someone, furious with its tinkling sound, had stomped on it.

ELEVEN

THE THREE OF US sat in the emergency room. It was mid-afternoon and only two other folks were waiting to be seen. One was a small boy with what looked like the kind of head injury that young boys tend to get when they fall out of trees, attempt a wheelie or try out in-line skates without a helmet. My injury would have to wait—he had the more serious bleed.

The other prospective patient, the guy hacking up a lung on the far side of the room, looked as if he'd never make it to the examining room. My guess was that he'd be taken first, but I was wrong. As it turned out, he wasn't even the one waiting to see the doctor. The woman with him, who looked just fine to me, was the prospective patient. I guessed the guy was just a heavy smoker. The boy went first.

"Uh, Madeleine," said Alex, "could I have a few moments with Eve alone. There's something I've got to tell her in private."

Madeleine did her best not to look surprised. She nodded, claimed a need for the ladies' room and strolled down the hallway, only stopping to inquire for directions at the sign-in counter.

I watched her leave. "I'm not so certain she should go off alone," I said. "This is a hospital, and there's no telling what trouble she might get herself into."

"She's a big girl," said Alex.

"No, she's not. She's tiny, but powerful like a bull-dozer."

"Eve." He took my uninjured hand in his. I remembered the two of us having this handholding encounter once before, that morning when I had figured out that he was using me for information. I tried to jerk my fingers away. He held on tighter.

"I'll call security if you don't let go," I whispered between clenched teeth. "I'll make a scene."

He dropped my hand, and I immediately regretted my words. His touch was so, *so* sensuous, as his hands caressed my fingertips and moved down onto my palms. I was willing to bet he gave a great foot rub, too.

"Okay, fine, but I really am worried about you."

I made as if to get up out of my chair, but he held up one finger, asking me to wait a minute before I turned away.

"Let me get to it. I know why you and Valerie fought. Mr. Sanders told me. I think he's going to tell Frida. If you haven't leveled with her yet, you might want to tell her the truth."

"You believe Sanders' story? Why would you take his word? Looks to me like he's simply trying to pin his wife's murder on somebody."

"Jerry confirmed the story."

I jumped out of the chair and stood as firmly on my teetering stilettos as a wounded girl could. "You told Jerry about what Sanders said? *Jerry?*"

"No, Jerry told me about the feud on his own."

I sat abruptly, but at that moment the nurse called my name. I had to pop out of the chair again.

"Stay here. I'll be right back."

"I could come in with you."

I considered his offer, along with the possibility that they might want me to change into one of those white hospital gowns. If Alex was going to see me naked, I wanted it to be on my terms, preferably in a bedroom of my choosing and in one of my sexy nightgowns.

I shook my head and followed the nurse. Before I stepped into the examining room, I turned and waggled my finger at him. "Stay put."

I LIKED TO believe I wasn't a big baby, but when it came to pain, I was a wimp.

"I don't really need stitches, do I?" I asked the doctor after he examined my thumb.

"You do. Otherwise the cut won't heal properly. It'll keep opening up. Chance of infection is greater." I watched as he reached for a syringe.

"I don't want to look." I didn't. The shot hurt like hell, but my hand quickly went numb. After the stitching, I asked the nurse for a lollipop. I thought I deserved something for undergoing the procedure.

"No, no. Too much sugar." She swept her hand toward an array of small action figures lined up on a shelf. "You can choose one."

I carried the Minnie Mouse figure in my unbandaged hand and looked for Alex in the waiting room. He was gone. *Damn.* I hadn't taken him for the type to flee the impending wrath of a tall, blonde woman. I twirled Minnie in my fingers. "He certainly wouldn't deserve you," I told her.

Madeleine had to be around here someplace. She'd take me home.

Down the hall from the waiting room came a

woman's scream, the sound of metal falling onto the tile floor and the crash of a large object against the wall. That had to be my ride.

A wheelchair came flying through the swinging doors at the end of the hallway, pushed by an elderly man dressed in a tropical shirt and plaid Bermuda shorts. In the chair sat a woman, probably his wife. There was familiar terror written all over her face. She kept turning her head to peer down the hall from which she had come. "Faster, Harold. The mad woman's gaining on us."

I expected to see Madeleine bolt through the door. I wasn't disappointed.

"I'm so sorry," she shouted to the couple. "I'm just clumsy, you see."

Madeleine had somehow wrapped herself in the tubing of a portable intravenous apparatus and was attempting to disentangle herself while pulling and pushing the mess toward the retreating couple. A few steps behind Madeleine came Alex, who grabbed her by the arm, held her still, and removed the tubing. By now the couple had alerted the security guard, and he was approaching Madeleine.

"That's her," said the old woman. "My husband was wheeling me down the hall for a spin when this crazy woman, arms flapping like a windmill, grabbed my tubing and pole and ran off with it."

"That's not true. I saw you remove the drip lines and abandon the apparatus in the hallway, but when I tried to return everything to you, you pushed me into that cart of bedpans. I got twisted up in the tubing. Don't you know your medication is in that bag?" Madeleine was working herself into a frenzy. Who could blame her? Apparently she had been trying to help this lying old woman.

"You ripped the needle out of my arm. I could have bled to death."

The man nodded, supporting his wife's statement.

The security guard turned his head back and forth from the couple to Madeleine with a look that said he wished he had the midnight shift when only druggies and gunshot victims came in.

"Madeline is telling the truth." It was Alex's voice, issuing from behind me. "She was trying to return the apparatus." Madeleine beamed with gratitude. The couple shook their heads. "Look at her arm," Alex continued. "The needle hasn't been torn out at all."

The doors to the hallway swung open once again and a man in surgical scrubs walked through. "There you are, Mr. and Mrs. Flynn. You're not trying to take a hike again, are you?"

The couple's mouths opened. No sound came out.

"They like to run down to the Twisty Cone for ice cream. Mr. Flynn, I told you she shouldn't be off her drip."

"It was her idea." Flynn pointed to his wife. "She made me do it."

"Well, now, let's get her back into her room, and we'll see what we can do." The doctor put his arm around Mr. Flynn's shoulders.

The old woman's eyes shot daggers at her husband and Madeleine. "We would have made our escape from this place," she said. "I'd be having a chocolate and peanut butter soft-serve twist right now, if you hadn't interfered." She wheeled her chair past Madeleine.

"Next time, mind your own business. Who do you think you are? A doctor or something?"

I could hear Mrs. Twisty Cone berating her husband and Madeleine as they accompanied the doc through the swinging doors and down the hallway.

"It really wasn't my fault this time," Madeline said.

"I know, honey, but you do manage to find trouble, don't you?" I put my arm around my friend and hugged her.

"Let's go home," said Alex.

"No. First I need to talk to Frida. Then I want to talk to you." I poked my finger into his chest. "No more lies."

"I haven't lied to you."

"Okay, then, no more prevarications." I should have been more direct and told him to just tell the truth.

"I don't think I know what that means."

"Yes you do. Don't play dumb. We need to talk more about what you've been telling me." Or haven't been telling me.

Alex and I walked out into the hospital parking lot and headed toward his car.

"Hey, what about me? Can I come along, too?" Madeleine called from behind us.

Alex looked at me for approval. I nodded.

"Sure, but could you stay a block or so behind us? I've seen what you can do when you get too close." Was Alex really worried or just teasing Madeleine? Maybe he was prevaricating again.

"YOU'RE RIGHT, OF COURSE." Alex steered the car through the evening traffic and into my subdivision. Madeleine was right behind us.

I was about to ask him what he meant, when I remembered what I was supposed to be doing.

"Hey, I want to talk to Frida." I reached for the steering wheel, but Alex shoved his muscular shoulder toward me, blocking my hand.

"You just had stitches, and the anesthetic will wear off soon. The best place for you to be is at home, lying down."

That sounded lovely.

"We'll call Frida from your place. After I get you settled in bed."

Even lovelier.

"What about Madeleine?"

"She can make you a cup of tea while I get Frida on the line."

We pulled up in front of my house and Madeleine jumped out of her car to help me through the door.

At that moment, as if on some predetermined medical schedule, the anesthetic wore off and my next sentence, which I intended to be "I'd prefer scotch to tea," came out something like, "Fraggle postle mag."

"You're white as a magnolia blossom," said Madeleine.

That might've sounded like a compliment, but I was a sun worshiper from the Northeast. I should have been as golden as a ripe papaya. Alex pulled me out of his car, took me in his arms, and carried me into the house.

He deposited me on the couch.

"Scotch." I pointed across the room at my liquor cabinet. He ignored me.

Keeping his promise, Alex dialed Frida. Madeleine busied herself in my kitchen.

"Get out of my kitchen," I yelled. Too late. The

sound of breaking dishes, followed by the ringing of my pots and pans hitting the floor, assaulted my ears. Silence followed. "Everything all right?"

"Fine. How would you feel about iced tea instead?"

"Okay, I guess."

I had no intention of drinking any kind of tea. I pulled myself up off the couch and walked with grim determination and wobbly legs over to my liquor cabinet.

"Not so fast." Alex grabbed the bottle out of my hand. Caught. "Nope. Frida will be right over. I explained your little accident to her."

"My little accident?" Madeleine said. "You told Frida about the hospital incident?" She handed me a glass of the weakest tea I'd ever seen.

"No," I said, "he told her about my hand." I waggled the bandaged thumb in the air to remind her.

"Oh, good. I'd hate for her to think that I had molested an old man and his wheelchair-bound wife."

"Alex wouldn't say that."

Madeleine looked relieved for a moment. Then her face scrunched up with concern. "I could only find one tea bag, and I used tap water. It comes out faster. You're giving her booze?" Madeleine looked at Alex with accusatory eyes.

"No. Tea should be enough. She's had quite a day."

"I can relate," Madeline said. "First those geriatric terrorists in the hospital and then I get here and can't reach the tea cups in the cupboard because stilts here has them on the top shelf." She paused and turned in my direction but didn't raise her eyes to meet mine. "Listen, hon, I think you could use some cups or mugs if you want coffee in the morning."

That was odd. I had plenty of cups and mugs.

Madeleine threw herself onto the end of the couch, grabbed the glass of tepid tea and took a sip. Then she looked me in the eye with one of those defiant I-dare-you-to-say-anything looks on her face.

The doorbell rang, saving Madeleine from injury by my good hand. Frida stood there.

"What's this about a knife?"

I told her about finding the blade and cutting myself.

"Let's have a look at it."

I held up my bandaged hand.

"No. The knife."

"Someone came into the shop while I was in the bathroom trying to stop myself from bleeding to death."

"Who?"

"I have no idea, but the person went out the door just as Alex entered. I think the bell startled her, so she smooshed it flat to keep it from ringing again. Alex saw her leave. What did you tell me she looked like?"

I took a sip of the tea. Not so bad. Actually, I was feeling pretty fine. The throbbing in my hand was letting up a bit, and I felt buoyed by the knowledge that Alex could identify the visitor. This case was fast coming to a close.

"I didn't. I'm not going to be much help. She looked like every other rich matron from the coast. Above average in height, I guess, although she was wearing heels. She had on huge, round sunglasses. Her hair was blonde, but she might have been wearing a wig. She had on a pleated navy skirt, red blouse, and white blazer."

He was right. An APB put out with that description would have netted the authorities every patron in the Neiman Marcus store at City Place.

I sighed. We were no further along on this case than we had been the day Valerie died. Only now, because Jerry had blabbed to Alex, I also had to worry about Alex telling Frida what he knew about our relationship.

"I think I might be able to clear up some of the questions about Valerie and Eve." Alex cleared his throat, as if nervous.

Here we go. I sank back into the couch cushions and yawned. Inwardly my nervous system was on high alert.

"I don't know what Eve has told you." Alex looked at Frida. "She sometimes likes to parcel out half-truths."

I perked up. "And you don't?"

He ignored me. "I was hired by Mr. Sanders, who was concerned about his wife. He paid me to follow her."

"Why was he concerned?" asked Frida.

"He didn't say. I originally assumed that I was dealing with a divorce case and that I would be gathering evidence against her. Then I met Eve. Mr. Sanders saw the two of us at the funeral and thought we seemed too friendly for his taste, so he fired me. With Valerie dead, I wasn't surprised that my services were no longer needed, but I was shocked at his rabid dislike of Eve. I wouldn't be telling you this—client confidentiality and all—but I got an interesting story from Jerry, very similar to the one I heard from Sanders."

Frida looked interested. "Go on."

"Please do." If I put anymore acid in my voice, I'd be spitting lemon seeds.

"Sanders invested some money with Jerry and lost it. The fault wasn't Jerry's, for once. The investment opportunity looked good in the beginning, but proved to be much like the Bernie Madoff Ponzi scheme. Sanders knew that Jerry had been cleared of any criminal involvement. Valerie, however, found out that Eve was Jerry's wife and, well, that set her on fire. There was Jerry's wife in her sights. She even threatened to pull her clothes out of the store. That's what the fight was about."

I breathed an inward sigh of relief and told my heart to stand down. The investment scheme gone bad was a part of what Valerie and I fought about, but it wasn't the important part. I smiled.

"Well, that's kind of what I told you." I looked at Frida.

"No, it's not at all what you told me," she said. "If Valerie was planning to pull her items out of your store, that would mean a loss of income for you."

"Not a reason for murder, if that's where you're going with this. She didn't threaten to pull her stuff out of the store. She couldn't. We had a signed contract. All our clients do."

Outside the front windows, I saw a car pull up. A woman with white hair got out. Oh, oh. Now things were going to get interesting.

TWELVE

"GRANDY!" I JERKED OPEN the front door. The short, rotund woman standing there threw her arms around me.

Worry lines etched her forehead. "What's wrong, Eve? All is not well here, is it?"

Whenever my grandmother shows up, I wonder if she is there to rescue me or cause more trouble. We have very similar personalities. Why wouldn't we? We are blood relatives, and she raised me from the day my parents' sailboat went down in the Sound. Their bodies were never recovered. I was nine then, and I can hardly remember a time before she came into my life. To me she is my Grandy and my mother.

Madeleine took one look at the woman in the doorway and flew across the room to embrace her.

"It's my little Madeleine." Grandy enveloped her in a hug. "You gotten into any trouble lately?"

Madeleine stole a glance in the direction of the kitchen, blushed and shook her head.

Grandy bore a striking resemblance to Paula Dean and was often mistaken for her, but once she opened her mouth, everyone could tell my Grandy wasn't the famous television cook. Her accent was pure Connecticut blueblood. Her secret was, she wasn't gentry at all. She had worked most of her life as a servant to the wealthy and was very good at imitating their speech.

"Max and I just got back from a week-long trip and

nothing was on our calendar," she said, "so I thought I'd drive down here to see what was wrong in your life."

I introduced her. She wiggled bejeweled fingers at everyone in the room then approached Alex with her hand held out. He reached out as if he meant to plant a kiss on her plump fingers, but instead he softly patted it. In return for his gallantry, she gave him one of her famous coquettish smiles. Even at seventy-five my Grandy oozed allure.

"So I see not everything is amiss." She continued smiling at him. Then she turned her attention to Frida. "But something is. A police detective, huh?" She grabbed the glass out of my hand and took a sip of it, wrinkling her nose at the taste. Plopping herself onto the couch, she patted the cushion next to her as a gesture for me to join her.

"Max isn't with you?" I asked. "I thought you said there was nothing on the schedule for a while."

Her eyes slid away from my gaze for a moment, then reconnected. "He's doing an overhaul of the boat engine. He said I should get out of his way and, since I had a dream about you last night, I thought I'd stop by."

Max was Grandy's third husband. The two of them ran a charter fishing boat out of Key West. Like all the Key West men over fifty, Max sported the Hemingway beard and mustache combination. He even entered the Papa Hemingway look-alike contest, which he had won several years in a row. Not lately, however. For, while "Papa" never aged, Max did, and the loss of hair put him at a disadvantage against the younger competitors.

"Enough about me." Grandy said, turning her attention to Frida. "What kind of trouble has Jerry gotten Eve into now?"

"Jerry?" asked Frida.

"My Eve is a good girl, within reason, of course. She does have her playful side, as I'm sure you've discovered, Mr. Montgomery." She threw a suggestive look his way.

"Call me Alex."

"Alex. Anyway, having a husband who plays as loose with the rules as Jerry does is bound to bring on a load of trouble."

"You'll be happy to know I divorced him."

"When?"

"Yesterday. He's getting married again, though. Soon."

Frida, Alex, and Madeleine filled Grandy in on Valerie's death, the car bombing and my more recent encounter with the knife.

"So how's the black SUV fit into this?" she asked.

"Huh?" I said.

"The one that keeps driving by here. There it goes again."

We all ran to the window and, sure enough, a black SUV with chrome wheels slowed in front of the house then sped up again, probably because of all the faces staring out through the glass.

"Half of the people in this town own a black pickup or SUV. Anybody get the plate number?" asked Frida. "I couldn't see because the sun was reflecting off of it."

No one else had even thought to check.

Frida got out of her chair. "I'm going out to the cruiser. If the vehicle comes by again, I'll follow it. You guys stay away from the window so we don't scare him off. Before I go, Eve, I've got some information about your car."

"Faulty wiring?"

"In a manner of speaking. Someone planted an incendiary device under your car, but whoever planted the bomb was incredibly stupid. That was the worst homemade bomb the arson boys had ever seen. It was dumb luck that it went off when it did. It was just as likely to blow when they were planting it as when you were driving."

Oh, now, that was comforting.

With the words "incredibly stupid" and "dumb luck," an image of my ex-husband flashed through my mind. Why was that, do you think?

"I can give you more details later." Frida dashed out to the police car, got in, and slid down in the seat. After a few moments, her head popped up and she signaled us to get away from the window.

Speaking of "incredibly stupid." We all took the seats that we had occupied before, except Madeleine, who slid beneath the window so that she could peer over the sill every few seconds.

"Go make some coffee." I waved her away from the window.

Madeleine looked at me with hurt in her eyes but stormed across the room and into the kitchen. I remembered the earlier episode with the iced tea just a little too late. By letting her roam free in my kitchen, I was just asking for more trouble, but I didn't have the heart to tell her not to bother with the coffee.

Alex turned his attention to Grandy. "Are you psychic? You said you felt something was wrong here?"

She chuckled at first, and then erupted into rumbling laughter. "I wish I were. I had a dream about you, darling, but that was after I got the message from you on my cellphone."

"I left that days ago."

"We get lousy cell service when we're out on the water. What's up? Something to do with Jerry, right?"

"Kind of." I wanted to talk to Grandy about Valerie Sanders, but I didn't want to have the conversation in front of the others, not even my best friend Madeleine, and certainly not Alex. "Madeleine. Come out here."

"I'm making coffee like you said."

"Never mind the coffee. I could use a pizza or some ribs. I'm starved. Maybe you and Alex could do a run to the Burnt Biscuit and get us all something." I turned my attention to Grandy. "I'll bet you're hungry after your drive, right?"

"They deliver. I'll put in a call." Madeleine grabbed the kitchen wall phone. "What does everyone want?"

I gave up. "Grandy and I haven't seen each other in months. We can catch up while you two do the hunting and gathering thing."

I thought that was pretty direct, but Madeleine persisted, trying to fill my shoes as a good hostess and oblivious to the request for privacy.

"I'm sure you have a lot to say to each other, but you need food, Eve. Besides, they deliver. We can save gas…"

Alex grabbed the receiver out of her hand and led her gently to the front door. "We'll be back soon," he said, waving.

Madeline protested, "We don't even know if they want ribs or pizza. With or without fries or slaw. Coke or Pepsi—"

"We'll get a little of everything." Alex opened the door and nudged her through.

I watched them drive off in Alex's car. Frida's head appeared over the top of the seat of her cruiser. She shot a look of disgust my way and shook her head, then disappeared once more below the level of the car window.

With everyone gone, Grandy and I could talk girl stuff, but she surprised me.

"I've got some news for you. Max and I have decided to downsize a bit."

"What's wrong?" I was suddenly aware of my Grandy's advancing years and worried that she and Max might be having health problems. "Are you and Max okay?"

She laughed, but I saw worry in her eyes.

"Oh, we're fine. It's the economy that's the problem. We've been running charters out of Key West for over twenty years now. The dock fees are killing us. They go up every year and our boat keeps getting older, just like us. In order to pick up enough charters to pay our fees *and* make money, we'd have to re-equip the boat or get a new one. We're just too damn old for that." She sighed. "Besides, we don't have that kind of money. To compete with the other charter companies, we would have to buy a much larger boat."

She shifted about on the couch and added, "Folks nowadays want to fish, yes, but they also want an up-scale experience—Jacuzzi tub in their room, gourmet meals three times a day, fancy dining area, fully equipped bar. We can't afford that." She jumped up from the couch and walked over to the window.

I steered her back toward the couch.

"I thought having a clean place to sleep and tasty grub for a few days was all anybody could want on a fishing charter," she said. "I always put together tuna salad sandwiches or burgers and sometimes we even cook the day's catch or steaks out on the grill. Now they want a flat screen TV and cocktails delivered to them in the lounge. We don't have a lounge and we're not getting one, either."

She gave me a defiant look. "We can't pay our docking fees any longer. We're busted, honey."

I put my arms around her soft, sloping shoulders. I'd never seen my Grandy beaten by anything. This was a first. She was always the one who led the way out of any trouble—financial or otherwise. She had been my compass in all the storms of adolescence. She was the only one who had warned me that marrying Jerry would be a mistake. Everyone else had agreed with her, but none had the courage to say so to my face.

"What will you do?" Any troubles I might be having seemed miniscule in comparison to the idea of Grandy without hope.

She shook herself free of my embrace.

"Now, let's not get too maudlin here. We'll manage."

"You could live with me."

"Have you lost your mind? We're not land people. We like a boat under our feet. If I can't feel the rock of the waves, I can't get to sleep."

"So, what are your plans?"

"We're heading for the marina in Key Largo, where a vacancy recently came up. Got a deal there. We'll only be doing day trips. Anyways, it's a lot closer to you than Key West. You can come down for a week-end to visit."

She reached up, patted my cheek and smiled. There was still concern written on her beautiful, cherubic face, but I could tell that she was finished talking about her woes for the evening.

"So, in your message you said that Valerie accused you of being a thief."

"Actually, she said that she never would have brought her items to our shop if she had known that I was married to Jerry. Then she put two and two together and realized that I was your granddaughter. That seemed to bother her just as much as my relationship with Jerry. She accused you of being a thief, saying that the apple didn't fall too far from the tree. I kind of popped her in the puss."

"I suppose you want to know what that remark was all about." Grandy fixed me with her round blue eyes.

"I didn't believe her for a moment. But, now she's dead, and I keep thinking that her comment might be relevant somehow. Alex thinks that whoever killed her was really after me."

"I can see how he might arrive at that conclusion, given the similarity in looks."

"How do you know that we looked alike?"

"Oh, come now. Even as children, you looked alike, age-difference aside. Valerie's nanny used to take her to the park in West Hartford, the same one I would take you to when the weather was nice. Your parents lived just a few blocks away."

"How did you know Valerie's family?"

"I worked for them when I was a young woman. I was one of their maids."

A quick smile created a tiny dimple, indicating a half-truth.

"Valerie's grandfather was my lover."

THIRTEEN

THIRTEEN

"YOUR *LOVER*?" I almost choked.

Grandy thumped me on the back.

"Surprised you, didn't I?" Her eyes twinkled with mischief.

She had a story to tell. I was eager to listen, but before she got started I ran to the kitchen to fetch us both some water. Storytelling can be dry work if the tale is long, and it usually is in our family. When I returned, Grandy was fast asleep on the couch.

"Grandy, Grandy." I shook her, but she put her hand on my arm and pushed me away.

"Later, Eve. I'm bone-tired. Wake me when the food arrives."

I slipped a lap robe over her and took my glass of water to the porch to await Alex and Madeleine's return. Yawning, I lay down on the chaise lounge and watched the sun set across the street. The next thing I knew someone was shaking me awake.

"Are you hungry?" asked Alex.

"Where's Madeleine?"

"She had me drop her at Wal-Mart. Said something about needing to buy cups. She told me she'd walk back when she was finished."

The land-line phone rang.

"I have to get that before the noise wakes Grandy."

I got there too late. Grandy was already speaking into the receiver.

"Where are you, dear?" She handed the phone over to me. "I think it's Madeleine, and she sounds upset, but I can't make out a thing she's saying."

"I've been kidnapped!" Madeline shouted, but before she could explain, another voice came on.

"This woman is crazy. I haven't kidnapped her. I just wanted to know where you lived, that's all. Jerry told me you were best friends with a little redheaded woman, and here I was at the store behind one. She mentioned your name to the cashier. I figured she had to be the gal. So I asked her polite-like if she was your friend. When she said yes, I offered her a ride to your place. When she saw my car, she went kind of crazy, took out her cell and punched in your number."

The accent was anything but Florida. It wasn't blue-blood Connecticut, either. I was reminded of some of Jerry's old poker buddies. The guys who were connected with the Family, with a capital "F."

I walked into my Florida room, out of earshot of Grandy and Alex.

"Put Madeleine back on the phone."

"He's the one in the black SUV who's been surveying your place all day. I think he's a gangster." Her voice trembled with fear or excitement. I couldn't tell which.

"Calm down. He probably is a gangster, but I don't think he means you any harm. If he did, I doubt he'd have let you call me. I guess we've got some unfinished business. I'll talk to him. You just chill for a bit." My voice shook with barely controlled terror as I said, "Mr. Napolitani, I believe?"

I may have believed he didn't mean harm to my friend, but me? He wanted that loan repaid. Now. No telling what he meant to do to get the money. If my little Miata was any indication, his methods weren't subtle.

"Am I interrupting something?" he asked.

"I have company right now, and I can't get away, so can this wait until another time?" I knew it couldn't. Why had I chanced making him mad?

There was a moment's silence.

"Why not? Is there a good place to eat around here, somewhere they serve Italian food?"

"I'm afraid you're stuck with steaks, catfish, pizza, or pork chops. I wouldn't say the pizza is very Italian."

I gave him directions to the Burnt Biscuit and agreed to meet him there as soon as I could get away. I knew I had no choice, but I wasn't going anywhere without backup. A rendezvous in a public place meant my friends could keep an eye out, and, if necessary, testify in court against him when he was tried for my murder.

The first question that came to my mind was whether I should bring Alex in on this conversation. Probably not. Maybe I should have Frida wire me. The thought of Frida reminded me of her whereabouts, and made me wonder why hadn't she intervened when she saw Napolitani and Madeleine together. She must have tracked the SUV to Wal-Mart...

When Madeleine got back on the line, I asked her not to mention any of this to Grandy or Alex. I hadn't decided how to handle the situation and I didn't want to add to Grandy's concern. As for Alex, well, I just got out of a relationship with a man who had proved unfaithful and unreliable and might have had a hand in arranging for my death. My need for another man was at an all-time low just now. I was a grown woman. A coward, maybe, but still an adult. I'd take care of myself.

Dummy, he's a crime boss, not an annoying neighbor.

Madeleine entered the house several minutes later, looking rather pleased with herself and not at all rattled, despite her encounter.

"He really was a gentleman," she whispered to me as she began stacking new cups and saucers in my cupboard.

"Are you all right, my dear?" asked Grandy from the other room.

"Oh, sure. I was concerned about the color of the cups I just bought. I couldn't remember Eve's kitchen décor." She winked at me, a movement Alex must have caught. He raised one eyebrow as if to ask me what was going on. I feigned ignorance.

After our feast, where everyone but me had seemed to have an appetite, we all helped clear the table. Madeleine offered to make coffee, but I suggested perhaps Grandy would like to make an early night of it.

"Oh, I'm fine. I had a little nap on the couch. I feel invigorated."

"Great then. I have an appointment after dinner. Maybe Alex and Madeleine can stay here and the three of you can play a couple of games of Pitch."

"I don't think I know how to play Pitch," said Madeleine.

"What appointment?" Alex looked suspicious.

My cell rang. I looked at my caller ID. Frida.

"You'll never guess who was driving that black SUV," she said. "It was Babs Cassidy, the ex-wife of the guy who loaned you his truck. Seems she's the jealous type."

"Frida." Here was someone who could help me. "Oh good. I'm glad you found out about that and yes, I do remember our appointment tonight in fifteen minutes at the Biscuit. I'll meet you in the parking lot."

"What are you talking about? We don't have a meeting tonight."

"Sure, I understand. I've already eaten, but the Biscuit serves their *Italian* specialty tonight, you know, *Napolitani* spaghetti. You love it. I'll just have a glass of Chianti or some other *Italian* wine while you eat. *Ciao.*" I flipped my phone shut.

"What meeting?" Alex's nosiness was beginning to irritate me.

"Um, Frida is helping put together a neighborhood watch program. I'm one of the organizers. Gotta run."

Alex followed me to my rental car. "Are you sure you're okay going out, after the day you've had?"

"I'm good. Besides, I forgot to tell Frida where I think the murder weapon came from, and it wasn't my store."

"Where'd it come from?"

"I think the knife that killed Valerie came from her house. If Frida can get a search warrant, she might find that one is missing from the Sanders' kitchen."

"Why do you think someone in the Sanders family was responsible for Valerie's murder?"

"I don't like the family. They give me the creeps. I didn't much care for Valerie, but there was something desperate about the woman. She was flawed enough to make me believe that she might be human under all that snobbery. The rest of them make me want to take a shower."

Alex seemed to consider my words for a minute.

"It's an interesting lead, but if you're right, whoever came into the shop today and took the knife from the back has already thought it through and is trying to cover up their tracks."

"We're too late, huh?"

"Yeah, I bet that knife has found its way into the Sanders' kitchen already." He sounded more certain about my Sanders lead than I had expected.

"I wonder who might have put the knife there. Damn. We lost all that time at the hospital getting me bandaged up and extracting Madeleine from her mess." I opened my car door. "Well, bye for now. Got to save the neighborhood from criminals."

Alex came closer to me, so close that I could feel the heat emanating from his body. He reached out and turned me around to face him. Could he read the lies in my face? He lifted my bandaged hand to his lips and kissed it. I giggled.

"You be careful, crime fighter."

I slid into the seat. He closed the door and rapped on the car's hood as I started the engine. Breathing a sigh of relief, I drove off to meet my crime boss.

FRIDA WAS SITTING in her unmarked police car, which she had parked toward the rear of the Biscuit's lot. She rolled down her window as I approached. "What in the hell is going on?"

I explained that I was meeting Nappi Napolitani and that I wanted her there for protection. "I think he's going to threaten mé with something unpleasant if I don't pay back the loan to Jerry. Apparently he's trying to tie up loose ends before Jerry marries his daughter."

"Did he threaten you over the phone?"

"No."

"Madeleine?"

"He just offered her a ride, but I think he's responsible for blowing up my car."

"You think, but you have no proof. Besides, the bomb was a real amateur job. I can't see a crime boss hiring someone so inept to do the job, can you?"

"Well, no, but—"

"Look, I'll try to get a table close to yours so that I can listen in on the conversation."

"There's another thing." I told her my suspicions about the knife.

She shook her head after I suggested that she get a search warrant.

"I can't see any judge granting that request on such flimsy information. Cannot do. Sorry. We'd need a lot more to get into that house."

"Hey, that knife belongs to the consignment shop. If it's in the Sanders' kitchen, it's stolen property."

"No, no, no. What if the knife is in the house? What does that prove?"

"The murderer put it there so there'd be a full set of knives. So you wouldn't think the knife came from the Sanders' set. So the murder weapon wouldn't be traced to the their household, implicating someone there—a family member."

My logic was impeccable.

"Eve, all the members of that household—Sanders,

his stepson, Valerie's daughter, and her husband—are already implicated, don't you know that?"

"This is additional implication."

"No."

"Okay, but could I have another look at the knife that killed Valerie?"

"Why?"

"I don't know. Maybe I'll know when I see it."

Frida scrutinized my face as if to find an answer she could believe. She waited a moment, then nodded her agreement.

"Tomorrow morning. Stop by my office before you open the shop. You only get to *look* at it."

Fine. I'd find another way to examine the second knife, the one I was certain had found its way back into the Sanders' kitchen.

I entered the dining area of the Biscuit and looked around at the diners. Two men wore boots and cowboys hats. Not them. Another man sat with a woman. The attire of both screamed TOURIST—shorts, shirts with fish and palm trees on them and sandals. White socks on the guy. A lone diner sat in the back of the room. It had to be him. I was aware of Frida entering after me and taking the table to his left.

I headed that way. He rose from his chair, smiled, and shook my hand. Then he held out a chair for me.

"Something to drink?"

He had dark hair, which he wore long, but that was the only characteristic that might have marked him as an Italian crime boss. No shiny black suit, no black shirt, no white tie. He wasn't short and fat. He was clean-shaven and was wearing gray pants, a red polo shirt and an expensive-looking ecru silk-blend jacket that he had tossed over the back of one chair. And he was handsome, very handsome.

I stared at him. Not at all what I expected.

"I've been wanting to meet you," he said.

"*Me*?"

"Yeah, Jerry has told me a lot about you. I couldn't believe most of it, so I had to see for myself."

"Look, I signed the divorce papers yesterday, so in my mind Jerry is free. Now, about the loan. I can pay him back on some kind of graduated schedule, if that's—"

"I don't care about that." He reached into his pants pocket.

I jumped, expecting him to pull out some kind of weapon. Instead, he extracted a roll of Life Savers and offered me one. Poison? I shook my head no. He took a cherry one, looked at the candy and sighed, then put the roll back into his pocket.

"My favorite is pineapple," he said.

"What?"

"My favorite Life Saver is pineapple, but there aren't many of them in a roll."

He sucked quietly on his candy and continued to stare at me.

"If you don't want the money, what then?"

"Just tell me about yourself."

"What do you want to know?"

"Oh, the usual stuff. Where you were born and went to school, your family, your work, stuff like that."

I was so relieved I wasn't going to be killed in my favorite cowboy bar that I began to babble about myself and continued for the next half hour. His eyes never left mine, but they did seem to twinkle a little brighter when I mentioned my grandmother. "Is that enough?"

"So you're Sarah Armitage's granddaughter. Very impressive."

"You know my grandmother?" I was surprised.

"Anybody who's anybody in Connecticut knows of your grandmother. In her day, she was by far the smartest, most beautiful woman in the state. Then she ran off with some sea captain and cheated us all of the joy of her company. Connecticut's been a little dull since then. No, I never met her, but I heard tell of her from my father."

I looked at him with suspicion. "They didn't date, did they?"

"Oh, no, no. She was already married when he met her. I heard a story about trouble in Connecticut. She left to escape some sort of suspicious controversy. That was a long time ago, and I never heard the details."

"Well, me either, but I know the trouble had something to do with Valerie Sanders and her relatives. I sure would like to know if Valerie's death is somehow related to me and my family."

"Well, you may not know it, but your meeting me here tonight has helped me immensely. If there's anything I can do to return the favor... I do have connections."

"I don't understand. What did I do? Why are you being so nice to me after you went to all the trouble of blowing up my car?"

"I'm sorry? *I* blew up your car? No, no. I wouldn't do that."

"Somehow, after meeting you, I can't believe you would, either. Now, back to how I helped you."

"My daughter is hell-bent on marrying your ex-husband."

"I know. I can't figure that out."

"Well, I can't either. Jerry seems like a boat without a rudder, or motor, or sail, or paddle."

"Not a lot of ambition. He does get ideas every now and again. Not much carry-through, though."

"My daughter thinks I can help him with that," he said.

If anyone could do it, it would be him. After all, he had the two things that Jerry craved most—power and money. Who knows, maybe becoming part of the Napolitani Family would be his making.

"Meeting you makes me realize Jerry can't be all bad, not if you married him. You're quite a gal. I like what I see, so, like I said, Jerry can't be all bad."

What could I say to that? "Don't give Jerry too much credit because he was drunk when we said our I dos." I didn't think that was what he wanted to hear.

"Um."

He reached across the table and took my hand. "Anything I can do for you, I will."

Fine then. I had just the thing. "I'd like help breaking into someone's house."

He offered me another Life Saver. It was lime. He got the pineapple one, finally. We plotted so quietly that even Frida couldn't hear us.

FOURTEEN

Mr. Napolitani and I left the restaurant together. Frida followed a few steps behind. "Goodnight, my dear." He shook my hand and then turned to face Frida. "There's no need to worry about your friend, Detective. I mean her no harm."

"She told you I was shadowing you?" Frida shot a look of disgust at me. I shook my head.

"I have a keen nose for the law. How could I believe that a woman of your good looks and deportment would be dining alone?" His smile displayed some very expensive white teeth.

Frida's mouth formed a round "O" of amazement, and, when the compliment finally penetrated, she smiled at Napolitani and chuckled. "You rogue."

He drove off in his black Escalade, probably heading back to the coast to settle into the condominium in West Palm he had told me about.

"What about your loan?" Frida asked.

"Oh, I arranged a payment schedule."

"That's what you were whispering about?"

"Yeah, sorry. He didn't want anyone to hear the details."

"You're going to tell me, right?"

"Oh, sure. I pay Jerry monthly for the next two years and then we're good."

"That's a big secret?"

I tried to look insulted. "Look, if Mr. Napolitani doesn't want anyone to know our financial arrangement, then I'm good with that. Don't say anything. Okay?"

"I don't get it, but fine. See you tomorrow at the office. About seven or so? I'll have the knife for you."

GRANDY WAS ASLEEP in the spare bedroom when I got home. Madeleine had left, and Alex was sitting in the living room in front of my television.

"You can go home now." I tried to make the suggestion sound as if it was his choice, but I knew it came out as a demand. "Sorry, but I'm beat."

"I can see that. I wasn't going to hang around. I just thought I'd let you know that Jerry called and wants you to call him back. Something about his father-in-law."

"You could have just left a note."

"I'm not stupid. I know who his father-in-law-to-be is. Not the kind of man you want to do business with. What's your interest in the man?"

I didn't like Alex's inquisition. He and Jerry had spent too much time together the other night bonding, regardless of whether one was a great guy and the other a bum. Boys will be boys, and they can find something in common, even if it's just testosterone.

"Alex, I really appreciate your, uh, friendship and support, but right now the only thing I want is a close encounter with is my pillow."

"Sure. How about dinner tomorrow night then?"

"Uh, I've got a meeting."

"Neighborhood watch?"

"Right."

"I'll call you."

"Great."

"You can tell me how the meeting went and how you like taking a leading role in making your neighborhood safe."

Was he being a smart ass?

"You and Frida, taking a bite out of crime."

"Get the hell out of here."

"You're a bad liar, Eve."

GRANDY INSISTED ON coming with me to police headquarters the next morning. Honestly, I liked the plan, because the only food I had in the house was some leftover pizza from the night before.

"I'll take you out for breakfast after, and I'll show you our shop," I said on our drive over.

"Breakfast first, then we buy some food for the house. Don't you ever eat in?"

"We ate in last night. It's only called 'takeout' because you take the order out of the restaurant and then eat the food at home."

"Right," she said. "I like Alex."

"Oh, I like him, too."

"Not as much as you should."

"I got divorced two days ago. Give me a break, will you?" I swung into the left lane to pass a trailer with two horses in it.

"Watch your driving. I think you scared those horses."

"Nothing scares cowponies. They're fearless. They share pastures with bulls and alligators."

She continued to watch the country go by. "This is

a whole new world around here. I didn't even know that this part of Florida existed."

"Rural Florida's beauty won't exist for long if the developers and big agribusiness players have their way."

"Money talks."

I nodded.

When we walked into Frida's office, the knife was laying on her desk.

She gestured to the chairs across from hers. "So, look, although I can't see what's so interesting. It's just a kitchen knife that was used for something that kitchen utensils shouldn't be used for. This is the murder weapon, the knife we thought came from your store. Now you're saying that it's not the right one, that you discovered *that* knife when you were throwing away packing material yesterday. But *that* knife somehow disappeared."

"I told you. I was crumpling up packing material and cut myself with a knife. When I examined it, I realized it had to be the knife that belonged to the set in our store. This knife, the murder weapon, wasn't from our set, but from another. Perhaps Valerie carried it into the store to defend herself. Maybe she knew her life was in danger."

"A lovely theory, but where is the *other* knife, the one that actually belongs to the set? Who took it? You say someone came into the shop besides Alex."

I leaned forward and bent over the knife, examining the rivets in its handle.

"Um," I said.

"'Um' is all you have to say after making such a fuss about seeing it?"

"Sorry. It sure does look like it came from the set in our shop."

Grandy reached in her purse and pulled out her reading glasses.

"Let me see that." She stuck her nose a few inches from the weapon. "Fine quality knife."

I SHOWED GRANDY around our shop and encouraged her to try on whatever she liked.

"Quality merchandise." The same word she'd used to describe the knife. "I'm not sure I can afford any of this, despite the fact that you have priced it all very fairly. Besides, I never have occasion to wear anything other than tees and cut-offs."

"You never know what you'll be doing now that you've moved the boat to another marina. There could be parties or, with your new schedule, time to dine out."

Grandy chuckled. "I'm imagining me in a cocktail dress and Max in flip-flops and swim trunks."

"Take care of yourself now and see to Max later," said Madeleine.

It was hard to tell what Grandy thought of the suggestion. She gave Madeline a "We'll see," and wandered off through the store. She stopped at a rack of matching skirts and tops.

"Wow, Dana Buchanan." She pulled a set from the rack and held the shirt up to examine it.

"Try it on. Oh, here's a really cute black velvet warm-up suit in your size. For those northern Keys nights," I said.

"I'd never have anywhere to wear that," she said. But after donning the outfits, with a little encouragement from Madeleine and me, she bought both—at a substantial discount, of course. She was my Grandy, after all.

Madeleine left the shop early to get ready for a date. She was on Yourperfectpartner.com and, of course, she had a line-up of men vying for her attention. She was trying them all out. It seemed safer that way, she confessed, because no one on the site knew she was a disaster magnet…yet.

Business was slow that afternoon. At least that gave me the opportunity to pump Grandy for information about her relationship with Valerie's grandfather. There was more to our family ties than Valerie's accusation of theft, and I wondered what the story was. Maybe I would find a link to her murder. I hadn't given up on the theory that someone had killed Valerie, thinking she was me. And although I was pretty certain that Mr. Napolitani wasn't interested in doing me in now, that didn't mean he hadn't tried in the past.

I was trying to think of the best way to approach Grandy about the Sanders family when a customer came into the shop. I busied myself by taking her selections back to the dressing room. While I was hanging up her clothing, the shop phone rang.

"Let it go to voice mail," I said. I stepped out of the dressing room and saw Grandy grab the phone. My customer handed me some additional choices, and I was momentarily distracted by her demand that I help her unstick the back zipper of a dress. When she left several minutes later—having bought none of the size 8 to size 12 dresses she had tried on (she was a 14, at least)—Grandy was still on the phone. She laughed several times and when she hung up, she was still smiling.

"Now I have an occasion to wear my new warm-up suit."

"Really?"

"Yup. I'm going out tonight."

Ah, I thought to myself, *that's perfect*. I didn't have to leave her alone all evening while I tended to my business. Wait a minute. Whom did Grandy know in Sabal City aside from me and Madeleine? Grandy and I were family. Not only that, but she raised me. She was the queen of plotting, and I was merely her lowly apprentice.

However, my need to find out more about how theft and love connected Valerie's family to mine caused me to shove any suspicions about tonight from my mind.

"About this relationship between you and Valerie's grandfather…"

She plopped down in a chair. "Now that's a sad story. He was my first love."

"I didn't even know you were acquainted with the Sanders family."

"To be accurate, the name was Warton. Sanders is the family that Valerie married into. Anyway, I worked for the Wartons for several years as their downstairs maid. Franklin was their eldest son, and his father wanted him to take over the family business. They were in transportation—trains, mostly, then planes. They designed, built and owned several railroads and later, airline transport companies. Now they've diversified, I guess." She shifted her round frame in the chair.

"If this is too painful for you…"

"No, it's this chair. Despite all the padding on my rear, it's like sitting on a concrete block. No give."

I ran into the office and rolled my desk chair out for her. "Try this."

"Better. Now, where was I?"

"Telling me about you and the Warton boy."

"Nothing much more to tell. We fell in love, a love that was impossible, of course. What prominent Connecticut family would allow their son to marry a lowly servant?"

"They found out about you two?"

"Oh, yes. Franklin insisted on telling them. He thought he could convince them that we should be together. I knew he wouldn't win. He didn't. They threatened to write him out of the will. He wasn't cut out to be poor. I saved the poor dear from himself by leaving and marrying an old friend—your grandfather."

She raised her hand as if to put a halt to what I was about to say. "He was the best man in the world, and I loved him fiercely. Have no doubt about that. Soon, Franklin married the woman his family selected for him. I believe he was very happy, too. Only his family always harbored bad feelings toward me."

"Why?"

"That's where the theft comes in. Franklin gave me this." She pulled a gold chain from beneath her shirt. Hanging from the chain was an antique gold locket, heart-shaped, a large diamond in the center, nine rubies outlining the shape. I counted them.

"It opens." She inserted her nail between the front and back of the locket. I expected to see two pictures inside, and I wasn't disappointed. Looking at the figures in the photos I saw two women. Not what I was expecting at all.

Grandy watched my expression with something akin to amusement. "You thought the locket might contain a picture of Franklin and me."

I nodded.

"Eve, dear, I can remember a time when you loved Jerry to distraction. Am I right?"

I thought back to when Jerry and I met, to when I thought he was the most exciting man in Connecticut, maybe in all the world. Somehow, at that time he had seemed smarter, sexier and even taller than I saw him now.

"I did love Jerry. Then."

"I loved Franklin, but some loves don't last for a lifetime and they probably shouldn't. I found your grandfather, and you'll find someone else, too."

I nodded. "Why did the family accuse you of being a thief?"

"The locket had been in the family for a long time. It's worth some money, and the family viewed it as theirs, not as Franklin's to give to whomever. Certainly not to a maid."

"Did Franklin have the right to give the heart to you?"

"Debatable, both ethically and legally, but they never took action. Instead they just spread rumors that I had stolen some property of theirs. Most of them viewed the locket only as property, never saw the beauty of it or its emotional significance. Except, perhaps, for Valerie. She came to me once and asked to see it."

"That's an odd request."

"I thought so."

"Weren't you worried that she might try to steal the locket from you on the spot?"

Grandy shook her head. "Your grandfather was in the next room."

"Ah."

"Valerie stared for the longest time, then said, 'It's beautiful. Guard it with your life.'"

"A threat?"

"Maybe. I couldn't tell."

Grandy and I sat in silence for several minutes. "Valerie was a bundle of contradictions," I said.

Grandy nodded.

"The pictures?" I leaned closer to the locket.

"Your mother and you, of course."

"Oh, Grandy." I threw my arms around her and hugged her as if I'd never let her go.

"Hey, you're squeezing me too tight. You might leave permanent indentations, girl." She was hugging me back, though.

"I love you."

"That's good. Then you won't mind if I come along with you and Mr. Napolitani on your adventure tonight."

FIFTEEN

"THIS IS A very bad idea." I steered my rental down the Beeline Highway heading for West Palm. Grandy sat beside me in her new black warm-up suit. I could feel her wriggle with excitement in her seat. "Stop that jiggling. This isn't a party we're going to, you know."

She ignored my comments, just as she had ignored all the pleading, begging, and threatening I had directed her way since learning that Mr. Napolitani had invited her along on our evening exploration. If I had his cell number, perhaps I would have called off this jaunt. He had cleverly avoided giving me any way to contact him, and he blocked his number when he made calls to my phone. That was why he was rich and feared and I owned a secondhand shop.

I had to go ahead with my plan. I knew I couldn't get Frida interested in searching the Sanders' house. She wanted to do things the legal way. I didn't. Although, my actions could get me caught, and I *could* spend time in jail. As much as I liked having Grandy as a roomie, I didn't think she'd welcome sharing a cell with me. I'd start to whimper the minute the jail door closed. She was tough. I only thought of myself as tough. I'd never been tested. Well, tonight was the night.

"Mr. Napolitani has some experience in these

things. I can't believe he'd do anything to jeopardize your life or mine," said Grandy.

That was comforting, but not necessarily true. His risk-taking threshold had to be a lot higher than either of ours. What we saw as dangerous was only an evening's entertainment for him.

I pulled into a strip mall a mile from the Sanders' house and parked at the side of the building under an oak tree. It cast shadows onto the car and made me feel as if we were somewhat hidden from other vehicles in the lot. The mall held a dry cleaners, a tile shop, several empty storefronts, and at the far end, a convenience store. At this time of night, all the shops were closed, with the exception of the convenience store.

Napolitani's black SUV backed in next to me.

He rolled down his window. "I brought backup." The interior of the car was too dark for me to see who was in his passenger seat. "We'll take my car and leave yours here. Get in."

Grandy and I hopped out of my car. The overhead light in the SUV didn't come on when I opened the back door.

"Hey, your light's not working," I said.

Napolitani turned in his seat. "That's the way I like it." A smile lifted the corners of his mouth.

I didn't. I still couldn't identify the passenger, who remained shrouded in the deep shadow of the tree.

Napolitani ratcheted up his grin. "Perhaps after we finish our business, we can have a drink."

Grandy nodded. Fine, I thought. A drink, if we're not in West Palm's city lock-up.

"So, everyone knows everyone now," Napolitani said.

The passenger in front shifted his body slightly, and I caught his face in the streetlight.

"Jerry! No way." I grabbed Grandy and reached for the door handle.

The door wouldn't open.

"I suppose this is the way you like your door handles too, right?" I tried to keep my tone light. My heart was in my throat. I could barely get the words out of my mouth. Why had I decided to entrust our lives to a Mafia don, especially one who employed my ex as his assistant? I lost it.

"Let us out." I hammered on the door.

"Evie, honey baby, calm down." Jerry turned and reached into the backseat for my arm.

Napolitani hit a switch and the door suddenly swung open, catching me off balance. My body pitched forward and, if Grandy hadn't grabbed my shirt, I would have fallen out onto the ground.

"Eve, you need to get a hold of yourself." Grandy pulled me back onto the seat. "I'm sure Mr. Napolitani means no harm."

"No harm? Why does he have to lock us in then?"

"This is the family car," he said. "I have two grandchildren, both under the age of five. I always have the doors on automatic lock to make certain the kids are safe."

"Oh." I could feel a flush of embarrassment spreading up my neck and into my face. Suddenly I was grateful for the darkness, as it hid my reddening cheeks. "Sorry I overreacted, but why is Jerry here? What help can he possibly be?"

"He can wait with the car, keep it running, while we search the place. I didn't have time to bring another man down here. Jerry was available and eager to help out."

Eager? Only because he wanted to impress his future father-in-law.

"Okay, but he stays in the car." I had no faith in Jerry's ability to stay calm if anything went wrong at the house.

NAPOLITANI'S INFORMATION SAID the house would be deserted. Sanders and his family were at a charity affair and the house staff was off for the night. I hoped his sources were reliable. They appeared to be. With the exception of a dim light in one of the windows, the place was dark.

Napolitani parked the car around the corner, leaving Jerry inside. Grandy, Napolitani, and I walked past the residence and turned down a path that led us along the side of the house. Our way was blocked by a wrought-iron gate—the only potential opening that I had seen in the high fence around the back of the building.

"How do we get over that?" I asked. "I guess I could climb onto your shoulders and…"

Napolitani pushed on the gate. It swung open.

"How did you…" I didn't want to know how he had managed to get the gate unlocked. If we were caught, Grandy and I would be safer being ignorant of Napolitani's arrangements. The smile on his face told me that keeping us ignorant had been part of his plan.

"I can't imagine what you think you'll find here, Eve," he said.

We approached a set of French doors leading to the kitchen. I remembered its location from Madeleine's and my consignment trips.

Napolitani straightened his tie as if he expected to be invited in for a drink. "I said I'd help you, but maybe you can fill me in on what you're looking for so I can search also."

"A missing knife. Anything else that looks, uh, suspicious."

That sounded so lame.

"No, no, my dear." Grandy almost faded into the night in her black warm-up gear. "You're looking for a particular knife."

I turned to Grandy. "So you say. I can't figure out…"

At that moment a car turned into the driveway, its headlights illuminating the front and sides of the house. The three of us pressed ourselves against the stucco siding, hoping that whoever was in the car wouldn't explore the backyard.

No lights came on, but we heard the front door open and footsteps echo through the entryway. The sound came closer, getting louder as a door opened. Through the darkness, we could see a spot of light bouncing around the kitchen. It was someone with a flashlight, no more eager to be spotted than we were.

Something dropped onto the tile floor. "Damn," a voice said from inside.

Grandy stuck her head above the window frame to the left of the French doors.

"Get down." I pulled her out of sight.

"Was that a man's or a woman's voice?" asked Napolitani.

"I don't know, but I saw someone in there messing around on the counters and the island. I think…"

Grandy's head popped up once more over the window ledge.

I grabbed her again. "Will you stay down, please?"

I took a chance and looked over the window ledge. Grandy's head joined mine.

"Somebody's on the floor looking for what was dropped," Grandy said. "Now they're fiddling around with something, maybe the knife set. C'mon, we can catch them in the act." Before she could move, the flashlight went out and the footsteps retreated from the kitchen back into the hallway. We heard the front door opening and closing. The car in the driveway started up and drove off.

"That was close. What were you thinking, Grandy? We can't barge in there. It's against the law."

"You think breaking in *after* the culprit gets away is legal? That is what we're going to do, right?"

The appearance of someone in the Sanders' supposedly empty house had frightened me enough that I was reconsidering my plan—what I had of one, anyways.

"We could just shine the light through the French doors and see if the knife is there or not. Grandy thinks she saw the knife set on the center island." My earlier resolve was gone, despite Napolitani having assured me that he was the best man around for breaking, entering, and disarming alarm systems. He could do it so well that no one would even know the system had been tampered with.

"I need to see it up close." Grandy sounded insistent.

Napolitani turned to me. "I thought you wanted a look, too. Otherwise, why am I here?"

"Fine. Let's go." To my own ear, my voice sounded as weak as fast food coffee.

"I'm right behind you." The voice came from our rear.

Who? Then I realized. "Jerry, what the hell are you doing here?"

Napolitani didn't even act surprised, merely shook his head and sighed deeply.

"I saw a car pull up and thought I'd warn you."

"That's not your job." Napolitani seemed to think little of Jerry's appearance. "What the hell. C'mon then. I can keep an eye on you."

"We already know about the car. We saw it pull into the drive and we watched as someone rifled through the kitchen drawers. Whoever was in the house is gone now, so you're a little late with your news." My sigh was identical to Napolitani's. Jerry was such a loser.

"Not *that* car," he said. "The one with Madeleine and Alex in it."

Why was I not surprised?

"Where are they now? You did manage to make them go away, didn't you?"

"And miss all this fun?" Alex's mouth was only a hair's breadth away from my ear. "You're such a bad liar, Eve. Neighborhood watch. Ha!"

"Hey there," Madeleine said.

The two of them stood behind us, stooped low to hide their presence from anyone inside, looking as if they really did belong in our burgling gang.

"I thought you were on a date. What happened?"

"He chickened out and cancelled, the coward." Madeleine sounded depressed.

Alex chimed in. "Whatever you're planning, stop and think. This is illegal and—"

I whirled around on him. "Oh, shut up. We really don't need your PI take on this."

In the heat of our argument, we had forgotten about Grandy, Napolitani, and Jerry. While the three of us were discussing the hows and whys of our presence here, the three of them had entered the house.

"C'mere, Evie," said Grandy. "A complete knife set, yet…"

"Damn, Alex. You told me that whoever had taken the knife would put it back here, and you were right. Now I've got nothing. I can't prove it was ever gone or that it's not the right one," I said.

Alex tried to hold me back, but I walked through the open door to join the others at the island. Napolitani pointed his flashlight at the knife set. Grandy was standing so close to the set that her nose almost rested on one of the handles.

"Be careful, Grandy. You'll cut yourself or leave a nose print." I grinned, although I knew she couldn't see me in the dark.

Grandy's head popped up from its inspection. "Does the FBI have a database of nose prints, too?" She dropped her head once again to the knives. "Very interesting." She continued to stare at the set.

"Forget it. This trip had been for nothing." I turned to leave.

"I don't get it. What's going on with the knife thing?" Madeleine entered and paused behind me. "I can't see a damn thing in here. I'm afraid I'll trip over something."

"Just walk slowly. I'm right in front of you. Watch your step. You know how you are."

"You don't have to remind me. I'm doing my best. I'll hang onto the wall for balance."

"No. Don't touch anything." My warning came too late.

"Oh, there's a box of some kind here. What—"

The house alarm began blaring.

"She tripped it somehow. We'd better get out of here. The cops will be showing up any minute." Napolitani herded all of us outside, but he stayed behind. "I'll reset the alarm. Maybe they'll think it was a malfunction."

Madeleine and Alex ran out and jumped into the car that they had arrived in. Grandy and I headed for the SUV, but had to wait there until Napolitani arrived to unlock the doors. Then it hit me. One of our merry band of house breakers was missing.

"Where's Jerry?"

SIXTEEN

"SOMEONE HAS TO go back and look for him." It was my suggestion. I knew he'd get himself into trouble.

"Where?" asked Grandy.

"In the house. Maybe he took a tour of the place while we were busy in the kitchen. He could be trapped. The cops will think he was the one who broke in."

"He did break in…with us," said Grandy.

We both turned to Napolitani.

"Don't look at me. I'm not going. You're not either. Jerry's on his own."

As if to underscore the danger of remaining any longer, the distant sound of sirens filled the tropical night.

"Get in." Napolitani opened the car door.

Grandy slid into the backseat. I hesitated. "Let me take a peek through the kitchen windows. I'll just be a minute."

I ran down the pathway leading to the rear of the house and pressed my nose up against the French doors. No Jerry. The sirens were getting closer. I worked my way around the house, checking the inside rooms from each window, but I saw no one. At the window of what appeared to be a dimly lit study, I thought I caught movement. I leaned in closer. Jerry. He was opening and closing the drawers of a massive desk that stood in the middle of the room. I banged on the glass and his head shot up. He moved toward me and raised his hand. There was a gun in it.

"Jerry." I didn't want to yell, but I hoped he heard me over the house's air-conditioning. "What are you doing? Get the hell out of there. The cops are coming."

He recognized me, shook his head and opened the window. "Here, take these." He handed me a sheaf of papers. Before I could reply, the window closed and Jerry moved away.

The sound of the sirens seemed to be holding at the same level now, as if something had stopped them in their progress toward the house. Was that good or bad? I didn't have time to think about an answer. I had to find a way into the place so that I could get Jerry out. Somehow. I'd have to break the glass in one of the French doors. I tucked the papers Jerry gave me under my shirt and turned toward the kitchen once more.

The sirens continued wailing but they still weren't getting any closer. *Stay there, stay there.* As I bent to pick up a small landscaping rock to break the window, a hand grabbed my shoulder.

"Don't do that." It was Alex.

I stood back up.

"Now turn around," he said.

"What are you doing here?"

"Rescuing you, as usual."

"Jerry's in there. I need to get him out."

"He's a big boy. Let him figure it out. Besides, he's not your responsibility, not anymore."

The sirens stopped blaring.

"What's going on?" I asked.

"Napolitani just heard it on the police scanner. Apparently Sanders' son entered the house earlier, just as the three of you were about to break in. He thought he punched the wrong code into the alarm and made it go off. He notified the police and they called off the alert. I'll bet they'll be here anyway, just to check on his story. So let's go, Eve."

"Jerry."

"If you're so hung up on the guy, why did you divorce him?" I heard disgust in his voice.

"It's not what you think. It's just that he gets into messes and…"

"You get him out." Alex grabbed my arm and pulled me toward him. I fell against his chest. He looked down into my face through the moonlit shadows, his azure eyes made opalescent by the night.

"I don't know why I bother." He pulled me closer and kissed me, his lips moving insistently against mine. I opened my mouth to protest, but my silly objection turned into a sigh of satisfaction as I kissed him back, my arms moving around his neck, my fingers playing with the tendrils of hair that fell loose on his collar. I wanted to remain there longer, but reality intruded, in the form of Napolitani.

"You kids might want to do that someplace else. Sanders, his son and a few cops are on their way. No rush, but wrap up the romance, would you? Soon."

Alex and I broke away from each other. He headed toward his car, and I went in the opposite direction, following Napolitani toward the SUV.

"Jerry's in the house." I caught up to Napolitani.

"I know. We couldn't have planned it any better, I guess."

"Planned what?"

"I guess you could say it was serendipitous. Mr. Sanders had something of Jerry's. He took this opportunity to get it back."

We reached the car, and I slid into the empty passenger's seat. Napolitani drove off.

I turned around and looked at Grandy in the backseat. "Hey. You doing okay?"

She nodded. "Did you find Jerry?"

I hesitated. Napolitani knew what Jerry was up to. I didn't, but I had some papers under my shirt that might help me find out. "Nope. He's on his own."

"About time. That boy needs to grow up."

"That boy is about to become my son-in-law and the father of my grandchild." Napolitani didn't sound altogether happy about it.

"All the more reason for him to become an adult."

"Well, we'll see what tonight brings." He sounded even less happy than before, but nevertheless resigned to whatever might happen.

I tried to relax in the comfort of the leather-clad seat, to let my mind wander a bit, to ruminate over the night's events while the two of them talked. I could feel the heat rising in my face and neck again. This time it wasn't embarrassment, but anger.

"You weren't trying to help me." I interrupted their conversation. "You were running your own game, one that somehow involved Jerry. You lied to me. I trusted you."

He said nothing but looked straight ahead, carefully driving the speed limit. At the strip mall he pulled into the space beside my rental, shut off the SUV's engine, and faced me.

"I didn't lie. There were details about tonight's program that I didn't tell you about, yes. You didn't need to know everything."

For the first time since we had met, I could see the danger that lurked beneath his smooth appearance. I'd said enough. He stared me down for a few extra beats before shifting in his seat to address Grandy.

"My pleasure." He kissed her hand. "I hope the evening was entertaining, and that you found what you were looking for."

"We didn't." I kept the anger out of my voice this time.

His smile didn't falter. "So sorry, then. Don't think too badly of me, my dear. I find that I quite like and respect you. I wouldn't have taken you along on this trip if I didn't, but my first responsibility is to my family. Jerry understands that. I hope you will, too."

"You did just fine." Grandy reached out and patted his cheek much as one would a child's.

"THAT WAS FUN, EXCITING." Grandy pulled down the visor in my rental and looked at her face. "I think I look a little tired. I'm hungry."

In the rearview mirror, I could see Alex's car following us. "Let's pull over at one of these bar and grills before we run out of places to stop."

"You look like you could use a scotch, honey."

"I could, but I'm not taking a chance on driving with a couple of drinks in me."

"I'll drive."

"You're on."

"I can drive Madeleine and me in this car," she said, "and you and Alex can return in his. How about that?"

I ignored her suggestion, slammed the car door and

started up the pea rock walkway to the restaurant's entrance.

"I could also stay at Madeleine's for the night. I'll bet she wouldn't mind."

"Leave it. I'm not sure where Alex and I stand just now."

"Well, I am." She sounded so certain, so pleased.

We entered and chose a booth across from the bar. Madeleine and Alex joined us. Everyone except me ordered burgers and cokes. I asked for a scotch.

"Nothing to eat?" asked Grandy.

I shook my head.

When our order arrived, the others discussed the evening in hushed tones while I contemplated the amber liquid in my glass.

"I'll be right back." I left my scotch untouched on the table, grabbed my purse, and got up. Alex did, too.

"Don't return there. There's nothing you can do for Jerry."

"I know that, but I have to see what's happening. It's not just Jerry. There's something that's bothering me."

"I'll come with you."

"No, I want to go on my own."

"And snoop around again, with the cops there?"

"I won't be snooping this time. I'm going to take the direct approach." I started across the parking lot. Alex stood at the bar's entrance for a moment, then came after me.

"If you ever want me to kiss you again, you'll stay here."

I hesitated a moment, then continued to my car. In the outside mirror, I saw his reflection in the moonlight, hands in his pockets, his head down, any expression on his handsome face hidden by the shadows.

I started the engine and pressed down on the accelerator, leaving Alex behind. I was going to be direct. No back door entry for me this time. I was going in the front.

WHEN I ARRIVED at the Sanders' house, all was quiet. No cops, but there were two cars parked in the circular driveway—a Cadillac I recognized as the one Valerie had driven and a Lincoln Navigator. I stepped up to the door and rang the bell.

Mr. Sanders' son, Dwight, answered. For a moment he seemed not to recognize me, then a look of angry alarm came over his face.

"You. What do you want?"

"I wanted another look at you. You were standing by your stepmother's Cadillac in front of my store the day she was murdered. I saw you."

"You're crazy. I was here at home. With my sister. I told the cops that already."

"I think sis lied for you. I might ask why she'd do that, but the family must stick together, right? Even if one of you is a killer."

I saw movement behind him. Valerie's daughter, Constance, appeared at his side.

"Who's a killer?" She leaned against the doorjamb, a cigarette in her hand. "Oh, it's you. What do you want?"

"I want to find your mother's killer"

"Why should you care? Your family and mine have never been on good terms. Mother told me all about it."

"She accused me of murdering Mom," Dwight said.

"I saw your stepbrother in the parking lot the day of your mother's murder. I don't understand why you covered for him."

Her nonchalant pose slipped a bit as she threw a nervous glance in his direction. "We don't need to talk to you." She closed the door in my face.

The nervous reactions of the two siblings told me all I needed to know. It had taken me a while to put it together, but there was a lot going on in my life right now—the murder, my attraction to Alex, the consignment shop, my car's destruction and finally, the theft of the knife. Whew! No wonder I hadn't remembered seeing Dwight by Valerie's car the day of the murder until tonight.

I never forget a face. Sometimes it takes a little time, but if I let the image cook in the recesses of my brain, I can eventually place it. In this case, seeing Dwight at the funeral had triggered something for me, but I hadn't been able to place it until tonight. The figure in the kitchen, too shadowy for me to identify outright as the son, had flipped a switch in my mind. When I had walked up the drive and seen the Cadillac, my suspicions had been confirmed, especially now that I'd gotten another look at Dwight.

I flipped open my cellphone to call Frida. I could identify Valerie's stepson and place him at the store. I was certain that Frida could now get a search warrant for the Sanders' house. What I had forgotten to take into account was that all of my snooping around might have made some people angry. The last thing I remembered was something hitting me on the head. Then everything went black.

SEVENTEEN

THE SMELLS IN my small prison were familiar, gasoline and oil and something else I'd rather not think about, something more organic and…rotten. I was hogtied, hands in back of me connected by a rope to my feet. I moved a bit and managed to rub a hand against my back pocket, hoping against all odds I'd find my cellphone there. No such luck. It must have slipped from my hand when I was hit.

Maybe someone in the Sanders' house had seen what happened and called the police. Then I remembered that someone in that house was a murderer. They didn't want to see me rescued by the police. I was the witness who could put the killer, Valerie's stepson, at the crime scene. Would the family protect him? Would they kill me to keep him safe? Yeah, likely. These people were rich. Grandy was right. There was something seriously twisted about that clan.

The motion of the car changed. It slowed, and I felt the tires gripping gravel, not concrete. Odors from the country came to me, the moldy stench of brackish water and a sweet fragrance, probably from burning sugarcane fields. Where were they taking me? Stones crunching beneath the tires gave way to a softer noise, a dirt road. The car stopped and in the silence, frogs croaked. Then a terrifying bellow ripped apart the night—the mating call of a bull alligator.

The trunk lid opened. Someone grabbed me and dragged me out. I hit the ground with a thunk. The only sound my captor made was a low "humph," then I heard the door close. The idling car shifted into drive and pulled away, the sound of the departing engine soon engulfed by the chattering of birds, frogs, and wind blowing through swamp grasses and palms.

I lay there for a few minutes. The alligator roared again. This time I thought his bellow was closer, fuller, more menacing. I wondered, was that the call for a mate or the dinner bell for me?

If I could get my blindfold off, maybe I could see where I was and, from there, how I could escape. I rubbed my head against the ground working to dislodge the material from over my eyes. After a while, I was able to move the blindfold away from my left eye. Not much help. Everything was pitch black.

I knew that the car had come down a road, dirt to be sure, but a road nonetheless. If I could wriggle toward it, maybe someone would find me. I worked my way like a sidewinder snake in what I thought might be the right direction, but ended up in a swampy area instead. Wrong way. I reversed my motion and soon hit what felt like earth. More wiggling and I hit another dirt patch. Had to be two tracks. Now what?

I was exhausted. My wrists were chafed and aching, and my legs were beginning to cramp. I lay there. This might be the end for me, an ignominious finish for a girl from the Northeast—eaten by alligators in a Florida swamp.

That wasn't even the worst thing I could imagine. I remembered reading about a number of Burmese pythons and anacondas that had recently invaded Southern Florida. I'd read an article in the *Sabal Bay News* about a constrictor measuring over seventeen feet that had been killed in the area. I shivered despite the hot humid night. Could a snake that size swallow a person of my height? Maybe not, especially the way I was tied up. I tried to position my body so it formed more of an angle from my head to my feet, but that only made my neck and legs spasm more. I couldn't hold the pose. Was I doomed to become some reptile's dinner? I had to get a grip on my runaway imagination.

After an indeterminable amount of time had passed, I saw headlights. Friend or foe? Was my captor checking back in to see if I had been snatched from the swamp's buffet table yet? If I rolled off the road, the car might pass me by. Oh, the hell with it. This was my only chance. I remained where I was.

The vehicle—a truck with a roof panel of lights switched on—slowed and stopped about ten yards away.

"Well, lookee here. We got ourselves a woman. All wrapped up like a Christmas gift," yelled the driver out his window.

Pure idiocy. I had no wrapping paper on me, and the rope could hardly be construed as ribbon.

Two men got out and approached me. Both wore dirty, beaten-up cowboy hats and equally old, probably manure-covered boots. Just my luck. I'd run into a couple of good ol' boys cruising the back roads for wild pig or… Well, I might just do.

"Would you mind? This is really an uncomfortable position." I looked up into a set of eyes as cold as a Minnesota winter.

"I'll bet." The driver pulled a knife out of a sheath on his belt and strolled toward me.

I groaned inwardly. I was wrong about my demise. It wouldn't be an alligator that got me but rather—dum-de-dum banjo music playing in the background—a *Deliverance* style movie scene, featuring a cowboy from Florida.

He stooped and held the knife in front of my face as he licked his lips. Then he reached out, put his hand on my cheek, and pushed my face to one side.

"This is a very sharp knife."

He reached around to my back and slid the blade under the ropes, cutting through them as if they were pudding. "I didn't want you to look over and flinch. You could have been hurt."

He grasped my arm and helped me to stand.

"I called it in," said the truck's passenger.

"Who are you guys?"

"Who are you?" the driver asked back. "Got any ID?"

I backed up a few steps. "You first."

"We're Drug Enforcement Agents. We got a tip that someone was out here waiting for a shipment of coke."

"If you're thinking that's me, you're wrong. Someone kidnapped me and left me here as alligator feed."

The radio from inside the truck crackled. The passenger reached into the cab and took the call.

"Headquarters got an alert from the state police. She's right. A woman was taken from outside a home in West Palm. Name of Eve Appel or Eve Taylor."

"That's me." I reached into my back pocket and extracted my license.

"Connecticut, huh? Yep, she's the one."

The driver kicked his boot into the dirt and swore. "Blew the whole damn deal. Might as well take her back. Nobody's gonna show now."

Neither of the men said much as we traveled down the dirt road, which eased onto a gravel connector and eventually became pavement, just as I had suspected. From there we took I95 South and turned on an exit I was unfamiliar with. Several lefts and rights later, we drove up to a gray four-story building in a section of West Palm that looked more like a slum than the opulent east coast you see advertised in the Florida tourist brochures.

I walked through the front entrance of the building and into a small foyer. Its walls were painted the most depressing shade of green I had seen since science class in college. My driver, who had introduced himself as "Bud," opened an inside door that led down a hallway and into a room filled with metal desks peopled by agents with the DEA insignia on the back of their jackets. Everyone looked up as I entered. No one greeted me, merely gave me the steady cop eye, the same cold dispassionate look worn by my two rescuers.

"You can use the phone over there." Bud gestured toward a desk piled high with papers.

"Thanks. Uh, can I ask you something?"

He gave a miniscule nod of approval.

"Did I do something wrong?"

"You messed up a drug bust. We had been working on it for two months, then you came along and scared the guys off. Yeah, you could say you did something wrong."

"It wasn't my fault, you know."

"Find us the guy who dumped you out there and

we'd be glad to transfer our pissed off feelings onto him."

I thought better of trying to argue with him or his partner, who looked even more peeved. The rest of the agents didn't appear likely to be won over to my side, either. What a bunch of grumps. I could have died out there. I *would* have died out there.

I felt a shiver run down my spine but shook it off. So. Who to call? Alex, Grandy, Madeleine, Frida? As much as I wanted my friends to be assured of my safety, I needed Frida to get into the Sanders' house with a search warrant so that she could arrest the son-in-law for murder. Then there was my kidnapping. This seemed a matter of police importance. When I got her on the phone, Frida agreed.

"Where are you? We heard that the authorities found you and that you are alive, but that's all."

I told her the entire story, minus the part about breaking into the Sanders' house.

"Sit tight. I'll get the warrant. I know a judge who stays up watching HGTV all hours of the night."

"That's great. How long before she can sign it?"

"She? It's a he."

"Sorry."

"Well, his wife isn't. She loves the ideas he gets for decorating their house from *Design Now*. Think you can get someone to give you a lift back here?"

I looked around the room at the scowling faces. "No way."

"Right. I'll have Alex or Madeleine pick you up."

"Please don't send Madeleine. You know how she is. I might never get home."

"Alex it is then. Oh, by the way, is Bud around there?"

"You want to talk with him?"

"Nah, just tell him I said hi."

I did, and his frown seemed to defrost a bit.

After I had hung up the phone, I told him that someone would be picking me up. He grunted and gestured toward a chair at an empty desk.

"I could wait outside." Where the climate wasn't so icy.

He laughed. I think it was a laugh, or perhaps he had some kind of throat condition that made him sound like a parrot on amphetamines.

"Aaarugh, awk, awk. Did you take a look at the neighborhood we're in? The folks that live around here aren't fond of our enterprise. They'd jump at the chance to strip you naked, take your wallet and then, well, let's not even think about what would happen next. Even if we were to hear you yelling—on the off chance that someone cared enough to run outside to save you—we still couldn't get to you in time. Sit."

I sat.

By the time Alex pushed through the door, the sun was coming up, and I was nodding off. There was a little drool on my shoulder.

Alex dashed over and gathered me up into his arms, slobber and all. "Hey, babe. Am I glad to see you. We were worried sick."

I untangled my arms and legs from his embrace.

"It took you long enough." I tried to look angry, but I felt tears filling my eyes. Before I could do anything about it, I was bawling harder than I had since my steady, Mick Sawyer, broke up with me in the eighth grade.

"You're with me and safe." He pushed my hair back off my sweaty forehead and kissed it. "You smell kind of…"

"What?"

"Funky."

"*Funky*?"

"Funky, like an auto repair shop and something else, maybe dead frogs."

"I was in a trunk, you know. A damn trunk. You have no idea." I felt the need to tell him everything I had encountered since I had left the diner, a kind of catharsis of angst over the evening's events. Alex's sympathetic face loosened my tongue, but before I could say much, he stopped me.

"Uh, I have bad news for you."

I gave a dismissive wave of my hand. "How bad can the news be? It can't be worse than my brush with headline news. You know, tomorrow's *Post* could have read: 'Bright, sexy entrepreneur nabbed and fed to swamp inhabitants.'"

He shook his head. "Mr. Sanders called in your kidnapping."

"Not what I expected, but that was nice of him. Seems like the least he could do after dragging me out there."

"Maybe not. He told the cops that he saw Jerry hit you over the head and throw you into his trunk."

EIGHTEEN

"I DON'T SEE WHY I can't talk to Mr. Sanders. Jerry can't be the one who hit me and dumped me in the swamp. Sanders must be mistaken."

Alex drove me back to the Sabal City Police Department. I sat across the desk from Frida. Her detecting buddy, Trevor Timble, was absent. I was glad for the privacy. Alex's presence didn't count. Apparently he was becoming a permanent fixture in my life, always showing up when bad things happened.

"It's police business and the West Palm cops are covering it. They believe Sanders, and that's all there is to it. You stay out of it. I know you've been up to something. Why else would you have been at Sanders' house at that hour?"

I couldn't tell her that I had been trying to rescue Jerry, or even why Jerry needed rescuing. But I didn't believe that he was the one responsible for nabbing me. I would have known. I would have felt it.

"I had to get another look at Sanders' son to be sure he was the one I saw in the parking lot on the day of Valerie's murder."

"Now, because you alerted him, we can't find the son. Why can't you let the cops do their work?" The pencil Frida was holding in her fingers snapped in two. I had pushed her too far.

"I'm sorry. Sometimes I get carried away and don't

think. It's my impulsive nature, I guess. Really. You're doing great work here."

Frida picked up the two halves of the pencil and threw them into the trashcan. She took a moment to center herself and release the tension before speaking again. "You know you're making my job more difficult, don't you?" she said, her voice much calmer. "Please stay out of this. Take a break, a vacation or something. You've had a rough couple of days."

"Now there's a great idea." Alex looked pleased. "A vacation."

"The shop—"

"Madeleine can manage," Alex broke in. "Maybe you could go to Key Largo with your Grandy when she returns. I'm sure she'd love to have you on the boat."

"That Jerry, trying to feed you to the alligators." Grandy shook her curls. It was the next morning, and she was piloting her SUV south on the Florida Turnpike.

"You don't believe that, do you?"

"He's a bad boy, but, no, he wouldn't do that. I do think there's something fishy about Sanders' story. It looks like Valerie married into a family as bad as her own."

"It's more likely that Sanders sent his stepson after me because I had placed him at the crime scene. But that seems kind of crazy, too. Unless he wanted his wife dead for some reason. This murder is making me nuts." I leaned against the window and watched as we rushed past the stucco walls of wealthy homes.

"The cops are looking for both Jerry and Sanders' son. How long can they hide?" Grandy set the cruise control and rested one hand on the wheel, the other on her knee.

My cell played its tune. It was Frida.

"Tell your Grandy she was right," Frida said when I picked up the phone.

"About what?"

"We executed the search warrant for the Sanders' house. She'll know what I mean." The line disconnected.

"Frida says you were right. About what?"

"That knife. I got a good look at the set of knives when we entered the Sanders' house."

"Yeah, I remember. I thought you were going to kiss them, you were so close."

"One didn't match. It looked like it did, at first, but it was much cheaper. I think that was the one from your shop. Someone must have placed it there in case the cops came looking for an incomplete set. I've got a good eye for cutlery, and I know the wealthy would never consider buying anything but the best. Carbon steel. One of them was stainless. Now all they need to do is compare the murder weapon in the evidence locker to the Sanders' carbon steel knives."

I slapped my knee. "Ha! I knew there was something different about the murder weapon, and that if I could just get into that house to look at those knives, well, something would click. It did."

Grandy glanced at me. "Honey, something clicked for me, not you."

"Me. You. Whatever. You didn't tell Frida how you knew all this?"

Grandy chuckled. "I told her I found out from one of the Sanders' help, and that I had to keep my source anonymous or the person could get fired. Frida doesn't need to know the details. The cops are looking at the real evidence now."

"You're so smart." I reached over and patted her arm.

"Well, you are too, in a way. It was dumb of you to go back to the house for another peek at the stepson, but your ability to identify him led to the search warrant. The knife clinched the deal. Now he's wanted for murder."

"Frida said he wouldn't have run if I hadn't showed up on the doorstep."

"Maybe," said Grandy. "Stop for a bite?" We flew by a sign announcing a rest area ahead.

"Let's just get to Key Largo. I want to sit on the boat's deck and soak up the sunshine."

For the first time since Valerie's murder, I felt at peace. Well, almost. Jerry's role in all this bothered me. After leaving Frida last night, I had taken a quick look at the papers he had thrown to me. Based on what I'd read so far, Jerry had sold me out again. This morning I had tucked them into my overnight bag, vowing to find time to examine them in more detail once we got to Key Largo.

THE BOAT WAS riding up and down on her lines and the rain was slashing at the windows in the galley. You could get quite comfortable inside if you had the stomach for rolling and pitching. I did. Our family had always owned some kind of boat, motor or sail, and I was used to rough weather on any vessel, as long as it was bigger than an inner tube.

Max was up on deck making sure that the lines were secure so that we could leave for dinner.

"Sorry about this weather, dearie," said Grandy. "I guess you won't be getting a tan this weekend."

Record cold was being predicted for tomorrow. I had managed to select one of the Key's few chilly weekends for my vacation. I didn't care about cold, wind and rain. I just welcomed being surrounded by people I loved and who felt the same about me. Not that Madeleine and I didn't love each other. We were the best of friends, almost like sisters, but Grandy had been there all my life, through some very tough periods.

"I'll be down another time when I can soak up some sun. For now, I'm just happy to be here with you and Max. We haven't had family time for so long."

The boat was small compared to many of the local charters. There was one head, a small galley, and three cabins—two in the bow and a larger one, occupied by Grandy and Max, in the stern. I took the one on the left of the companionway ladder. The room barely had enough space to turn around in, even if you were careful to tuck your arms to your sides. I stashed my overnight bag under the berth, then, thinking twice about the action, pulled it out again to extract the papers that Jerry had given me. I wanted to take another look at them before we departed for the local eatery.

The only way to read in the small room was to lie down on the bed, so I lowered myself onto the firm mattress and turned on the small light above my pillow. By the time I had digested the contents of the documents, my suspicions had been confirmed. I wanted to join the manhunt for Jerry, and I hoped that I'd find him before the cops did. When I did, I wanted to shake him silly, then kill him. My murderous fantasy was interrupted by a knock at the door, followed by Grandy's voice.

"Let's go, sweetie. You know there'll be a line, and I'm starving."

I placed the papers under my pillow and turned off the light. Through the port window I could see only rain and palm trees bending in the wind. *Where's Jerry?* It would have been a fine night for his murder.

When I opened the door, Grandy looked at my face and scowled. "This is supposed to be a vacation. I know the weather is rotten, but you look like you have your own storm brewing inside. What's up?"

There was no sense in making Max and Grandy pay for Jerry's actions. "I'm sorry. I guess I'm just letting this cold get me down." Grandy didn't believe me. She threw me one of her 'You're lying' looks.

"We'll talk over food." She took my arm and pushed me toward the companionway. "Take one of those rain slickers on your right. You'll need it."

THE THREE OF US arrived at the restaurant looking like Cape Cod fisherman in our yellow raingear. The locals in the place hardly glanced in our direction. We clearly belonged there.

The tourists entered with their best tropical wear beaten by wind and rain, their Jam's World regalia so limp and weather-beaten that it had lost all its resale value. I felt sorry for them. This wasn't the weather that they had packed for. Some of them had obviously wised up and purchased sweatshirts and jackets from the local merchants with "Key Largo" logos.

Family Kitchen, the restaurant we chose for dinner, was frequented by Key Largo residents and occasionally discovered by tourists. It had atmosphere, but not the kind usually associated with Keys dining. There was no sandy beach seating where one could sit outside and listen to the wind in the palms. Oh, you could eat outside if you wanted, but you had to do so under an aluminum overhang within inches of the gravel parking lot, where the insistent roar of automobiles racing down Highway 1 would interfere with intimate conversation.

Inside, the two small dining areas were filled with cracked vinyl booths, mismatched chairs and wooden tabletops that had been marked by the initials of many impatient diners. The entrance to the dining rooms was partially blocked by a large bar and the double-hinged doors of a tiny kitchen. You could either put your name on the waiting list or hover at the crowded bar, where you were almost guaranteed to touch butts with an eager stranger trying to push through to the counter.

The food was that good.

A table opened up and an employee yelled Max's name. We ran over, and Max waved away the menus the waitress offered.

"There's only one dish to order here for dinner. Fried whole yellowtail. Three." He held up as many fingers. Grandy and I nodded our agreement.

This was where we ate every time we were in Key Largo. You could find fine gourmet dining, but this was just great eats. We drank local ale with dinner and ate with little conversation until I pushed away my empty plate, sat back in my chair and sighed. I was relieved that Grandy was as swept up in her food as I had been. I wasn't eager to talk about my mood, since Jerry was the cause of it. I wasn't off the hook yet.

"There's a lull in the storm," Max observed. "Quieter."

The hot food and the ever-growing number of patrons in the small dining area were creating enough warmth to chase away the damp and cold. Our abandoned slickers lay in a shiny vinyl heap on an empty chair. Max swallowed the last of his beer and, seeing that the two of us were finished as well, ordered another round. Extracting a handkerchief from his pocket, he wiped perspiration off his sunburned brow and cheeks. He really did look like Hemingway—well, at least like a computer-aged version.

The waitress set three full bottles on the table.

Grandy ignored hers and skewered me with one of her 'fess up looks. "Now. Tell."

"Uh-oh, sounds serious," said Max.

"Something's aggravating Eve. She doesn't look happy. What do you think, Max?"

"Maybe the weather's getting her down. It certainly doesn't make for that sunny vacation we promised her."

Two pairs of eyes fixed on me without wavering. They were kind and friendly, and I knew I couldn't lie to them. I took a quick sip of beer.

"It's Jerry."

"It's always Jerry," Grandy said. Max nodded in agreement.

"When I went back to Sanders' house, I saw him inside the study with a gun in his hand. He opened the window and shoved some papers at me. Now I know why he was so interested in getting into that house and why Napolitani let him wander off while we were examining the knife."

"Napolitani was in on this?" asked Grandy.

"Yep, I think so."

Max reached out and patted my hand. "It's okay, honey. You can tell us. We know you've got a soft spot for Jerry."

I exploded. "Soft spot? Don't be silly. Jerry and me, that's water under the bridge, especially since he signed away all of our assets, the idiot."

"He did what?" asked Grandy.

"He sold the house in Connecticut, the sailboat, his condo in the Bahamas and the Jag to Sanders. Oh sure, they were his to sell. His name was on those properties, but our divorce agreement stipulates that he owes me a percentage of the sale value, and he sold them to Sanders for peanuts. Now why'd he do that?"

"It's simple. If it's only a percentage of the value and not a fixed amount that he owes you, it means he won't have to pay you much. A typical Jerry move." Grandy moved her bottle around and around, creating a pattern of wet circles on the table.

"I don't think so. Something else is up. He gave me the papers for safekeeping. He had to know I'd look at them. It was some kind of message, but I'll be damned if I can figure it out."

They looked first at me then at each other, expressing pain and sympathy. "You need to get over that man."

Max nodded. "Maybe, because you signed those papers without a lawyer, something can be done to alter the terms of the divorce."

"Maybe." My mind was somewhere else. Jerry couldn't be as bad as recent evidence was making him out to be. If only I could talk to him.

NINETEEN

THE WIND CAUGHT our raincoats and whipped them around our knees as we ran from the restaurant to the car.

"She's not letting up any." Max unlocked the car doors, and we slid into the warmth of the interior.

From the passenger seat, Grandy twisted around to talk to me. The beads of water in her white hair twinkled in the parking lot lights like dew on a foggy morning.

"I hope you won't think I'm being nosy," she said, "but I'd sure like to see those papers Jerry gave you."

"Sure. Why not? Maybe you and Max can tell me what I'm not seeing." I leaned back into my seat and watched the halos of light pass by my window.

We dashed from the car to the boat, crowding down the companionway and into the small galley.

"I'll make coffee." Grandy grabbed the old aluminum drip pot from the overhead cupboard. "You fetch those papers."

I hung my slicker back on its hook and entered my cabin. When I moved the pillow aside, I found my hiding place empty. A quick search of the bed and the small storage space below revealed nothing. I was more than a little creeped out. Who had gotten in, and why would they take those papers?

I stuck my head out of the cabin. "They're gone. Somebody took them while we were at dinner."

"I locked the hatch door. How could anybody get in here without a key?" asked Max.

I thought immediately of Mr. Napolitani and his expertise with locks. My eyes met those of Grandy, and I knew she was thinking the same thing.

"We were followed," I said. "I'll bet Jerry has those papers back in his possession."

"Helped by a future relative." Grandy slapped the pot lid closed and placed it on the stove.

"I guess for Napolitani, family is everything." I sank into the gallery bench seat.

"Look, girls," Max slid in beside me, "we're all tired from the day and the weather. We can talk this through tomorrow. Let's just get a good night's sleep."

"After coffee," said Grandy.

"I'll pass. I'm too bummed out and exhausted to stay on my feet another minute. I'm going to make friends with my berth." I kissed both of them goodnight and entered my cabin. I'd just turned off the overhead light when my new cell rang.

I hit the answer button. Hard. "This better be important, like natural disaster important."

"It's Jerry."

"Isn't it always?"

"What do you mean?"

"Whenever I feel like I've bottomed out, you show up and make things worse. Go away."

"Okay."

"No. Wait. First tell me why you took those papers."

"What do you mean?"

I sat up in the bed and switched on the light, as if

illumination might help me deal with my aggravating ex-husband.

"I know what was in them, and I don't appreciate having our divorce settlement taken away so easily."

"That's the whole point, Evie. The property sales were never registered. I've got the only existing copies."

"How was I supposed to know what you had in mind? Anyway, you gave them to me, yet you didn't trust me enough so you had to break into my Grandy's boat and steal them. Napolitani helped you, didn't he?" I slammed my pillow across the small cabin in frustration.

"Are you saying you don't have them anymore, that someone stole them?"

"You. You took them." Now I was yelling into the phone, my voice loud enough to alert Grandy and Max. I hesitated. "You did steal them, didn't you?"

"I did not."

"Well then, do you know who did and why?"

"I've got a good idea."

"You know the cops are looking for you, right?"

"Looking for me? Why?"

"For attempted murder and kidnapping."

There was silence on the line. "I'm shocked. And innocent." He sounded genuinely taken aback, but Jerry was a master at feigning surprise.

"Who did I kidnap and attempt to kill?"

"Me."

More silence. The only way I could tell that he hadn't disconnected was that I could hear breathing interspersed with gulping noises.

"Now that's crazy. Why would I do that? Who said I did?"

"Sanders told the police you were the one who threw me into a car trunk and drove me off into the Everglades."

"Figures."

"Is that all you've got to say. Don't you want to hear what happened to me? I could have been killed."

"Sorry, honey. Listen, I'm parked in a strip mall in Ft. Lauderdale and… Cops. Gotta go." He clicked off.

"You okay in there?" Grandy tapped on my door. "I thought I heard you yelling. Are you having a bad dream?"

A bad dream? That would have been nice.

MAYBE IT WAS the quiet descending on the marina that woke me, a startling silence after a long night of rain lashing against the windows and palm fronds rattling in the frenzied wind. Then I heard soft footsteps on the deck above. A tap on my door soon followed.

"I heard it, too," whispered Max through the door. "I'll take care of whoever's up there."

Max was seventy-eight years old and in good shape for a man of that age, but handling an intruder would take strength as well as stealth. I opened the door and grabbed a heavy skillet from the galley. Max might require support.

When I stepped onto the deck, I could see that my help was superfluous. Max was standing against the cabin with a spear gun in his hands, pointing the ugly thing at a man in the bow.

"This guy says he knows you."

Grandy came up the companionway, a flashlight

in her hand. She pushed around me and pointed the beam of light at our intruder's face.

I expected Alex or Jerry, but the face I saw was a complete surprise.

"Dwight Sanders. What are you doing here?"

"Hold this." Max handed me the spear gun. "I'm going to search him."

I handed Grandy my frying pan and took Max's weapon.

Dwight didn't move while Max thoroughly patted him down. When he was finished, I handed the spear gun back.

"The cops are looking for you. They think you killed your stepmother. I think you kidnapped me and left me in the swamp to die. I'm puzzled. Why are you here? Trying to get another shot at me?"

"No. No." He held out his hands and moved toward me.

Max menaced him with the spear gun, and he backed away again.

"Could you tell the old guy to put that thing down? Do you have any idea what that could do to a man if it went off?"

"Yes, I do, son." The spear gun remained pointed at Dwight's chest. "Eve, call the cops."

"Wait. Give me a little time here. I didn't kill anybody. I can prove it, too."

"How?" I asked.

"In my car. I've got a tape of a conversation between my…"

Suddenly an explosion ripped through the air, and a fireball shot into the night sky.

"That was close. It looks like it came from the parking lot of the Mariner's Motel," said Grandy.

Dwight groaned. "That's where I left my car."

Grandy, Max and I watched as flames shot into the air. Charred and burning pieces of debris fell onto the dock nearby.

Another sound, like hands clapping, rent the air.

"Get down," yelled Max. "Someone's shooting at us." The three of us hit the deck.

"Oh, crap!" yelled Dwight. "They must have followed me here."

I heard a splash and Dwight was gone.

We waited but heard no more shots. The fire lit up the marina, and many of the boat owners who had moved up to their decks when the commotion began were now running down the quay toward the conflagration.

I peered overboard, expecting to spot Dwight's body, but there was nothing there except the eerie reflection of undulating orange and red flames in the black water.

The sound of fire engines and emergency vehicles filled the night air. The fire was now giving off mostly sooty smoke. As firefighters and EMTs flooded the scene, my thoughts were carried back to Sabal City and the night my car had met a similar fate.

BY THE TIME the police had finished interviewing us and the firefighters had completed their work on the burned car, it was close to morning. A wedge of sun appeared for a moment on the horizon, but a line of gray clouds slapped it away. The rain began again and the temperature dropped another ten degrees.

Instead of going back to sleep, we stayed up and drank several pots of coffee to kick our brains into gear. Seated around the galley table, we were playing yet another hand of Pitch, probably our fiftieth of the morning.

"You think he got away?" Grandy shuffled the deck and dealt.

"Absolutely, or we would have found a body this morning floating in the canal," said Max.

"I still don't get why he came here to talk with me. How did he know where I was?"

"It was no secret that you were coming down here with me." Grandy threw her ace onto the table and took my two of trump.

"It sounds to me like he was trying to finish what he had messed up by leaving you in the Everglades." Max examined his hand and scowled.

"I just don't get any of this. Once he had botched the kidnapping and I had the opportunity to identify him as the man by Valerie's car at my shop, he should have stayed out of sight. There was no reason for him to come here and try again."

"You don't believe he's innocent, do you?" Max tossed a junk trump card when Grandy led with her jack. "You better come back at me with trump, honey." He waggled his bushy eyebrows at her.

"Forget it. I've made my three points."

I sat at the table, looking at my cards but not making any sense of what was in my hand. I had thought for sure that Dwight was the one who'd kidnapped me and killed his mother. It all fit so nicely. Except for motive. Why would he kill her?

"You still playing, Eve?" asked Grandy.

"I got nothing. I'm just marking time here."

Several minutes later, Grandy made her points, for the fourth time in a row, while Max and I both sat empty handed. At least Max had some points on the board from other hands. My score was minus eight.

"Time for lunch." Grandy busied herself making tuna sandwiches while I put the cards away and wiped the table. Their moods were absurdly buoyant on this lousy day, and I couldn't figure out why.

"You beat the pants off both of us at cards, Grandy, so I can understand your cheerfulness. But, Max, you surprise me. No charters in this weather, and it doesn't look like it'll clear soon. Yet you're as chipper as she is. What's going on?"

Just then someone yelled, "Permission to come aboard."

"Aha. Come on. We're below," Max yelled back.

The companionway door opened with a rush of wind and salt water, and Alex's head appeared.

"What the hell are you doing here?" I asked.

"You didn't tell her you called me?" He removed his jacket, held it back out the door and shook the rain off.

"We wanted to surprise you, Eve," Grandy said. "You seemed so down, we thought that Alex might cheer you up. He can give you a ride back to Sabal City. He'll be much more interesting company than I would be." Grandy's eyes twinkled.

Their heightened spirits irritated me. If I wanted to be upset, I had the right. After all, someone had tried to kill me. More than once.

"If you didn't want to drive me back, you should have said so. I can take a bus."

Three faces settled hurt looks on me.

"I'm sorry. I'm sorry." I felt bad about lashing out at them. After all, they were just trying to help.

"No, honey, we're the ones who should apologize. You put on such a brave front, I guess we didn't realize how shook up you were over what happened," Grandy said. "I assumed you were out of sorts because of the weather. We wanted to make this weekend better for you, so we called Alex."

Part of what she had said was true. She did want me to have a good time. The Alex part? Well, that was the matchmaker in her surfacing. It had nothing to do with what I wanted.

"I can leave," offered Alex.

"You can, but I bet you won't." I bit my tongue. I *was* in a foul mood. "Anyway, I think I'd like to get back to the shop."

"Why? It's Saturday. By the time you arrive, it'll be closing time. Tomorrow is Sunday. You aren't open," Grandy said. "Let's take in a movie at the local cinema and have dinner out. You can leave early tomorrow."

My shoulders slumped in resignation. Then I glanced at Alex. I'd forgotten how appealing he could look. It was absolutely yummy the way his damp hair curled over his forehead and ears. "Sounds good."

THE MOVIE WE SAW was a romantic comedy and it would have been funny had it not been for the temperature in the theater. Nobody invests in central heating in the Keys, and the movie theater was no exception. On the other hand, the cool temperature did have its perks— Alex wrapped his arm around me to keep me warm. I wanted to stay for another showing.

Instead of staying for a double feature, we decided

to go to a local eatery for wings. For some inexplicable reason, that place had a furnace, and, to my disappointment, it was on. I sat next to Alex and the warmth from his body made the place even toastier.

It was after eleven by the time we got back to the boat. Alex took the cabin across from mine. I thought that I might have difficulty sleeping, that his proximity would send out waves of attraction, luring me toward his berth, but I fell quickly into a dreamless slumber. I didn't even stir until the next morning when Max shouted that he had the Sunday paper.

"You're gonna want to see the headlines." He tapped on my door.

I threw on a tee shirt and a pair of jeans. Running a hand through my hair, I appeared in the galley, where my shipmates were already devouring the news.

"Let me see that." I grabbed the paper out of Alex's hands and read.

"Looks like our murderer got murdered," he said.

TWENTY

"BODY FOUND IN CANAL," I read aloud from the head-lines then quickly perused the front-page article. "It says here, 'The man, who was shot in the head, has been identified as Dwight Sanders, a prominent West Palm Beach businessman.' Businessman? Dwight? It goes on to say that he was a person of interest in the murder of his stepmother and that he was last sighted in Key Largo."

"I guess that's the end of that," said Alex.

"The end of what? Somebody killed him, wanted to keep him from telling what he knew about Valerie's murder. It's not the end of anything. It's merely another piece of this confusing puzzle." I tossed the paper on the table.

"You mean, you believe what Dwight said?" Grandy turned to Alex. "This girl, sophisticated in so many ways, is dumb as swamp water about men, especially bad boys like Jerry and Dwight."

"Motive, Grandy. Why would Dwight want to kill his stepmother?"

Max shrugged. "The usual. Money, maybe."

"She didn't have any." Alex said it quickly and with certainty.

"How do you know?" I asked.

"Uh, Jerry told me. We talked about the investment

thing that he had gotten the Sanders into and how they had lost millions."

He looked so guilty when he said it.

"Now why would Jerry confess that to you? He lied to me about any involvement with Sanders and his family."

"He was drunk when we had the discussion."

"See. What did I tell you? Here she is cross-examining the wrong guy," said Grandy.

"Oh, I intend to have a chat with Jerry, too. When I find him. Hopefully that will happen before the cops get to him."

Grandy set a plate of sandwiches on the table and ordered us to "Eat up." I continued to eye Alex with skepticism, but he was too busy engaging Max in boat talk to notice. Grandy kicked me under the table and whispered a "Be nice" in my direction. I screwed up my face but kept my mouth shut.

I ate only half of my sandwich, then left everyone at the table to finish their coffee and Key lime pie leftovers while I packed my overnight bag.

Grandy handed me a brown paper bag. "There's a piece of pie for you in here. Another one for Alex, too." Then she hugged me goodbye. "Call me when you get home."

Alex and I drove the "strip," the twenty-plus miles between Key Largo and Homestead, without speaking. As we turned onto the Florida Turnpike, Alex broke the silence.

"Why do you dislike me so much?"

I couldn't tell him that I distanced myself to protect my poor abused heart, broken years ago by Jerry and jump-started every time the man had cheated on me.

He would have said that was irrelevant. Maybe it was.
I didn't know the rules for having a relationship with
anybody other than a bad boy. What did one do with a
nice guy who treated you with deference and respect?
One you wanted to wrestle into bed every time he so
much as looked at you. So I told him part of the truth,
the part that kept me from throwing myself at him.

"I don't dislike you. I just don't trust you, and I
think I have good reason for that, don't you?"

"Do you? Like what?"

"You know. You've had relations with the Sanders family."

"As a private investigator only."

I gave him a long, hard look. "Really? You kept the
PI job even after Valerie was murdered. What was that
about? Didn't Sanders believe the police were good
enough to solve the crime? Then when he found out
that you and I were friendly, he fired you. Why? See,
I've got a lot of unanswered questions about you. Are
you going to answer them for me? I don't think so."

As if on cue, my cell rang. Good old Jerry, but
would *he* tell me the truth? Or was I just going to hear
more lies?

ALEX AND I waited in front of a Starbucks in the West
Palm Service Center. After a half hour of swiveling
our heads each time a lone man entered the center, I
told Alex I had to use the ladies' room. "You know
Jerry. You can spot him as well as I can."

"Yeah, but you lied to him. You told him you were
alone, driving a rental back to Sabal City. I don't think
Jerry will be happy to see me."

"I gotta pee. We'll have to take the chance." I turned my back and ran for the restroom.

I felt immeasurably more relaxed when I left the stall. I was washing my hands when a woman wearing far too much makeup pushed up to the sink next to me, shoving me off balance.

"Sorry, honey. I tripped. How you can balance on those heels is beyond me."

I shot her a dirty look, but she shouldered me out of the way, reaching across the sink to grab a paper towel.

"What's your problem?" I asked. Then I took a good look at her. "She" was no "her."

"Hi, Evie. Pretty good get-up, huh? It got me past Alex. Say, what's going on between you two, anyway? How come he got an invite to the boat, but I got left out?" Jerry's smile revealed lipstick-covered teeth.

"Alex is not wanted by the police. Grandy seems to prefer her guests that way."

Jerry pulled me away from the sinks and into the corner by the changing table. He was wearing stiletto heels as high as mine and a coral dress that clung to curves I knew he did not have. A pair of oversized sunglasses sat atop a blond wig. I reached out to touch it. It felt like real hair. Catching my gesture, the washroom attendant rolled her eyes. With Jerry's hand on my arm and mine in his hair, this must have looked like more than a casual conversation.

"I've got a few questions for you," he said.

"Oh, no, not until you answer some of mine. Like, why did you sell Sanders our condo, house, and boat?"

"You got the papers on you?"

"I told you. I don't. Someone snatched them from under my pillow back at the boat."

Jerry groaned. "Don't you know better than to hide important stuff in the most obvious place?"

"I guess I didn't take the same 'How to be a Clever Criminal 101' course as you."

"Who do you think took them?" he asked.

"My first guess was you."

"Wrong. Sanders must have sent someone down."

That made sense.

"The papers, Jerry. Why did you sell the stuff at such a reduced price?"

"He threatened to go to the Securities and Exchange Commission and tell them that I had known the investments I recommended were part of a Ponzi scheme. You know, where the early investors make money because the consultant pays them from the later investments."

"You didn't know about it, did you?" I leaned in, as if getting closer to his heavily mascaraed lashes and pancaked face would allow me to discern the truth.

"I didn't know squat about that scheme, but Sanders was rightly pissed when he lost all that money. Someone had to pay. He made that someone me."

"I don't see how taking those documents changes anything."

"Mr. Napolitani recommended that I get them back. He said it would give us some wiggle room when talking with Sanders."

"Wiggle room? What kind of 'wiggle room'?"

"Never mind. Listen, I've got to go."

"One more question. What's the relationship between Alex and the Sanders family?"

Jerry hesitated just a moment too long, then applied another layer of paint to his already thickly powdered face. But this layer wasn't cosmetic, this one was the illusion of innocence. "I don't know what you're talking about," he said. Then he walked out.

After he had left I let myself fall back against the baby-changing table, wondering why it was so damn difficult to get a straight answer from either Alex or Jerry. They were so different in so many ways, yet so alike when it came to acting sincere and avoiding the truth.

I had found out something from Jerry, however. I now knew how easily a clever man could dress up like a woman in order to blend in. Dressed like that, any man could go unnoticed in a public toilet, or perhaps, a shop full of customers. A man could get away with murder dressed like that. They could also reenter said shop at a later date to cover their tracks, maybe steal a knife to replace the one that they had lost in the heat of the moment. How fortunate for them that I'd dropped one on the back room floor. Oh, it wouldn't have been Jerry, of course, but someone else. I felt even more certain now that Valerie's killer had access to the Sanders' house. That meant both family and friends were suspect. Maybe not Dwight. Poor dead Dwight.

"WHAT TOOK YOU so long? I was about to send in a mounted patrol."

"That's not the kind of question you ask a lady," I said, feigning offense. "No Jerry?"

"Nope."

"I guess he chickened out then." I looked around the crowded area but saw no sign of the "woman" who had accosted me in the restroom.

"Yeah, well, I've seen Highway Patrol officers

going in and out. If he wants to remain a free man, he should start picking better meeting places. Let's go." He gave the area one last look, then grabbed my hand.

An hour and a half later, we pulled up in front of my house.

"I'll come in and take a peek around. To make certain no one's here," Alex said.

"Like who? Dwight's dead and Jerry's not going to show his face here." I reached for the car door handle. Alex put his hand on my shoulder.

"We should talk."

"Oh?" About time. But being inches away from his full lips made me forget how important the truth was to me. Talk could wait. Gravity was pulling me in.

There was an untimely tap on the car door.

"Hey. I'm not interrupting anything, am I?" Madeleine's perky face appeared in the window.

Alex looked peeved. Whether that was because he really did want to talk or because he was about to communicate in another way, I couldn't tell. My face must have shown relief because now I didn't have to wrestle with my conscience. The furrows on his forehead deepened.

I rolled down the window. "Hey there. No, we just pulled up and were considering dinner. Want to join us?"

Alex slammed his palms on the steering wheel. "Oh, damn. I forgot. I have some paperwork to do. I'll carry your bag in, and the two of you can catch up."

"Never mind the bag. I've got it." I reached back and grabbed my duffle, then hopped out of the car. "Thanks for the lift. Sorry the weather wasn't better."

"Maybe next time." He saluted me and then shifted into drive.

Madeleine and I watched the car zoom off, its back wheels spinning out on the loose gravel.

"What did you do to him?" she said. "Any faster and he'd have ripped the tires clean off that car."

"Let's go to the Burnt Biscuit, eat steak and get crazy with some cowboys. I need a little fun."

THERE WAS A bass tournament in town and the anglers seemed to have chased all the cattle jockeys back to the range. I like fishermen, but, when you want to have fun, there's nothing more annoying than having to listen to fishing stories that grow longer and more absurd as the night wears on. We ate our steak and wandered home. Madeleine offered to spend the night, but I assured her that I was fine.

"You're not saying that because you think something would go wrong if I stayed here, are you?"

I considered several possibilities: an unexpected hurricane, a cattle stampede through my neighborhood or a plane dropping out of the sky and landing on my roof. I couldn't see how she could cause any of those. Well, maybe the stampede, so I decided not to chance it.

"No, honey. I just want to be alone tonight."

Madeleine and I opened the store together Monday morning. It was after noon when the first customer appeared. The initial rush of murder-inflated interest had definitely subsided. Trade was down, and not for a lack of classy inventory. I had to get to the bottom of this murder or we'd be filing bankruptcy in a month.

I hadn't heard from Alex since he had left me to

wrestle with my hormones. Madeleine insisted that I was too tough on him, too suspicious of his motives for being around me, too distrusting of one of the good guys. I wasn't certain. I needed another opinion, so I called Grandy, who agreed with Madeleine's appraisal of the situation. That wasn't what I wanted to hear. I shoved their assessments to the back of my mind and considered other issues.

Suspicions of the Sanders family and their circle of friends bothered me. Dwight's death had made it easy for the authorities to wrap up the case, but I was still pondering the issue of motive. Since nothing was happening in the store, I made several phone calls to acquaintances in Connecticut. We talked about old money, old families, and those individuals who skirted the edges of the law. I had no contact number for Napolitani, but I thought I might be able to get in touch with him through his daughter, my soon-to-be-replacement, Jerry's new fiancé.

"Hi. This is Eve. You know, Eve Appel. Do you have a minute?" Friendly, casual, as if we knew each other better than we actually did.

Her voice was bitter. "I know, and I'm not interested in speaking with you unless you tell me what you did with Jerry."

"I didn't do anything with him. He did things with himself."

"What's that supposed to mean?"

I was tempted to tell her he dressed like a woman on at least one occasion, maybe more, but I stopped myself.

"Nothing. Could you tell me how to get in touch with your father?"

"Why?"

This conversation wasn't going as well as I'd hoped. "Never mind. Just tell him I'd like to talk with him."

"I'm not telling him a thing." The line went dead.

The conversation had gleaned more than I thought it would. Now I knew Jerry hadn't been in touch with his fiancée and the soon-to-be mother of his child. Why not?

Madeleine and I were about to close early when a black limousine pulled up in front of the store. Goodie. Patrons from the coast.

I couldn't have been more wrong.

The chauffeur got out and walked around to open the back door. Madeleine and I stood transfixed in front of the window as Leon Sanders, Valerie's husband, got out and walked into the shop.

"Mr. Sanders. I'm sorry to hear about your son."

The expression of doubt and anger on his face told me didn't believe me for a minute and even if he did, he couldn't have cared less about my condolences.

"Let's dispense with the pleasantries." He stopped mid-sentence, as if he had realized that there was nothing pleasurable about a death in the family, condolences or not. He made a dismissive gesture with his hand. "I'd like to talk to your grandmother."

"Grandy?"

"Yes, I believe that's the one."

"About what?"

"That's between her and me."

I wasn't going to let this man bully me. "Mr. Sanders, you're in my shop. On my turf. You're asking me to do you a favor. One I'm not certain that I approve of. I love my Grandy, and I'll do anything to protect her, especially from you and Valerie's family. So, whether you like it or not, you'll have to go through me if you want to speak to her."

Valery . . .

ac . . .

TWENTY-ONE

LEON SANDERS CAST his gaze up at the ceiling, as if it
held the answers to our predicament. Finally his eyes
met mine. He heaved a deep sigh then sighed again,
as if he needed more air than my tiny shop provided.

"Must I tell you why I want to see your grandmother?"

"Yes, I insist."

He veered away from me, as if to leave. Then he
doubled back again, a look of stubborn determination
on his features.

"The locket. You know what I'm talking about?"

I nodded, not trusting myself to say anything about
Franklin's gift to Grandy.

"Valerie loved that locket. Now it's the only thing
that I have left from her family."

"Valerie loved the *idea* of the locket. Grandy's had
it since long before Valerie was born. Besides, I find
it very difficult to believe that the locket is the only
remaining jewelry from the Wartons. Both your families were neck deep in jewels. There are hundreds of
pictures in the society columns to attest to that."

"They're gone. All gone."

"Stolen?"

"Uh, no. Apparently, Valerie was in such despair
about our financial state that she pawned them."

"You found the pawn tickets, I gather."

"No. I hired PI Montgomery to follow her and he quickly learned what she was doing. He told me shortly before her death."

"The entire family knew of this? That she was pawning your family heirlooms?"

He nodded.

Could that somehow have been a motive for Dwight to kill her? It didn't make sense to me.

"Did you confront her?"

"No. I was going to, but before we could talk, someone killed her."

"Someone? So you don't think it was Dwight?"

Mr. Sanders' face reddened. "Of course not."

"Fine. I don't think Dwight did it either, but the authorities seem happy to wrap up the case by saying that Dwight was murdered by a drug deal gone wrong."

"Dwight wasn't involved with drugs."

Now that was the song sung by all clueless parents.

"I don't see what this has to do with the locket and Grandy unless you think she'll take pity on a jewel-less family. Maybe that's a tragedy in West Palm, but it's not where we come from."

Sanders' face told me he was weighing his options. Option "A" had been the sympathy plea, but that didn't seem to be working. So this time around, he opted for plan "B."

"I'll find the money to pay for it."

I laughed hard enough to bring tears to my eyes. He certainly didn't know my Grandy. Money couldn't sway her.

"Sure." I wiped my eyes on my shirtsleeve. "I'd be happy to hook you up with Grandy." This story seemed typical and arrogant. Both Valerie's family and the Sanders clan had underestimated what the locket meant to Grandy. It wasn't about the money. It was about love.

I thought Grandy needed some humor in her life right now, given the miserable weather, so I flipped open my cell and left Sanders standing in the front of the store while I wandered out back. To my surprise, I didn't get the chuckle I had expected, but she did me one better. A loud toot like an auditory sneer came through the phone. "Well, we sure can't fish in this weather. We'll head on up there."

"Hold on a minute." I turned to Sanders. "She'll be here in three hours."

"Make it two," he said. "We can meet at my house."

Imperious man. He wanted a favor yet thought he could dictate the terms.

"Fine. Give me directions," said Grandy, who was still waiting on the line.

I whispered into the cell. "This guy makes me nervous. Are you sure you want to meet on his turf?"

"I'll have Max with me. Why don't you call Alex?"

Because I don't trust Alex either, I thought. I didn't say it out loud because Grandy would have just given me the lecture on good guys and bad guys again.

SEVERAL HOURS LATER, I pulled into the Sanders' drive and parked my rental alongside several other cars— a Beemer convertible, a Lexus, and two Mercedes. I hadn't had time to shop for another car, and my rented Ford Focus looked like Cinderella's pumpkin a day after the ball. Grandy and Max's car wasn't there yet. Should I wait for them before going into the house? Another vehicle pulled into the drive, one that was familiar to me. It was the black SUV owned by Mr. Napolitani.

The driver's-side window went down and the dark, handsome head of Nappi Napolitani appeared, gleaming smile and all.

"I have something I'd like to give to you." He handed me a large manila envelope.

I opened it and pulled out Jerry's ownership papers.

"So you were the one responsible for nabbing these from under my pillow. Why? I thought we were on the same side."

"Of course we are, but I was worried that your hiding place wasn't as secure as the one that I could provide, so I was just holding onto them for you."

"Why not give them to Jerry?"

Napolitani's face darkened. "He hasn't contacted me or my daughter. I'm looking for him."

"You know the police are, too."

He waved a dismissive, manicured hand at me. "Police. Ha."

"Sanders told them he was the one who kidnapped me."

Napolitani gave a derisive snort. "You show these papers to Sanders and tell him that you got them from me. He'd like to get them back, and we might even agree to that if he changes his story about Jerry. Right?"

"No, we wouldn't agree to that. Jerry sold my divorce settlement, tiny as it was, by turning that property over to Sanders."

"We'll work out something." The window rolled up. Napolitani drove off.

I stood there, dumbfounded, holding the envelope.

I didn't know much about what was going on with Napolitani, Jerry, or the Sanders family so I hoped that
Grandy and Max would be better than I was at dealing
with the rich and the criminally inclined.

Alex's car pulled into the drive. *Hey, hey, the gang's
all here.* I hadn't called him. *Wonder who did.* Or was
he just getting accustomed to popping in for visits
every now and then? "You," I said.

"Me. I guess you're not too happy to see me."

That wasn't true. I loved seeing those eyes, imagining the feel of his sun-streaked hair against my fingers
and dreaming of his hands on my shoulders, his lips
on mine and… But, no! I wasn't happy about seeing
him here, despite my daydreams of us being together,
in bed. The real-life Alex had too many secrets.

I ignored his comment and rang the bell. To my
surprise, Cory Burnside answered. Beyond her, in the
large living room, I could see Randolph, Leon, his
daughter Constance, and her husband Eduardo. That
other woman, Marie Someone—the one I saw at the
funeral, who looked like Eduardo's female clone—
was also there. I walked past Cory, my heels making
a click-clacking noise on the marble floor.

"The wealthy plead their case. Great title for a reality show." I threw my purse on the couch, fell into the
leather chair next to it and crossed my legs.

Leon raised his arm and looked at his Rolex. "Your
grandmother's late."

"I think your watch is fast. I set mine by the short
wave radio in my house. It's accurate. Maybe you need
to have your battery checked." I tapped my Timex with
the black faux-leather band.

He made a sound that sounded much like a "hurrumph." Good. I had provoked him.

The bell rang again. This time Randolph went to the door. He showed Max and Grandy in. I hugged them both and whispered in Grandy's ear, "Careful of these vultures." She patted my cheek with a look that said she'd handled worse.

Leon didn't even ask them to sit down before he started making demands. "I want you to return the locket you took from Valerie's family."

Randolph cleared his throat. "I don't think that's the best approach to use, old man. Let's everyone sit and we'll discuss this." He gestured to the couch. Grandy and Max sat. Randolph introduced everyone, including himself, Cory and Stella, the clone, who turned out to be someone's personal secretary.

"Why are you here, Randolph?" I asked.

"Leon is upset, given the recent events—you know, the murder of both his wife and son. He asked me to speak for him."

"You should have spoken first then, before he could piss everyone off."

Randolph smiled and nodded. "I'm sure Leon is sorry he acted so…"

"Imperious?" I said. "Demanding? So much like an ass?"

Randolph chose to ignore my words. "The jewels from the Warton family and from the Sanders family are gone, pawned by Valerie in a desperate attempt to raise money. She was, of course, trying to repair the damage inflicted by your husband." He shot me a look of contempt. And here I had thought that Randolph liked me.

"*Ex*-husband. And he was cleared of all charges," Grandy said.

"Whatever." Randolph waved away her remark in that oh so irritating manner that the wealthy often have. "Because Valerie loved that locket so…." Grandy and I both snorted. "Because her daughter would like something to remind her of her mother, we're asking you to consider returning it. For a price, of course."

I got out of my chair and wandered over to the bar, lifting the scotch bottle in order to examine it. Leon came over and pulled it out of my hand. He pointedly set it down beyond my reach.

"Why don't you take the money that Valerie got from pawning the jewels and just buy them back?" asked Grandy.

There was silence in the room. Randolph spoke. "May I tell them, Leon?" Leon nodded. "They don't have the money. It's gone."

"Gone? Gone where?" asked Max.

Leon shrugged. "We have no idea."

I looked around the room. Since I didn't believe that Dwight had killed his stepmother, I figured that someone in this room was probably guilty of her murder and might have had a hand in Dwight's as well. The money from the jewelry? From what Valerie had said to me and Cory, it would seem that she had invested it somehow, somewhere.

"Any ideas, Cory?" I asked.

"How should I know? I wasn't with her when she went to those awful places to sell the stuff."

"How about you, Alex? You were following her. Did she ever go to a bank or an investment firm?"

"No." If he felt like I was attacking him, he didn't

show it. He remained his cool self, leaning nonchalantly against the doorjamb by the pool area. "She kept her usual schedule in the afternoon, either going to the stables, to Sabal City, or out to lunch with Cory and her other friends."

Leon pushed Randolph aside. "This is getting us nowhere. Now what about that locket?"

Grandy pulled the locket from beneath her shirt and held it in her hand. "I came here to let you know face-to-face that I won't let the locket go. I can understand how you feel about losing the other family heirlooms, but this locket was Franklin's to give to me. It signifies our love for each other. That means more than money. The family took him away from me, but it can't take what he meant to me away. Not then. Not now. Not ever."

Constance exploded out of her chair, leaped across the room and grabbed Grandy's hand. "Give me that. It's mine. Take your fat maid's hands off it. I need it."

Alex took her by the shoulders and tried to pull her away from Grandy, but Constance grasped the locket and wouldn't let go. The gold chain broke and the locket fell onto the marble floor where Constance made a dive for it. Surprisingly, Eduardo stepped in and grabbed the jewelry out of her reach.

"Control yourself, my dear." He held the locket up and let the heart dangle from his hand. "This is not important." His cold eyes held her wild ones and his long fingers reached out and wrapped around her upper arm. His grasp was so powerful that I was certain there would be bruise marks by evening. She slapped his hand away and ran from the room. Eduardo tipped his head toward Ms. Clone, and she followed promptly after.

Eduardo handed the locket back to Grandy. "We're not finished yet, you know. The locket belongs in this family. I will find a way to recover what is ours."

Eduardo stood over Grandy, his tall slim body swaying slightly, like a cobra moving in time to a flute player's music. The hairs of my neck stood on end. The corners of his mouth turned upward and formed a smile, then he walked out of the room, leaving behind him a chill, as if someone had left the door to cold storage open. Another figure entered the room.

"Mr. Napolitani," said Grandy.

No one in the room asked who he was. Did Leon Sanders and the Burnsides know him? Or was Napolitani's appearance so imposing that they didn't dare question his right to be there?

He held out his hand. I knew what he wanted. He didn't trust me to do the deal with Sanders. I scrounged in my bag and pulled out the manila envelope. He took it and offered it to Leon.

"You may be interested in these. If it's money you need, we might make some kind of a deal."

"What about Jerry?" Now I understood. Napolitani had no interest in saving Jerry.

Leon opened the envelope and looked through the papers. "I didn't even know these were gone."

From the look on Napolitani's face, it was clear that he thought Leon was lying. He let it go. "If we make a deal, you will never, *ever* bother this woman about that locket again." His black eyes moved from Sanders' face and softened when they came to rest on Grandy's.

"I can't control what my son-in-law might do. His methods are, well, unusual."

"Figure it out. My methods are more unusual. I'll let you think about it." Napolitani turned and walked out the door.

I ran after him.

"Hey, buddy. You just gave away my divorce settlement."

Oops. I shouldn't have been so accusatory. I saw Napolitani's eyes flash once, caught in the porch lighting. He turned and walked back toward me. My mind considered for a moment what "unusual" methods he might use on the front lawn of a has-been multimillionaire's house.

He took my hand in his. I wondered if I would still be able to run the shop with several broken fingers. I couldn't back down. I had so little—the shop, a few bucks in the bank, and a loan from my ex-husband.

"This is what you meant by 'working something out'?" I gave him an accusatory look.

He drew me closer, putting his arms around my waist. His citrusy aftershave encircled my head. It was the smell of money with a hint of social climbing thrown in. "You're as interesting as your grandmother. If I was a younger man, I'd give Alex some competition." He touched my forehead with his lips. "You worry too much, Eve Appel. I said I'd work something out. Now you must trust me."

He walked toward his car but stopped before he opened the door. "Tell Jerry it's safe to come out of hiding. I think Mr. Sanders will recognize rather quickly that he mistakenly identified Jerry as your kidnapper. I'll bet he calls the authorities before morning and tells them so."

"How do you know I can get in touch with Jerry?"

"He'll be in touch with you, and this time he won't be dressed in drag."

Foolish me. Of course, Napolitani would know that Jerry and I had been in touch.

"Why would Jerry trust me?"

"If I was on the lam, you're the one I'd trust."

I smiled as I watched his taillights disappear into the sultry tropical night. Nappi Napolitani was an angel. I knew he'd rescue Jerry and Grandy. Somehow. I'd leave the dealing to him.

"Well, well. I knew you went for bad boys, but that's scary, even for you." Alex stood on the porch, arms crossed in front of his chest. There was little warmth in his eyes now.

TWENTY-TWO

THE DOOR TO the Sanders' house opened, and Grandy and Max walked out. I hugged both of them and told them to be careful on their drive back to the boat. Eduardo's threats about getting the locket made me uneasy. As for Constance, well, I thought the Sanders should have her locked up. The gene pool in these intertwined families was shallow and murky.

Although Grandy gave Alex a kiss on the cheek, she offered me nothing but pointed looks. Alex ignored me. I watched Grandy's car pull out of the drive and felt tears threaten to spill out. If anything happened to her or Max because of the Sanders family, I'd, I'd... I didn't know what I'd do, but the use of guns, spurs, knives, and ropes wouldn't be out of the question. I had friends who could loan me those items.

I thought about hanging around until Cory and Randolph Burnside left. Maybe I could waylay them for more information, but I couldn't think of what to ask. Randolph's smarmy manner also put me off. Even if they knew anything of value, I'd much prefer cornering Cory at home alone on her pool deck, a shot of their good scotch in my hand.

Alex, his back against his car, was staring at the night sky.

"Okay, look. I can't help it if Napolitani likes me."

"Of course not. You're such a babe." His tone was

far from light. "You seem to like him just fine. Your Grandy is right. You go for the bad boys, don't you?"

"If I went for you, I'd be going for what? The good guys? I don't think so." I'd had about enough of Alex playing the angel. There was something he wasn't telling any of us. Time to get to the bottom of this.

"I've heard you refer to Mr. Sanders as 'Leon.' Sounds like you're not just some private eye he happened to hire."

Alex slammed his hand hard against the car door. It must have hurt like hell, but when I saw his face, I knew that what he was about to tell me would hurt me even more.

"I was kind of like a cousin to Valerie." He put his hand on the door handle, as if he might want to make a quick getaway.

I remained cool. I was so frosty, in fact, that the evening air temp dropped at least ten degrees.

"Cousin Alex then. Where'd you get that PI card? Find it in the trash somewhere? Order the ID over the Internet?"

"I *am* a private eye. When Leon found out that Valerie was sneaking jewelry out of the house, he wanted to minimize the fallout by keeping it in the family. He hired me to do the job."

"Then you got too cozy with me and he backed off, thinking he'd deal with the missing jewelry in some other manner."

"Right."

"Do you know what he meant to do?"

"No."

"Do you think he has any idea how to handle this?"

Alex said nothing.

I pushed a little further. "Even after Valerie was killed, Mr. Sanders thought he could keep the issue of the missing jewels in the family. It's all about family with them, isn't it? Sanders may be delusional enough to believe that Valerie's actions had nothing to do with her death. Do you believe that?"

Alex ran his hands through his hair. "The pawning of the jewels and her death have to be related, but I don't see how. Do you?"

"I haven't a clue." I was lying a little.

GRANDY CALLED ME at home later that night to tell me that she and Max were back on their boat. "See, honey? Nothing to worry about. That Argentinean Lothario was simply showing off in front of his father-in-law,"

"Maybe. You keep a look-out." I wished them good fishing for the remainder of the week and then fell into bed, exhausted.

At the store the next morning, I got Madeleine up to speed on the events of the previous night. We were sorting through some clothing that had been on the racks since we first opened, marking them down ten percent to boost sales. When we finished, I put a SALE sign out front and opened the store. The bell, which we had replaced after our unidentified visitor smashed it, rang. Good, a customer. It was not even five minutes past ten. I looked up and groaned. Mavis Worthington, our gadfly lady-journalist, entered the shop.

She hadn't been back since the day of the murder, when I let her take home some items on approval. She had her daughter return them all later. Mavis was that tight with her money. I followed my groan with a sigh of resignation. She also liked to talk and talk and talk.

Madeleine must have seen the expression on my face.

"I'll get this one. You go ahead and inventory the items that were dropped off yesterday. Some are from the coast." She put on her entrepreneur's face and bee-lined toward Mavis. I hid in the back room, keeping busy with my inventory project.

Several minutes passed. Madeleine stuck her head through the doorway. "Mavis wants to talk with both of us."

I screwed up my face and set my work aside.

"I'm coming." I joined them in front of the jewelry counter.

"I thought I'd stop by to see how business is going. Not well, I gather." She looked around the empty shop. "You two don't know much about marketing."

I turned my head away from Mavis so she couldn't see me roll my eyes.

"Oh, Mavis," said Madeleine, "we'd appreciate your input. You know this town so well."

Thank God for Madeleine's social savvy. She knew what to say, and I knew when to keep my sassy mouth shut. Sometimes.

Mavis smiled and gave Madeleine a pat on the shoulder. "You should consider advertising on our local country radio station. That's what most folks around here listen to, you know."

Madeleine and I had discussed that possibility just last week. I nodded in agreement as did Madeleine.

"Get Slim, the morning DJ, to do a broadcast from here."

Also smart.

Then came the kicker.

"And take out a full page ad in the magazine, *Around Town*."

Ah, yes, the one Mavis wrote for.

"We don't have the money to do that," I said.

"I'll make you a deal. You give me my choice of duds, and I'll cut the cost by fifty percent."

Madeleine and I exchanged glances.

"We'll consider your offer and get back to you," I said.

"Great, but don't wait too long. Especially if you want to be in this month's issue. It'd be best to get in there before the snow birds go back north."

Mavis looked around at the merchandise for a few minutes longer, then waved goodbye and left.

"What do you think?" Madeleine sounded dubious.

Before I could answer, Mavis stuck her head back into the shop.

"Oh, and another word of advice... I know you like having the West Palm patrons in the store to class things up, but when they come in reeking of eau de pony, it adds nothing to the upscale ambience you are trying to create. People around here get enough of that smell in their own backyards. They clean up to go shopping, you know. Those women from the coast like to shove it at us farmers, wearing their fancy riding boots and duds, like they couldn't be bothered to change them before going slumming. Showing off their money, that's all. As if their sweat was more expensive than ours."

"What do you mean?" I asked.

"Didn't you smell them? The day of the murder? The woman who was stabbed and the other one who walked by me right after the victim went into the dressing room. They smelled ripe from the stables."

"You've got quite a nose," said Madeleine.

"I was close enough to them. The second one shoved me out of the way when she marched into the dressing room."

"Maybe the smell came from your boots." I looked down at them.

Oops. Me and my big mouth. Mavis shot me a look that said she'd like to rope and tie me like a yearling calf.

"My momma raised me right. I wipe my boots before I come inside." She lifted her foot and showed us the sole. It was clean. "It was more than manure on their boots. It was the smell a rider gets from being on a horse. You can change clothes, but if you don't take a shower, that pony smell stays with you. They were wearing it like it was designer cologne."

"What did the woman who pushed you aside look like?" Maybe I could get a description of the killer.

"Like every other rich bitch from the coast who thinks she's slumming in Sabal Bay. Designer jeans, a western shirt from Saks and sunglasses large enough to cover her entire head. Those expensive hoity-toity riding boots." She turned and left the store.

Hmmm. For once, I found Mavis useful. She hit on something I'd been playing around with for a few days. I shared my thoughts with Madeleine.

"You've been thinking about pony poop? What for?"

"Never mind for now." I walked to the front of the shop and stared out the window. What had Alex said about Valerie when he was shadowing her? She

stopped by pawnshops and then either went to lunch
or to the stables. That must have been her last stop
before she came into the shop, where she picked up
the aroma of horse and where her killer might have
done the same. Maybe Dwight wasn't the murderer.
Who then?

"What do you know about polo ponies?"

"Nothing." Madeleine shrugged. "Lots of people
around here are horse experts. Horses, ponies, what's
the difference?"

"THERE'S A BIG DIFFERENCE." Madeleine and I were
seated with Rob Cassidy at the Burnt Biscuit, drinking cold drafts. It was Karaoke night and a narrow-
hipped cowboy with brown eyes and a white straw hat
was singing "Tequila Makes Her Clothes Fall Off" and
doing a damn great job of it. His voice wrapped around
my head. I felt like my shirt and jeans might hit the
barroom floor soon, no matter how little I drank, as
long as he was singing.

"Pay attention, Eve," said Madeleine. "Rob says
polo ponies aren't horses."

"Hmmm? They aren't? Well, they're certainly not
cows."

Rob reached out and touched my arm. "Honey, I
deal in cow ponies and working horses, not horses
trained to chase a ball around a playing field."

The cowboy finished his song and left the stage
echoing with the applause of every woman in the bar.

"Encore!" I shouted. The singer smiled in my direction and shook his head. I waved him over.

He tipped his hat to Madeleine and me and shook
hands with Rob.

"For now I'll let somebody else get up there and sweat. I'll do another one later."

Rob introduced Madeleine and me to the cowboy vocalist. "Antoine Slater, not only a great singing talent, but the best bronc rider in this county. Tell these gals about horses. They don't know the eating end from the kicking end or a cow pony from a thoroughbred."

Antoine and Rob spent the next hour telling us about horses, bloodlines, and what each breed did best. It was more than I wanted to know but enough to convince me that these cowboys were just what I needed to trap a killer. Of course, I had to persuade them of that.

I was in the middle of outlining what I had in mind when we were joined by someone I wasn't eager to see. Well, maybe I wanted to see him again. Just not at that moment.

"What did I just hear? Eve's trying to get you to buy into a string of polo ponies?" Alex tilted his head in my direction.

"That's what you get for eavesdropping. Not the true story, and none of your business."

Rob gave Alex the up and down, who-the-hell-are-you look. "This guy a friend of yours?"

"Not anymore."

The tension created by my remark might have sunk my grand scheme if Madeleine hadn't come to my rescue.

"Alex, let's take a walk, shall we? I'll tell you all about the horsies." She looked up into his eyes with innocent appeal and took his hand in hers. They walked off. He could hardly protest being led away by one of the prettiest women in Sabal Bay.

"I don't want you to actually buy a string of ponies. I only want you to pretend to be interested in buying them."

The two men exchanged glances.

"We can do that," said Rob.

Antoine nodded in agreement. "What will you be doing?"

"I'll be in disguise as Rob's bored, over-indulged wife." I'd learned a lot about disguises and pretense over the past few weeks. I knew I'd be good at both.

The next time I saw Alex, he was leading a blonde in tight jeans and a western shirt out onto the dance floor. They were doing a two-step to Antoine's crooning. Good. Now that he'd got another honey, the man would leave me alone. I didn't trust him, but I still felt the flame of jealousy burn in my stomach and make its way up my throat. Or was that heartburn from the beer?

"I'd better switch to ginger ale."

Madeleine came up behind me.

"Where'd he pick that one up from?" I nodded toward Alex and his honey on the dance floor.

Madeleine leaned into the bar at my elbow and looked me in the face. "What difference does it make? You don't even like him."

I do like him. And that's the trouble. I like him too much. Grandy would probably say that I only felt comfortable admitting my feelings now because I had found out that he was duplicitous in his relationship with me. That made him prime bad boy material.

Antoine finished his song and was replaced by another singer.

"Dance?" Antoine held out his hand, and we walked toward the dance floor, where the two of us showed up the other couples by dipping, swinging, side-stepping and scooting our way through a series of complicated rhythm patterns and steps. Soon the other dancers were just standing back and watching us. At the end of the song, Antoine dipped me back in his arms and planted a kiss on my lips. His mouth held mine for a moment too long, and I found his touch a trifle too pleasant. The couples surrounding us must have picked up on the interplay because, when we parted, people were whistling and clapping. I looked around the dance floor, but there was no sign of Alex and his blonde.

"Sorry about that," Antoine said. "I was out of line."

"Only someone from Sabal Bay would apologize for a kiss."

He looked a bit offended. "What do you mean?"

I couldn't tell him that the kiss meant nothing to me—the brassy, bold, sophisticated, heartless gal from up north. I'd be lying, and I wasn't so heartless that I wanted to hurt his feelings.

"I guess I'm not used to men with manners."

He smiled. "Well, ma'am, my mama would box my ears if she thought I had insulted a lady and not apologized after."

Alex wedged his way onto the barstool next to mine. "She's used to the kind of man who would leave her for another woman and cheat her out of her own money."

I turned to him, a smart retort forming on my lips. I was silenced by what I saw. His eyes didn't look quite right. They kept sliding around in their sockets, and the color seemed closer to gray than blue.

Then it hit me. He was drunk. Then it hit him. In a surprisingly graceful move, he slid off his seat into a heap on the floor.

TWENTY-THREE

I STOOD IN my bedroom holding two cups of coffee. I took a sip from one and set the other on the table beside the man sleeping in my bed. With a groan he turned over.

"How ya feeling?" I smiled a big, shit-eating smile. It felt fine.

The front door slammed, and the house shook. Although the noise didn't seem that loud to me, Alex obviously thought otherwise. He grabbed his head and held on as if he expected his brain to explode into a million pieces.

Antoine walked up beside me and encircled my waist with his arm. "Need any help this morning?"

"Nope. Just getting my guest out of bed for his morning exercise."

Alex pulled the covers up over his head. "I don't want any exercise."

"Well, you sure wanted it last night, spinning that dolly all over the Biscuit's dance floor."

"What happened to her?"

"I rescued you. I didn't think you two were a good match."

Antoine looked at me with dismay.

"Oh, all right then. Tell him." Could my smile get any bigger without causing my lips to cramp?

"When we took you to my truck, we found her

draped over the front fender of your car, sleeping. I put her in Eve's car, and Eve dropped her off at her house."

"Well, I dropped her at somebody's house. I think it was her husband's."

"Husband?" Alex's voice came out as both a squeak and a growl, like a mouse with bronchitis.

I grinned. I was having fun. At Alex's expense. The house I'd driven her to was her husband's house, but she had acquired it as part of their divorce agreement. I knew that because she had told me, after she had sobered up some on the drive.

"I don't think hubby was home." I was loath to give up needling Alex.

"You're a cruel woman." Antoine left the bedroom.

"What's he doing here?" Alex said.

"Not your business."

"Was he here all night?"

"You mean like you were?"

"I was? Here? In your bed?"

"Yep. Well, since you're up, you'll probably want your clothes."

"Clothes?" He lifted the sheet and peered underneath. "I'm naked. Who took off my clothes?"

I smiled and reached over to snatch his briefs off the bureau. I dangled them from my index finger, swinging them back and forth in front of his face. He tried to swipe them from my hand but missed. Either he was still too drunk to be coordinated or too hung-over to focus his eyes. Or both.

The phone beside the bed rang.

"Oh, God, please make the sound go away. Make this woman go away." He clapped his hands over his ears.

I picked up the offending instrument and ended his torture.

"You ready?" It was Rob calling from his cellphone. "I'm out front waiting."

"Yep." I put the receiver back in the cradle and glanced down at Alex. He looked bad, real bad, but even in this condition, he looked good, real good.

"The keys to your car are on the bureau. Car's out front. Orange juice is in the fridge. Shower's that direction." I pointed at the door leading to my bathroom. "When you leave, lock the door behind you. Please leave. I don't want to see you here when I get back. I've got work to do."

"Work. Your shop?"

"Yeah."

"One more thing before you go."

"Yes?"

"I think I'm falling in love with you."

"You're still drunk." I slammed the door on my way out and heard a stifled groan from the bedroom.

ROB WAS DRESSED in black from his cowboy hat down to his boots. It was exactly the image I had in mind—a cowboy dude from an old Western, updated into GQ's version of bad. He reeked of understated wealth and influence. Antoine, seated in the passenger's seat, was clothed in a similar manner. He, too, exuded a kind of western charm and certainty of manner.

Earlier in the morning I had visited the shop and picked out an appropriate costume. I needed one, since I was the one pretending to be someone else—the tired-of-rural-life, pampered wife of a wealthy rancher. She had been born in rural Florida, I decided, but she didn't want to dress country, not today, not in this place. So I chose a straw hat with a huge, floppy brim and tied a coral scarf around it for a hatband. My dress was one we'd recently acquired from someone on the coast. It was sleeveless with a full skirt, brown with white polka dots, like the one worn by Julia Roberts in *Pretty Woman*. If it was fashionable enough for Julia's character to wear to the polo matches, it should work for a trip to Eduardo's stables. I also grabbed a long, brown wig to cover my blonde punk hair.

Rob got out of his Escalade and opened the back door for me. "Madam looks terrific. If I didn't know you were hung up on that detective, I might make a serious run at making you my second wife."

I ground my teeth at the mention of Alex. "What detective?"

Antoine turned in his seat and gave me a skeptical look. He was about to say something, but the expression on my face must have put him off. He shrugged and turned back around.

We drove down Route 441 into Port Mayaca and crossed the bridge over the feeder canal to the lake. The water showed not a ripple in the morning light, but it retained its murky color, looking like a giant cup of strong black tea. Not a lake to swim in. I wondered if the long dark objects on the bank were logs. One moved and slid into the murky water. Not a log. I shivered.

"Too cold? I can turn down the AC." Rob reached for the control, but I told him no.

After the bridge we turned left on the first Palm Beach county road. The pavement changed from asphalt to gravel then to dirt. This wasn't the classy section of the county, but what the location lacked in status and sophistication it made up for in cheap land. Eduardo was smart. Why waste money on landscaped roads and a respectable address when you could put your money into something with a better return? Besides, he was only several miles from the International Polo Club, close enough to draw buyers away from their Sunday games, tournaments, and gourmet dining and toward his paddocks filled with fine horses.

The entrance to his stables radiated simple elegance: a royal palm tree on either side of the drive and a wrought-iron gate with the name "Argentinean Pride" overhead in bronze. Very nice. Rob punched the button on a stone kiosk and gave his name. The arched gate opened. They were expecting us.

When I called earlier this morning to set up the appointment, I was told that Eduardo was on a business trip, but the stable manager could show us around. Still, I wanted to keep a low profile in case Eduardo unexpectedly showed up. Or in case any other member of the family happened to stop by. I pulled the brim of my hat lower over my face.

We drove a quarter of a mile down the road, pastures filled with sleek, graceful animals on either side of us. The stables came into view. There were at least three buildings, two that housed horses. The other looked like a ranch house with a porch running across the front. As our car stopped, a man who had been standing on the steps approached us.

"Leonard Spelling." He held out his hand and shook Rob's. "You're Rob Cassidy. Your secretary called to say you wanted to see some ponies."

"I hope the short notice wasn't a problem. This is my wife, Lydia, and my trainer, Antoine."

I nodded at Spelling, then turned away as if he wasn't worth my attention.

"No problem at all."

"Good. When Lydia gets a bug about something, she needs to do it right away."

"Oh, so the idea to buy a string of polo ponies was hers?"

"She gets kind of bored sitting on the ranch in Sabal Bay, looking out at nothing but cows and working horses. She attended a match last Sunday and thought she might like to get involved in the polo set, meet some new people."

I walked toward one of the barns, my back to Spelling. "I want to see some of these so-called ponies up close." The men followed.

"So, you like horses?" Spelling's question was addressed to me. "You ride a lot?"

I stopped and turned, my hat brim low over my forehead. "I do not ride. I don't particularly care for horses. They smell. I liked the people I met at the match, though."

Before continuing on my way, I saw Spelling look at Rob, who gave him one of those *women, who-can-figure-them-out* looks.

We entered the first barn. Eduardo had recently finished building the structure. I could smell freshly cut lumber as well as horse manure. The floor was covered with sawdust and dotted with pony droppings.

"Careful you don't ruin your shoes by stepping in that," said Spelling.

Shortly after he had warned me against it, I "accidently" placed my foot into one of the larger decorations.

"Is there some place where I can clean this off my shoe?" I held up the foot with the besmirched shoe and wrinkled my nose in disgust.

"Oh, right over there at the other stable. The bathroom in this one isn't finished yet. I'll show you."

"Never mind. I'll find my way. You go ahead and see the ponies, dear." I patted Rob's arm and waved at the men.

While Rob and Antoine took a look at the first barn and pumped Spelling for information on the operation of the place, I intended to do some exploring of my own. I walked to the other building and entered. Stalls lined either side of the structure. Horses turned their heads in my direction. Stable boys did the same. I scraped my foot against one of the boards that made up the wall of the first stall.

Farther down the aisle I could hear voices and a horse nickering. The sound of the animal intensified to an insistent neigh; then came a loud crash.

"Shit," said a voice from that direction. "She almost got me in the balls. Hold her still, would you?"

A lower voice with a soft Mexican accent said, "Sorry, Señor Doctor. She be still now."

"Got it."

I walked to the stall and looked in. The horse there, a mare, had turned her head to keep an eye on a tall man with thinning gray hair who was standing behind her. I don't speak horse, but I could read anger and distress on her long equine face. The same expression was on the face of the short, dark man who stood holding her bridle.

"If you can't handle these horses any better than that, you can find a job somewhere else," said the gray man.

"Hi there," I said.

Señor Doctor said nothing. He pushed past me with a satchel in his hand and walked out of the barn. The man attending the horse nodded to me.

"Are you lost, Señora?"

"Looking for the bathroom. She's a beautiful horse." I gestured at the animal. "She sure didn't seem to like that guy, whoever he was."

"The vet. None of the horses like him."

"Why not?"

He looked like he was about to answer me, when a voice outside caught our attention. "Carlos. You in here?"

I recognized the voice. Constance.

"I need to hide," I said. "Where?"

The stable man gestured toward a stall filled with hay and feed. I moved into it, pushing myself behind a stack of bales.

I wasn't alone in my hiding place.

TWENTY-FOUR

"JERRY," I HISSED. "What the hell are you doing here?" I kept my voice low. Constance's got louder as she moved into the barn and toward the stall where we were hiding. Jerry held his finger to his lips, making a "shh" sign.

"Is there someone else here?" Constance's voice was demanding, imperious, as if the man had no right to be speaking with anyone.

"I was talking to the horses, Señora."

"Well, stop it. Get to work. Where's Dr. Phillips? Weren't you supposed to be assisting him?"

"Si, Señora. I was. He left a minute ago."

I peeked around a bale of hay and saw him point toward the other barn. She strode off, striking her riding crop against her boot. *Slap. Slap.* I pitied any horse she might ride.

I left my hiding place and dragged Jerry out by the arm.

"Thanks," I said to the attendant. "You didn't have to do that. Hiding me."

He stroked the mare's flank with tenderness. "No matter, Señora. You expressed concern for this animal, and you don't even know her. They don't care about the horses." He nodded toward the other barn. "Only money." He shook his head, his chocolate-colored eyes filled with pain.

"I know someone who would appreciate a man who respects horses. I'll talk to him. Maybe you can get a job on his ranch."

"*Gracias.* You are very kind, but no. I need to stay here and give these animals the care they deserve. Who else would do it?"

"Your name is Carlos?"

"Carlos Rodriguez."

Our conversation was interrupted by Constance yelling from the other barn. "Hey, boy, over there. Come here. The doctor needs you again."

"I must go now." With a final pat on the horse's neck, Carlos ran from the stable.

I let myself relax against the front wall of the stall, crossed my arms and turned my attention to Jerry. "Now that we're alone and have a minute, I'd like to know what you're up to."

"That's quite a get-up. You don't look anything like yourself. I almost didn't recognize you."

"I learned it from you. What gave me away?"

"I don't know, old girl, but I've known you for years. Maybe it was the way you got yourself into trouble, as usual."

"I'm in trouble? How about you?"

"Evie, baby, let's not argue here. It's not safe. Constance could come back. Or that doctor."

I heard voices from the barn entrance. It was Spelling, Rob and Antoine. I shoved Jerry behind the feed and bales.

"I need to talk to you. Stop by the house tonight. Promise me."

"I'll be there as long as you don't have any other company."

"What other company? Oh, Alex? He's no longer in the picture."

"You think." He scurried to the back of the stall.

"Enjoying the horses?" Rob walked up to me and put his arm around my shoulder.

"This is a nice one, but something must be wrong with her. The doctor just left a minute ago. I thought he was being kind of rough with her."

"Doctor Phillips has to be firm with these animals," Spelling said. "They're fully checked out once they arrive here from Argentina and must get a clean bill of health before we sell them to anyone. I can assure you of that."

"What do you think, Antoine? How about this animal?" Rob gestured toward the mare.

Antoine moved into the stall and began to move his hands knowingly over the horse. At first she shied at his touch; then, encouraged by his gentle movements, she relaxed.

"I think we'd like our own vet to take a look at any pony we might buy," said Rob. Antoine nodded his head in agreement.

"Let's saddle her up, and I'll take her around the ring," said Antoine.

While Antoine took the horse out for a ride and the rest of us watched from the paddock fence, Spelling glanced at my shoe.

"Did you find the facilities?"

"No, I didn't. I got sidetracked by the doctor and the horse."

"You're showing a lot of concern for an animal you admitted earlier you don't even like."

"I don't much care for pit bulls, either, but I don't like to see them treated badly."

"Well, I can see you don't know a thing about handling horses. You have to show them who's boss."

Rob's attention turned from the ring to Spelling. "On my ranch we take the approach of convincing them that you're not a threat. Humans are meat eaters. A horse gets around us, smells that, and then we try to get up on their backs. They think we're looking for a meal. You have to win them over. Once you do that, they're loyal animals and they'll do just about anything for you."

"Polo ponies are different." Spelling's face reddened and his eyes narrowed in anger. "Most of them are mares, and they're just as difficult to handle as women," he added, looking directly at me.

Rob stepped between Spelling and me. "Well, I guess my experience with both women and ponies has been different from yours. It's really a matter of gaining their respect, human or equine. You don't do that, you're going to have trouble."

WE LEFT THE ranch soon after Antoine had taken his ride on the mare and Rob and Spelling had crossed swords.

"I don't like that man," Rob said. "The stable attendants are terrified of him. The horses are skittish and something about that doctor isn't quite right."

Antoine nodded his head in agreement. "Once she felt comfortable with me, the mare handled well. She'd probably be easy to train as a polo pony. Somewhere along the line, she has learned to be mistrusting of humans."

"You know," I said, "this visit was set up to gather information. The two of you sound serious about buying and training a string of ponies."

"Oh, we are. I told Antoine last night that I'd been thinking of expanding. I think it's time for the International Polo Association to see what we cowboys can do when we've a mind to."

"Are the two of you going to play?"

Rob and Antoine exchanged glances. "Maybe. Mostly we'll do the training, with a little help from someone who knows the game, and then I can sponsor some of the best players. I've played a little now and then. So has Antoine."

"I do pick-up for the rodeos around here, so I'm used to getting in close with the horses. I like it," Antoine said.

"Yeah, but with polo, you have a mallet in your hand and you're chasing a ball down a huge field." I shuddered at the thought of it.

"Seems easier than chasing a bucking bronc or a twenty-five hundred pound Brahma Bull around a rodeo ring." Antoine chuckled. "In any case, I'm not certain that I'd want to buy my ponies from that place."

"Well, Spelling said they were expecting the arrival of some new horses any day now. Said he'd give me a call. We can take a look at what he's got then." Rob turned off the county road and onto the highway leading back to Sabal Bay.

I told them what the stable attendant had said about the owners and others at the ranch.

"I'll keep an eye out when we go back there," said Rob. "I think you'd better not go with us. Eduardo and his wife will be there. I'm afraid they might recognize you."

"Right. I won't go with you then." I wanted to visit someone else instead.

WHO CAN I *TRUST?* Madeleine, sure, but her propensity for bumping into trouble made her more of a liability than an accomplice—I mean as a snooping partner. I'd all but thrown Alex out on his ear and Napolitani was probably back north. Frida was a cop, which meant she'd be great at undercover work, but what I had planned bordered on the illegal. I couldn't call Max and Grandy away from their work. That left only one person, and he was coming to visit me tonight.

I was working on a scotch when my doorbell rang. I looked through my peephole to make sure it was Jerry. The streetlight illuminated a stranger on my porch. Well, given that he was into disguises, it could have been Jerry, but only if he had managed to shrink about five inches since this afternoon. I switched on the porch light to get a better look.

"Turn off the damn light. Someone might see me."

"I'm not letting you in unless I get a clear look at you. Who the hell are you?"

I couldn't make out his features. From the concave lens of the hole, he appeared to have an animal perched on his rather small head.

"It's me. Don't you recognize me? I thought you were good at that."

It couldn't be, could it? "Dwight? You're supposed to be dead."

"Well, I'm not."

"Go away, whoever you are. Mr. Sanders identified

that body himself. You think he doesn't know his own son?" I looked at the scotch in my glass. I hadn't had that much to drink, had I? Maybe I'd lost the ability to hold my liquor.

"He said that to protect me. Now open up. I need to talk to you."

"What's on your head? It looks like an opossum."

The man pulled the furry mass off his noodle and pushed his face nearer the peephole. "It's a wig. See?"

Sure enough. The face of Dwight Sanders, the little weasel who might have killed his stepmother and surely dumped me out in the swamp, filled the lens.

"I don't care if you are Dwight. You're a murderer. You tried to kill me. Now get out of here before I call the police." I wasn't convinced that Dwight was the killer, but why take a chance on letting him into my house?

"I'm not scared of the police. Call 'em, but let me in first. I swear I wasn't the one who left you to the gators. You've got to listen to me. I know who killed Valerie and who tried to kill you."

"Me too. It was you."

"No. You've got to help me."

As he was speaking, a car turned the corner and drove down the block toward my house. Its headlamps swept across my yard and made the porch as bright as daylight.

Dwight turned to look at the car. "Oh shit. They found me. Listen, I saw you and your friends at the ranch this afternoon. You must have figured out what's going on. Meet me there tomorrow night at midnight. I'll explain everything. I can prove that what I'm saying is true."

"Wait. Dwight." I opened the door but he was already gone. Walking to the edge of the porch, I craned my neck around the side of the house toward my backyard. Nothing.

Dwight was wrong. He was giving me too much credit. I hadn't figured out what was going on, but after his visit I was even more intrigued.

The car that had frightened him pulled up in front of my house. It was a black SUV. Anyone could have been in it. With the exception of Madeleine, Alex, and me, almost everyone I was acquainted with drove a black vehicle of some kind.

Two men got out and approached the house. Rob and Antoine? Why would they be here? No. It was Jerry, accompanied by Napolitani. I'll be damned.

At that moment, Alex's car pulled up and parked behind Napolitani's. Hail, hail, the gang's all here. My admirers. Here to help me or to interfere with my plan. Which was it to be?

Alex didn't seem surprised to see Jerry and Napolitani. They, too, acted as if his presence was expected. I told Jerry I wanted him here tonight so he knew that I had something cooking. Since I don't ever cook, he also knew I didn't mean food.

Alex muttered something to me as I held open the door for him.

"What?"

"I said, I'm sorry I was sick in your house."

"That's it? That's all you're sorry for?"

Jerry and Napolitani followed Alex in the door and took seats side by side on the couch, watching Alex and me as if they had tickets to some great boxing match.

"Did I invite the two of you in? Did I ask you to sit down?"

"We're here to help you," said Napolitani. "You do need help, don't you? Jerry seemed to think you wanted to go back to the stables and take a better look at the place. He thought I might come in handy in case—"

"In case I need someone to take out an alarm. Or maybe to disable more than the electrical system."

"We called Alex so he could be in on the plan this time instead of just following us around," Jerry said.

Oh, crap. What if they had also called Madeleine? She'd just knock things over or let the horses loose. Who knew what trouble she might get into? Correction, get *us* into.

The horrified look on my face must have said it all.

"I didn't call Madeleine. Did you guys?" Alex looked at Jerry and Napolitani.

The guys on the couch shook their heads.

I hadn't realized that I'd been holding my breath, hoping that Madeleine might spare us her presence tonight, until that moment. I exhaled and chuckled in relief. "Too bad Grandy can't be here."

The gods must have heard me call Grandy's name. The phone rang. It was Max.

"Grandy's in the hospital in Tavernier. Someone grabbed her on her way back from the Laundromat and roughed her up. They warned her that she'd better give back the locket or next time you wouldn't escape becoming dinner in the swamp."

TWENTY-FIVE

NAPOLITANI DROVE. JERRY was in the passenger's seat. Alex and I sat in back. As we sped down the turnpike toward the Keys, I sputtered with rage. I contemplated the satisfaction I would derive from hurting the people responsible for putting Grandy in the hospital. I was certain that I knew who they were, or at least who was behind the attack. I was torn between wanting to hold Grandy in my arms and wanting to lay siege to the Sanders' house, taking no prisoners. Grandy came first. I needed to see her, make certain she was all right. Then I could play barbarian with the Sanders clan.

"Maybe we should have split up," said Napolitani. "You and Alex could have gone to your Grandy while Jerry and I took care of business in West Palm."

"Thanks, but your methods are—"

"They are effective. More so than yours. Right now, I'd guess that you're not concerned with the legality of thrashing the hell out of Sanders. Right? And you, my dear, want revenge. There's a more important issue here."

"Like what?" I didn't care about the other issues. I wanted pay back.

"Someone must be punished for what they did to Grandy," Napolitani said. "I'm good at that."

"I don't understand the difference. Revenge. Punishment. It's all the same."

"Not at all. Revenge is the sweet feeling the avenger gets when the criminal is punished. The punishment itself? It's to teach a lesson. This I know well. Later. Later we'll talk about what must be done." Napolitani peered over his shoulder to look at me and make certain that he'd made himself clear. He had.

Alex squeezed my hand. "I'm sorry."

"I know."

"I mean, I'm sorry for everything. For Grandy. For her pain and yours. For the hell you're going through wanting to get to the people who beat her up."

"Especially the ones who arranged for her beating."

Alex gave my hand another gentle squeeze. "About the other night. There's no excuse for my bad behavior, but I'm so crazy about you that my jealousy got the better of me."

"You sure have a great way of telling me how much you care. You lie to me, find another woman, then get drunk and pass out in my bed." I should have jerked my hand out of his, but the contact felt so good, so comforting. I squeezed his hand back.

"I shouldn't have kept my relationship with the Sanders family from you. It just never seemed like the right time to tell you."

He leaned closer to me and whispered in my ear. "Do I have any chance with you?"

Here I was, frantic to find out how my Grandy was. That should have been my only concern, other than the satisfaction that came from contemplating my revenge. Instead, what popped into my head was how

I could continue to make Alex squirm with guilt and jealousy. I guess I can be a difficult woman.

"Leave the poor guy alone. He's got a thing for you and he's not thinking clearly," said Jerry.

"Have pity on him," said Napolitani.

Now, I could understand Jerry's ability to read my mind—we had been married for over fifteen years—but how had Napolitani been able to tap into my brain waves?

Oh, the hell with it. I was too anxious about Grandy to give Alex a bad time. I filed it away on my mental "to do" list, which now read: Have fun. Bust Alex's chops.

"We'll talk some other time," I said.

Alex smiled. Was that an "I'm so happy" smile or a "Gotcha on the run, gal" smile. I didn't really care. I looked out the window and caught the reflection of my worried face in the glass. *Please let my Grandy be okay.*

SHE LOOKED SO SMALL propped up in the hospital bed. I could barely see her face through all of the bandages that covered it, but what I did see looked swollen and more colorful than the biblical Joseph's coat of many colors.

I was horrified at her appearance. If I could just get my hands on the people responsible, I'd—

"They overdid the bandages. It's not as bad as it looks." Grandy touched her face.

I rushed forward to give her a hug but stopped when I got next to the bed. I leaned over, then hesitated mid-bend. Where did you kiss someone whose face is covered in gauze? I chose the top of her head.

"Where's Madeleine?" Grandy reached for the others, hugging all of them, including Jerry. Now that we were divorced, she seemed more willing to see his good side, if there was one.

"She wasn't home when I called. I think she's on a date. I left a message. She'll be in touch, I'm sure. How are you?" I sat on her hospital bed and put my arm around her shoulders.

"Don't squeeze too tight, honey. I've got a couple of bruised ribs."

"When she first came in, they worried that her nose was broken, but it's not. That rainbow of bruises around her eyes will darken by tomorrow. Everyone's gonna think *I* gave her those shiners." Max made a rueful smile, but I could tell he was worried. There was no mirth behind his grin. Instead, I saw tense lines around his mouth.

"Grandy, you look terrible." It was Madeleine, standing in the doorway.

"Don't tell her that!" Madeleine was usually more considerate.

"Never mind, Eve," Grandy said. "It's true. White on rainbow is not my best color palette. C'mere, love." She reached out to Madeleine.

"How did you get here so fast?" I asked Madeleine.

"I heard your message when I got home from the grocery store, so I called Frida. She turned the lights on the cruiser and here we are. Made it in record time."

Frida stood in the doorway behind Madeleine, looking very official. She and Madeleine entered and sat on the other side of Grandy's bed. If any more people showed up, we'd have to get a parade permit.

"From your message, Eve, there's little doubt about who's behind this." To Grandy, Frida said, "Did you see the guy?"

"No. It was too dark, but I think there was more than one of them. After I was knocked down, a man delivered the warning. I thought I heard another voice in the background." Grandy tried to roll over in my direction. She grimaced with the pain her movement caused. "You're the one I'm worried about. They said they'd get you. Unless I give that locket back."

"I don't think you have to worry about me. As you can see, I've got friends. And not all of them are here."

"She's got cowboys, too." There was derision in Alex's voice.

"I'm going to talk with the Key Largo police. See if I can help them solve this one," said Frida.

I knew what that meant, and so did everyone else in the room. It meant that the eventual punishment of the assaulters was out of our hands and in those of my capable police friend, Frida. Napolitani looked disappointed, but I was relieved, relieved that neither Nappi nor I would be serving a jail sentence for assault and battery on the Sanders family.

Frida gave Grandy another kiss and then left the room to meet with the local authorities.

"I guess I'll have to grab a ride back home with you," Madeleine said.

"You can have my seat in Nappi's car," I replied. "I'll be staying here for a few days."

"You'll do nothing of the sort." Grandy tried to sit up straighter in bed but let out a groan and slid back down onto her pillow. "You've got a business to run."

"Madeleine can do that."

Madeleine bobbed her head up and down in agreement.

"No way," Grandy said. "You get back to Sabal Bay

and take your bodyguards with you. Down here you'd only have Max and me to protect you. Alex just said it. You've got all these guys and some cowboys back home. What could be better?"

"I'm not going."

"Then I'll be forced to send back this locket."

I was shocked. Grandy give up the locket? To those Philistines?

"You can't. That locket means too much to you."

"Not more than your life. Look in the bedside table."

In the drawer lay the locket, its ruby and diamonds sparkling up at me.

"What do you want me to do with this?"

"Give it to Jerry. He can return it to the Sanders family, and we'll put an end to all this."

Jerry looked startled. "Me? Why me? I don't think the family would let me back in their house."

"I'll do it. For you and your granddaughter." Napolitani held out his beefy hand. Grandy nodded her agreement. I dropped the locket into it.

"Now everyone is safe. I'm tired." Grandy closed her eyes.

"Maybe we should let her rest," said Max.

We said goodnight. Max and I gave her a final gentle kiss on her bandaged cheek and followed the others out of the room.

"She really wants you to go back home, you know," said Max. "I can take care of her when she leaves the hospital."

"I'm staying." I walked away from him and caught up with Napolitani to tell him that I wouldn't be joining him on the ride back. Jerry, Madeleine, and Alex stood at the elevator waiting for us. Max checked in at the desk to make certain that the nurse had his cellphone number, in case something came up with Grandy during the night.

I grabbed Napolitani's arm and pulled him into the visitors' waiting room.

"Are you really going to return the locket? Do you understand what she's giving up?"

"Do you have a better idea?"

"Let me borrow it. For a day or two. If things work out, you won't have to return it."

"What are you going to do? The people who beat up your Grandy will do the same or worse to you. You almost became a gator's dinner once already." Napolitani scowled at me and made no effort to reach into his pocket for the locket.

I mulled over the idea of bringing Napolitani in on my scheme. "If I tell you what I have in mind, will you help me?"

He smiled. In the darkened room his white teeth flashed almost as brilliantly as the jewels in the locket. "It would be my supreme pleasure to help you. Yet again."

"Help her do what?" Alex stood in the doorway. He was flanked by Jerry and Madeleine.

The game was on. The posse, if you could call our mismatched band of troublemakers that, was formed. I didn't intend to tell them that we'd be joined by a member of the Sanders family, Dwight. I seemed to be the only one who didn't believe he had killed his stepmother. I hoped I could trust him and that what he knew would help us bag a killer.

I WALKED DOWN the hallway and away from the others in search of privacy. It would be fine if the person I was about to call knew that I was in the hospital seeing Grandy, but I didn't want them to know anyone else was with me. I dialed the Sanders residence and waited for someone to pick up. In the meantime, I opened my hand and looked down at the locket that Nappi had dropped into it. Bait. As if I was going fishing for something big, like an old gator or a barracuda. But more dangerous.

The phone rang several times and then a machine kicked in, asking me to leave a message. Even better.

"You win," I said. "I'll meet you at the stables tomorrow night at eight. I have the locket. It's yours. I'll turn a blind eye to everything you've done. Now call off your dogs." I disconnected and smiled.

Nappi walked up behind me. "This is a dangerous game we're playing. What if we don't find what we're looking for?"

"In that case, I turn over the locket and walk away."

"That doesn't sound like you." He reached out and tilted my chin to look into my eyes. "No, not like you. You know something, don't you? Tell me."

"Not now. Later."

I gazed down the hallway toward the other members of our gang. Alex was watching Nappi and me with disapproval. I could almost feel the jealousy creeping toward us. I fluttered my fingers at him. He grinned at me like a teenager in heat.

Nappi rolled his eyes. "Poor guy. He's got it bad. I only hope he can keep focused. I would hate for his emotions to get him, or us, killed."

"He's a professional. He'll be fine." My cell rang. I glanced at the number and flipped it open.

"Come alone tomorrow." The voice sounded muffled, as if the person was trying to disguise it. I couldn't tell whether it was a man or a woman, young or old. I didn't care. My caller asked no questions about the meeting I had arranged, which meant that my message had made sense.

"Of course." I flipped the phone closed.

I turned to Nappi. "I'm not supposed to bring reinforcements tomorrow. Does that sound right to you?"

"Not really. I would rather our greeting party be made up of more than one person."

"It might be a bad idea to go against their request. They'll have their own gang to back them up."

"Of course they will. They're suspicious. They think it's a trick, and they also believe you know more than you do."

"I know enough."

He tapped my fist, the one that still clenched the locket. "If you did, you wouldn't need that much bait to pull the confession out of a killer."

It was good to have a man like that on your side. He was right. I shouldn't go it alone, not in this case.

TWENTY-SIX

NAPPI AND JERRY took turns driving during the three hours it took to get back to Sabal Bay. Everyone slept but me. I was worrying about Grandy and second-guessing my decision to return home rather than stay with her. Alex snored beside me, his warm breath caressing my ear as he rested his head against my shoulder. On my other side, Madeleine followed Alex's lead, only much louder.

By the time Nappi pulled up in front of my house, it was after two in the morning.

"Anybody hungry? I can scramble eggs and make some toast." I was wide awake and starving.

"I thought you couldn't cook," said Alex.

"It's just eggs and toast. I can do that."

"No she can't." Madeleine sat up, stretched and yawned.

"Let's go to the diner," said Alex.

Madeleine curled her top lip in disgust. "Not me. The diner's food is worse than Eve's."

Alex frowned. "You're kidding about Eve's cooking, right?"

"No, she's not," I said. "But it's not something I want spread around." What I meant was, I didn't want prospective romantic interests to find me wanting in the kitchen. It was a girl thing.

By the time they had finished their conversation

about my culinary klutziness, I regretted my effort to be generous. "I didn't make the offer to be insulted. Forget it. I'm going to bed."

Alex looked at me with a spark of hope in his eyes.

"By myself." I got out of the car and started toward my front door.

"Wait. I'll walk you." Alex rushed to catch up.

"Oops. Forgot something." I turned back toward the car, catching Alex off guard. I weaved around him, leaving him spinning on the walkway.

"Will you make up your mind?" I could almost hear his teeth grinding as he spoke through a clenched jaw.

"Meet here at eight tonight then?" I wanted to make certain I had the backup I required.

Napolitani nodded.

Alex grabbed my arm and steered me toward the house. "You act as if you trust that mobster more than you do the rest of us."

"I do. He was there for me when I needed him. I have no reason to believe that he won't be again. Where were you when I needed help? Playing footsie with your skeevy relatives."

He looked hurt. "I told you I was sorry about keeping that relationship from you. Why can't you forgive me?"

"Sure, I'll forgive you, but only if you come through for me tonight." I inserted my key in the lock and opened my front door.

"Napolitani doesn't mind crossing the line when it comes to the law," he said. "I guess you don't either. Whatever you're planning, I'll be there to see that you don't get into trouble."

"My knight in tarnished armor. We'll see." I closed the door on him.

In bed, I tossed and turned for several hours. There were two unknowns in my plans. One was Dwight. I believed him when he said he had nothing to do with Valerie's murder. Why else would his father identify the dead body as his son's? It had to be, as Dwight insisted, to protect him. Leon wouldn't do that for a murderer. But Leon also appeared to be protecting someone else—the real killer, perhaps. I doubted Dwight knew that or, if he suspected, that he wanted to believe it.

The other wild card was Alex. I wanted to trust him. I wanted to like him. I might even want to fall in love with him. But Grandy's beating had shown me the power of family ties—just how far members would go for one another—and Alex was one of the Sanders. What did that mean? Perhaps I was foolish to let him take part in tonight's activities. As frightening as it was to try and trap a killer, I liked myself better as a snoop than as a wealthy society matron sipping martinis at the club back in Connecticut. I smiled to myself as I snuggled down into my pillow. My business might fail and I might get killed, but I had more than cowboys here. I had friends.

After just a few hours of restless sleep, I got up and made a strong pot of coffee. I had a long day ahead, followed by a night that might be equally as long but was sure to be interesting, maybe life-threatening. I had to focus. My mind needed to be clear, not caffeine-riddled. I drank half a cup of the brew and threw the rest away. The phone rang. It was Rob.

"I got the strangest call a few minutes ago," he said.

"Someone with an accent. Spanish, I think. He wanted to talk with my wife. Not my ex-wife, but the 'señora who was with you at the stables.' That would be you. What do you think he wants?"

I thought back to Carlos the stable attendant, and his kind eyes and gentle hands.

"What did he say?"

"Only that he needed to talk with you. I told him you were out shopping and would be back in a half hour."

"When we talked in the barn, I told him I might be able to get him another job since he seemed so unhappy there. That must be what he wants." That's what I told Rob, although I knew that couldn't be it. Carlos told me he wouldn't leave the horses to people who didn't care for them.

"I'll be right over. I need to take that call."

"SEÑORA, I MUST talk to you. I can't stay on the phone long. They don't like us phoning from work. Can you come to the stables?"

"When?"

"Today."

"Won't that look funny, my showing up there for no reason?"

"No, Señora, you come with your husband. The ponies, new ones, they arrive today. Mr. Spelling will invite your husband to come. I…"

I heard angry voices in the background, followed by a click. He had hung up.

Rob entered the kitchen where I had taken the call. I explained what the stable attendant wanted.

"Sounds like trouble to me, something you should stay out of."

If only he knew what I had already gotten myself into.

The phone on the wall rang. Rob picked it up.

"Uh-huh. Sure that would be fine. Well, I can't guarantee that. She might have other plans. Oh, okay. We'll be there."

He hung up and turned to me with a puzzled look on his face. "That was Spelling. Your contact was correct. A shipment of horses just arrived. The vet should be through inspecting them by late afternoon. He asked me to come out around five and to be certain to bring you. Odd, don't you think, considering how unpleasant he was the last time?"

More than odd. Frightening. Someone must have overheard my conversation with Carlos.

"You're not thinking of going, are you?" Rob asked.

"I'm absolutely going."

"We talked about this. Eduardo and his wife, Constance, are sure to be there. They'll recognize you."

"Maybe not. They'll be so thrilled about having a buyer for the ponies that they'll hardly notice me. I'll wear a particularly large hat this time. I have to go. Carlos knows something he thinks is important enough to risk his safety, maybe his life, by contacting me."

"I'll have Antoine take him to one side to see what's up."

"No," I said. "I think he'll only talk to me."

My already full schedule this evening had just gotten busier. Someone at those stables was a killer. I had thrown bait into those unfriendly waters, and it looked as if I was about to toss my friends in after it. Was I really willing to risk their lives? My own?

I LEFT A message on Nappi's cell saying that if I wasn't at the house at eight, everyone should meet me at the stables. There was a good chance I could talk with Carlos beforehand, find out what he knew and, using that information, figure out what was going on and how it related to the murder. I might even be able to wrap this whole thing up by six. If not, there was Plan B, at eight tonight. Like all my plans, this one remained a little vague. What was I going to do? Goad whoever met me for the locket into admitting to my kidnapping and Grandy's beating? It sounded like an episode of *Perry Mason*, not real life. Oh yeah, throw in the identity of Valerie's killer as a bonus. And, of course, there was Plan C—Dwight to the rescue at midnight. Each half-baked scheme was a safety net for the one before. Unless…. What if the gang and I didn't make it through Plan A?

"Stay close to me. Don't run off by yourself. We'll find Carlos together," said Rob. He, Antoine and I pulled around to the barn where I'd met Carlos the first time. Spelling stood in the barn's doorway. There was no sign of Eduardo or Constance. Another man stood at Spelling's side, someone I wasn't eager to encounter again. Randolph Burnside. I hadn't seen him for a while. I could have gone forever without seeing him again and not felt cheated of the experience. I wondered what he had to do with this operation.

After Spelling made the introductions, Burnside turned his attention to me. Would he recognize me? Not many women are as tall as I am.

"This is your lovely wife?" Burnside looked me up and down. A process that, given the disparity in our heights, took some time.

"You remind me of someone."

Uh-oh.

"Valerie. My wife's dearest friend. She was tall like you. There was another woman." Randolph paused, a finger to his lips. "Well, no matter."

Probably most women looked tall to him.

I grabbed Rob's hand and squeezed. Maybe he wasn't certain of the message, but he seemed to realize there was something about Burnside that spelled trouble.

"I'm sorry," said Rob, "but I'm a little unclear about your connection to the stables."

"I'm part-owner. With Eduardo and his wife. They should be here soon. In the meantime, follow us and we'll take a look at those new ponies."

Antoine and I let Spelling, Rob, and Burnside get ahead of us. We followed, inspecting each stall, hoping to catch sight of my contact.

As we passed the feed room, someone called my name. "Mrs.... Mrs., Señora." It was Carlos. He looked terrified.

When Antoine and I turned to enter the room, Carlos shook his head. "Alone."

I told Antoine to walk on ahead.

"They say you're not who you pretend to be."

I opened my mouth to explain, but he interrupted me.

"Not much time, Señora. Come with me."

He grabbed my arm and led me through a back door in the feed room and out behind the barn. We ran to the far end of the second barn and entered. In the stall to our right, a mare, held by two stable hands, was struggling against a man whose hand was inserted into the poor animal's vagina.

"What the hell?" I whispered.

"Shh. Just watch."

"Hurry. This one's a real fighter, Doc."

"Hold still, bitch." The vet shoved his hand in farther. "Got it."

When he pulled his hand out, he held a plastic bag. It looked to be filled with some kind of powder. A very special, very illegal powder, it seemed. Carlos whispered in my ear. "Cocaine." It must have been smuggled into the country with the polo ponies.

The vet, Dr. Phillips, dropped the bag into his medical satchel. "Just in time. Here come our customers. Too bad they won't be buying. I'd like to get this nag off our hands." He roughly elbowed his way around the horse. Fear filled her eyes, but then something else appeared. If the stable attendants hadn't been holding her down, she would have charged him. Her front hooves left the stall floor for a moment, but she was pulled back, and the vet exited.

"Drugs."

Carlos nodded.

Voices echoed throughout the barn.

"Let's get out of here. I don't want you mixed up in this. These people are dangerous," I said.

"*Si*. I know."

We left the way we came and stood for a moment behind the barn. What was I going to do? We needed reinforcements. Could I reach anyone? I punched Frida's number into my cell and got her answering service. I left a message and prayed that she or someone from the police could get here in time. Next I tried Nappi. No answer. The same for Madeleine. And Alex. And Jerry. Where was everybody? Shopping for the appropriate clothes to wear to an eight o'clock breaking and entering party?

"I have to go find Rob and Antoine and warn them somehow. I'll try to keep calling my friends. Is there a phone you can safely use? Or a car?"

"One of the stable attendants has a cellphone. I can try to find him, Señora."

I wrote all the numbers of the eight o'clock gang on a scrap of paper I found in my bag. I kept my phone in case I could call again.

"Here. Call these numbers until someone answers. Tell them Eve needs them here. Now." I shoved him away from me and turned to enter the barn.

The entrance at the other end, the one we had just used, was darkened by two people. As I walked toward them, I recognized Eduardo and Constance. Hail, hail. Their gang was all here.

I was still wearing my disguise, full-skirted dress and brimmed hat with large dark glasses.

As I walked up to them, Rob turned and smiled.

"We lost you for a minute there, honey." He took my hand and pulled me close. "Let me introduce—"

"There's no need," said Constance. "She's Eve Appel and she has something I want. Hand it over." She pushed her face up close to mine and stuck out her hand.

I tried to look puzzled, innocent, confused.

"Don't play that game with me. Your family's made up of nothing but thieves."

Eduardo stepped forward and placed his hand on

Constance's shoulder, pulling her back. His knuckles turned white. How hard was he grasping her?

"Shut up. You're just like your mother. Like all American women. You talk too much."

Constance grimaced and reached up to grab the fingers digging into her shoulder.

Rob stepped forward. "You're hurting her. Let your wife go."

Eduardo merely gave his oily smile and looked at Randolph, who pulled a gun out of his pocket.

TWENTY-SEVEN

THE GUN RANDOLPH held was ugly. It looked huge, almost too big for his hand. Or was that just because Randolph was so small in contrast? It was clear from the way he held the weapon that he knew how to use it. I suddenly felt shorter.

The three of us stood very still, but I could tell that Rob and Antoine were poised for a fight.

Spelling pulled out another gun. No good. I saw Rob signal Antoine to stand down. Too much firepower.

"Put your hands behind your heads and get down on your knees," said Spelling.

We obeyed.

Eduardo, still grasping Constance's shoulder, barked sternly. "Go home. I'll be there soon."

"But she's got it. I know she does," Constance whined.

He looked at her and sighed, the kind of sigh that came from a man holding fury at his core. As fast as the strike of a coiled snake, he slapped her. I jumped as if he had hit me. Constance ran from the barn, holding her cheek and sobbing.

"Told ya. Women and horses. Got to get rough with them."

Eduardo turned his reptilian eyes on Spelling.

"Sorry, boss." Spelling said. He seemed to retreat

into himself, shrinking beneath Eduardo's cold gaze. Now there were two small men with large guns.

"Search her," Eduardo said.

Spelling leered at me. "Sure thing. My pleasure." He gave his weapon to Eduardo. His hands patted and fondled my body, then he dumped out my purse and looked through it. "Nothing here."

Eduardo narrowed his eyes. "I don't care, you understand, but my wife wants that locket you promised her." He sighed again as if bored with this game of hide-the-prize. "Where is it?"

"Tell him," said Rob. "Then we can get out of here."

Eduardo ran his fingers through his dark hair and shook his head.

"I don't think so." He signaled to Spelling, who dragged Carlos out of the feed room.

"I'm sorry, Señora."

"One of my more loyal stable boys found him using a cellphone. He was trying to contact your friends, Ms. Appel."

"Oh, that's funny," said Spelling.

Eduardo shot him another look of contempt.

"Sorry, Boss."

"According to my stable boy, this one," Eduardo looked at Carlos, "took Eve here to get a glimpse of what Dr. Phillips was doing to the mare. That's not something I'd like to get around."

Eduardo turned his back on us and walked a few steps away, then turned. His shoulders heaved in yet another one of his exaggerated sighs. His voice was soft, low and controlled, as if he were lecturing school-children.

"You see, Ms. Appel, I'm surrounded by idiots who

all think they have the right to say whatever pops into their heads. Not just the women." His eyes were hard. "No, the men, too. Stable attendants, my manager."

Spelling opened his mouth to speak but closed it quickly.

Eduardo flicked the riding crop he carried against his leg. His eyes darkened. When he spoke, the control was gone.

"Talking! All this talking. I need silence and I'm going to get it." He struck the crop again and again on the palm of his hand. The sound echoed throughout the barn's interior and it sounded like a whipping was taking place. My arms ached from holding them on my head, and the pain moved down into my neck and back as if each stroke of the crop had landed on my flesh.

No one spoke.

"Ms. Appel?" Eduardo said.

"You want me to say something? Why should I when you're only going to kill us anyway?"

"Yes, but it's how I do it that should concern you."

"Don't worry about us, Eve," said Rob.

Eduardo gave the king of all sighs. "Yes, yes. You must worry about her." Eduardo went into one of the empty stables and pulled out a bound and gagged Madeleine, her eyes wide with terror.

"That's why you didn't answer your phone." My tone sounded accusing. I didn't mean it to be, but fear was making me babble while I tried to think of a plan of escape.

"I'm sure your other friends are similarly occupied. Eh?" Eduardo looked at Spelling and Randolph meaningfully, but neither man would raise his eyes to Eduardo's. Did that mean one of them hadn't completed his job? My heart thudded with hope.

"You can't kill off the entire population of Sabal Bay just because you think I know something about how you run your pony business."

"I can't be bothered with what you and your friends know or don't know. I'm a busy man." He flapped his hand in a dismissive gesture. "Take care of them. I'm going home to my wife. Just make certain you find that locket. Use whatever persuasive techniques you deem necessary."

Dr. Phillips walked in. "Can I help? Maybe she has it hidden where we hide the cocaine on the horses. I could look for it." The suggestion made me quiver with loathing and terror.

"Whatever. Just find it." Eduardo walked out the barn door without a backward glance. I saw someone else join him at his car. The personal secretary, the dark woman I'd seen standing next to him at the funeral. She reached up to him, throwing her arms around his neck. He detached himself from her embrace and opened the passenger door. She hesitated a moment, then lowered her head in a gesture of submission and got into the car. Eduardo sure had a way with women.

Spelling's voice drew my attention from the car back to the barn. "I already searched her."

"Not as thoroughly as I can," said Phillips.

"I think we should tie up our cowboy friends. Then we can work on the little one with the red hair. Go get some rope." With Eduardo gone, Spelling assumed command.

"I don't run errands for you," said the vet. "There's

rope in the feed room." To Randolph, Phillips said, "Surely you're good for more than just standing there looking like an armed elf."

"I'm your boss. You wouldn't even have a job if I hadn't pulled those strings that allowed you to keep your license. That horse doping charge in Kentucky wasn't easily covered up, you know."

"If I leave, who's gonna do your ponies for you?"

Phillips took the gun from Randolph's hand and assumed the other man's position, his back up against the stall where the feisty mare was located. His movement caught her eye and his smell unsettled her. She began circling her stall nervously. Keeping his eyes on us, he ignored the mare's frantic head twitching and the pawing of her hooves on the straw. She was growing more disturbed. He must have heard her agitated snorts.

"Maybe I should throw your little friend in there and let the horse take care of her." He approached the stall and banged his foot against the boards, a cruel smile on his face. The horse whinnied and tossed her head, her eyes white with fear. She shied away from the noise, pushing herself up against the back of the stall; then, whirling around, she rushed forward. In a split second, she had reared up and brought her hooves down on the top rail of the stall, startling Phillips. He whirled about as she reared again, hooves careening toward his head. He jumped to one side, her hooves missing him by inches. The hand holding the gun came up and fired, but the bullet missed its target.

Spelling pointed his gun first at us, then at the horse, but it was too late, he had dropped his guard. Rob and Antoine jumped him. Spelling's gun flew through the air and landed at Randolph's feet. He reached down to grab it, but I kicked it away.

Now only the vet was armed. Phillips, pointing his gun steadily in our direction, stepped away from the stall and motioned us to take his place. The horse continued to rear, twist, and turn, her anxiety intensified by the sound of the shot and Phillips' aggressive posturing. Unbeknownst to Phillips—while Spelling and Randolph tried to locate the other gun on the barn's sawdust floor—I shoved the wooden slide that secured the stall door. The horse seemed to sense my intentions. She held back for a moment then rushed the opening, ramming through it and knocking Phillips down. I grabbed his gun. Antoine, Rob, and I stepped out of the angry mare's way as she reared, striking Phillips on the head. She raced toward Spelling and Randolph, who ran for the feed room. Phillips lay on the barn floor, not moving.

"Is he dead?" I asked.

Rob felt for a pulse. "No, but he's got quite a cut on his forehead. He might be out for a while. It's a wonder she didn't kill him."

"I would have," I said. The man disgusted me.

Carlos ran after the mare, who slowed at the sound of his voice. She nickered to one of her mates in an end stall. He grabbed her bridle and gentled her with soothing words and comforting pats.

Antoine and Rob dragged Spelling and Randolph out of the feed room. Randolph began a litany of denials.

"I was only trying to help poor Constance get back her family's riches. I thought Dr. Phillips deserved another chance. He's a fine horse man."

I was untying Madeleine and getting her to her feet when I overheard Randolph and I couldn't resist commenting on his lies.

"Randy boy, you are so full of it."

"No, no, it's true. I thought Phillips was giving the horses enemas after the long trip at sea."

I laughed. "You truly are a horse's ass. Enemas. How stupid are you?"

"Well, douches, then," he replied.

"With his fists?"

Then began the pointing of fingers, as Spelling and Randolph blamed each other for the entire illegal operation. I found it interesting that neither said anything about Eduardo, but then again, he was still free and who knew what damage he could do to the two of them. Once he was behind bars, they might open up.

Several minutes later, Frida appeared in the barn accompanied by her partner and several officers from the West Palm County Sheriff's office. Soon after, my gang arrived. I was relieved to see that they hadn't been harmed.

Apparently, when Madeleine learned about our plan from Jerry, she begged to tag along. Why he had to tell her, I don't know. They had stopped by her place only to find her missing, so they went to my house, assuming she'd be there with me. When they saw my house was empty as well, they headed for the barns.

An ambulance carted Phillips off to the hospital. Randolph and Spelling were taken into custody and, because of the international drug smuggling component of the case, Frida notified the federal authorities. They would be waiting for their prisoners in West Palm.

"Who gets to arrest Eduardo?" I asked.

"The Feds," said Frida.

"Do you think they'll take Constance into custody, too?"

"Maybe. We'll have to see what they do. I suspect that, between Eduardo's connections and his money, he'll bond out within twenty-four hours. The same goes for his wife, if she's arrested."

I had twenty-four hours. That was good. This time I would work alone. I didn't want to get my friends involved in the mess.

I RODE HOME in the back of Nappi's SUV, flanked by Madeline and Alex. It felt like a repeat of our ride up from the Keys earlier this morning. Had it only been this morning? It felt like days ago. The three of us were in the backseat, with Jerry and Nappi in the front. Nappi drove.

I looked at my watch.

"Why do you keep checking the time. Something up?" There was suspicion in Alex's tone.

"I can't believe it's been less than twenty-four hours since we drove back from the Keys. I didn't sleep well, and I'm beat. I need to hit the hay."

Nappi laughed. "Got horses on your mind?"

I nodded. "I'm glad they're going to be all right. That horrible Phillips." I hadn't shared with Alex, Jerry, or Nappi the details of how Phillips had intended to find the locket. They didn't need to know. Madeleine and I exchanged glances. I could trust her to keep silent. I was worried that they would counter violence with violence, and that was the last thing I wanted right now.

Alex tightened his arm around my shoulder. "I thought that maybe we could spend some time together, but I can see that this isn't a good time."

I reached up and patted his cheek. "Thanks, sweetie."

Alex walked me to my door and gave me a long, lingering kiss goodnight. My toes curled with passion and I almost gave in to my desire to invite him inside. But I was so damned tired that I'd probably fall asleep mid-foreplay. Plus, I had a previous engagement.

Once in the house, I stripped off my clothes, which smelled like hay, horse manure and fear, and stepped into a hot shower, lathering twice to remove the evening's horrors. Before I had a chance to really relax in the warm water, I turned the faucet to cold to wake myself up. A quick cup of coffee and I jumped into my rental. I had an appointment back at Eduardo's stables.

My drive to the ranch gave me a little time to think about what I was doing. I was certain I didn't want to involve any of my friends. Look at what happened to Grandy. Perhaps that wasn't directly my fault, but if I hadn't moved to Florida, Valerie wouldn't have been killed in my shop. The family's attention might have been diverted to other pursuits, such as reclaiming their lost money and drowning their financial woes in high-end shopping and maxed-out credit cards. They might have been too busy to remember the old family locket.

However, they probably wouldn't have been too busy to import horses with dope up their you-know-whats. I guess my nosiness had done some good. It had also almost got my friends killed. That's why I had given the cowboys and the gang the night off. I was after a killer.

I turned off the pavement onto the county road, then looked for the driveway leading to the ranch. Damn, it was dark out here with no lights. Okay, no friends, but was it smart of me to go meet a dead man? Or, rather, someone who was supposed to be dead?

TWENTY-EIGHT

Eve, I TOLD MYSELF as I climbed over the closed gate leading to the ranch, *you're quite safe now that Eduardo, Randolph and Constance are in jail.* I rued the decision to wear my signature stiletto heels as I slid from the top rail onto the drive. This wasn't a social occasion. It was simply a meeting with a dweeby little man who might have a lead on a killer.

I shivered a little at the thought of returning to this place. But who was left to bother me? Not Leon, Dwight's father. He'd called the cops and claimed that he had been mistaken about Jerry being my kidnapper. That was a good faith gesture, right?

One thing at a time. I had taken care of the locket issues earlier this evening. The people who were supposed to show for that wouldn't be out of jail until tomorrow, if ever. Now I had to consider Valerie's murderer. That meant my midnight meeting with Dwight. Why me? Because, as with Carlos, Dwight trusted me. Only me. Was it my compassionate nature or the generosity of my character? I shook my head. No. It had to be my tenacious and overbearing personality. Paired with my height.

I looked up at the moon, bright enough now to illuminate the way to the barns, but I heard thunder in the distance and knew that soon I wouldn't be able to count on lunar light to guide me. Besides, once inside the barns, I'd need a flashlight. I patted my pocket to reassure myself that it was still there.

The only person I expected to see was Dwight. Was I crazy to believe that little weasel? Maybe. Someone had tried to kill him, and I thought I knew why.

He had been standing by Valerie's car on the day of the murder and he must have seen something, something he had later decided to make the murderer pay for. Leon must have known that Dwight was in danger and that he would be safer if thought dead. Did Leon know who was gunning for his son?

The killer had to be Eduardo. If Dwight didn't already know that Eduardo was in jail, I wanted to tell him, so that he'd go to the authorities and tell them his story. Valerie must have found out about her son-in-law's drug dealings. That would have been motivation enough for him to remove her. So he stabbed her in my shop.

That sounded right. Now all I had to do was get Dwight to talk. Eduardo and associates would be in jail for more than drug trafficking. I still couldn't figure out the logistics of the stabbing, though. Well, that was up to the police.

I walked into the first barn, using the flashlight to find my way. All the horses were gone, removed by the authorities earlier tonight. Only the smell of manure, feed, straw and hay remained. I passed through the darkened stable and out into the night. Clouds rode across the moon, forcing me to rely on my flashlight as I headed toward the second barn. The same emptiness there. No horses. No stable boys. I strode through the barn to the other end, pausing in front of the spot where, earlier, a horse had saved our lives. On impulse,

I climbed over the wooden rails and leaned into the now deserted stall as if I could somehow capture the essence of the horse that had saved us.

A hand grabbed my leg. Startled, I lurched backwards and dropped my flashlight.

"Come down from there. You're already tall enough. I don't need to be talking to a giant."

"You scared the hell out of me, Dwight. Now I've dropped my light."

"What's going on? By the time I got here around eleven, all the horses were gone and everyone else, too."

I told him about the drugs and the pending arrests. "I guess that should make you feel safer, huh?"

"Eduardo will bail out by tomorrow morning, if he hasn't already. I need to get out of here and go someplace where he can't find me."

"You need to talk to the police. You could put him behind bars for a long time. Then you'd be safe."

Dwight gave a snort of disbelief. "He's got a long arm. He could easily leave the country and then send some of his goons to have at me. Again."

"Eduardo doesn't seem like the type to tolerate blackmail. You saw something the day of Valerie's murder. Instead of coming forth, you decided to make some money on the side. I hate to say it, but you brought all this on yourself."

"So how did Eduardo manage it?" I went on. "I mean, how did he get into my shop to kill Valerie? I can't figure it." Maybe if I got Dwight talking about what he had seen, he'd find it easier to repeat the story to the authorities. "Did he disguise himself as a woman? Use someone else to do the stabbing?" I was pushing him, but I had to know.

"Eduardo? I didn't see him there," said Dwight.

The moon came out from behind the clouds and lighted the entrance to the stable well enough for me to see his face. I didn't like what I saw.

"I thought you were a lot smarter than that." Dwight seemed disappointed.

"Me too, but then again, she's just the granddaughter of a maid," said a voice from behind me.

"Constance. What are you doing here? I thought you'd be in jail."

"No jail for me, the suffering little wife of the foreigner involved in drugs. We have unfinished business, you and I. So, after the arrest, I went to your house. You were just leaving. I followed. As for the drug thing, what did I know about it? Of course, I'll stand by my husband when he gets out. Our lawyer will take care of everything."

"Except the murder charge. Don't you care that he killed your mother? How can you support him knowing that?" I couldn't believe that she loved him enough to ignore murder.

She paused and then changed the direction of our conversation. "I'll tell you what, Dwight, brother dear. You help me get rid of the body, and I'll let you go. Deal?"

Had I made a mistake by trusting Dwight? He looked relieved at her offer. Her offer? Then I got it. Eduardo didn't kill Valerie. Constance did. Dwight had seen her leaving the store through the side door. What a fool I was.

I moved away from Dwight and toward Constance.

I could take the bitch. I knew I could. Then out came one of those ugly guns. It looked ludicrous in her manicured hand, but still deadly. Her finger on the trigger was steady.

"Drop the gun, Constance." Her father emerged from the feed room and walked toward us. I turned to look at him, hoping that he was also armed. I didn't like guns, but right now I'd have given my little red Miata for one. I searched his hands. Nope. No gun. I'd have to fake it.

"The three of us against you." I might as well assume that Dwight was on our side, even though he hadn't been much help so far.

"You can only shoot one person, maybe two before one of us takes you down." I hoped I was right. I wanted to be the individual left standing. I was anxious to wipe up the barn floor with her.

"You're not going to shoot your own father now, are you?" Leon held out his hands in a pleading gesture.

She'd already stabbed her mother, but I saw no need to state the obvious.

Without warning, she fired, hitting Dwight in the shoulder. She wasn't a very good shot, although she seemed determined. She let go with a second round. Her father grabbed his leg. Both men fell to the floor. I dropped to my knees beside them. To Constance it must have looked as if I was trying to offer aid. Instead, I snagged the flashlight off the floor and hurled it at her. It missed but was enough of a distraction to throw her off balance. I tucked and rolled, knocking her feet out from under her. The gun flew out of her hand. She scrambled to her feet and ran out of the stable.

A quick check of Leon and Dwight showed their wounds to be painful but not life-threatening. The shot had gone through Dwight's shoulder but the opening wasn't pumping blood, it was just leaking it onto the stable floor.

"I'm fine," said Leon. "Find my daughter before the cops do. You can talk her into giving herself up."

I flipped open my phone and called Frida.

"Better get out to the stables again. There's been a shooting here."

"Find her, Eve, before the cops do. I love her, no matter what she has done." Leon moaned and held his leg.

"Let me see that." I removed his hand to examine the wound.

"Go. Find her." He shoved me away.

I ran to the barn door and looked out across the paddock, now washed bright by moonlight. I could make out a figure fleeing toward the trees beyond the far fence. I ran after her. Once she reached the shelter of the trees, I'd lose her. After that, she could circle around and come back to the parking area, jump in her car and leave. My motive for finding her wasn't quite the same as her father's. The authorities would be on their way, and they could only ask questions if they advised her of her rights. With me, she had no rights, and I had a lot of questions for her.

I stumbled on the uneven ground. *Damn shoes. I should have worn sneakers tonight.* Then I remembered. I didn't own any. Constance would probably be faster. She was my height and younger. I removed my heels, my favorites—the ones with the slave sandal look in black alligator—and started to toss them away, but then I remembered that they had cost me a fortune. I was divorced now and on a tight budget. So instead of dropping them, I strapped the pumps together, then put on the steam and pounded across the paddock, wondering if that soft place back there had been soggy soil or something more horsie-processed.

I prayed that the clouds wouldn't move in to obscure the moon. I needed the light to see my prey and avoid placing my toes in nasty places.

I was gaining on her. In fact, I was only a few feet behind when she entered the trees. The terrain there was rougher and my feet were taking a beating. I made a vow to invest in some more practical footwear, like the two-inch open-toed espadrilles I'd seen in Stein Mart the other day.

We ran into the scrub palmetto and were forced to zigzag our way through the palms. A clearing opened up ahead. Beyond the open area, the trees grew thicker, and the night grew blacker. Heavy clouds were blowing in on the wind and a storm seemed to be rolling toward us. It was now so dark that I lost sight of her. My flashlight would have come in handy right now, but it still lay on the barn floor.

I stopped and listened but could hear nothing except the sound of the approaching thunder. A crack of lightning revealed Constance, standing to my side with something in her hand. Before I could identify the object, the darkness descended once more. Constance lunged at me, and I felt a sharp pain in my arm. A knife. She was holding a knife.

"You're not going to get away this time. Once I get that locket, I'm not just going to dump you in the swamp. I'm going to bury you in it. Eduardo should have sent *me* to handle the job, not some hit man."

What about my car? Were she and Eduardo responsible for that, too?

I shoved her away and, to my surprise, she didn't follow up her attack but, instead, fled deeper into the night, deeper into the palmetto, pines and cypress. I followed, aware now that she was capable of more than fleeing. She wanted me to follow. Then she'd turn and attack once more with her knife. I had only my Jimmy Choos to defend myself.

TWENTY-NINE

THE ROLLING CLOUDS broke for a moment, and the pale moon shone through. Constance stood at the edge of a swampy area. She looked back at me, and I saw indecision on her face. Kill or flee? Her internal battle waged only for a moment; then she turned to face me, her intent clear. Her shoulders were hunched over as if she were an animal about to spring.

"You might as well give up, Constance. I called the police and they'll be here soon. Listen. I think I hear the sirens now." We both froze. Thunder rumbled in the distance, but there was no other sound. Even the bullfrogs that had called from the swamp earlier were silent. We'd disturbed their evening's conversation.

The wind was at my back, traveling from the direction of the ranch into the woods and making the trees sway, then whip around as if stirred up in anger. As quickly as the moon had revealed Constance at the swamp's edge, the clouds gathered, leaving a darkness so inky black that my own body was lost in it. I felt dizzy and reached out to steady myself. I moved toward the place where I thought Constance was waiting. If I couldn't see her, then she couldn't see me. A flash of lightning gave a bluish glow to the clearing where she'd been. Gone! Had the light revealed where I was?

Something brushed my arm. Before she could wield the knife again, I struck out with the only weapon I had—the stiletto heel of my classy shoe. Then I ducked and rolled away from the attack and kept rolling into the brackish water of the swamp. The splash I made had probably given away my position so I worked my way along the shore. Wading hip deep in the opaque waters, I tried not to imagine all swamp things housed within.

"I'll find you no matter where you hide," Constance said. "We found Dwight, didn't we?"

"Yeah, but you missed the first time. He took out one of Eduardo's men, didn't he?" I was guessing, but I felt like I was beginning to understand the details, as my mind and Constance's threats provided the missing pieces.

"He saw you exit the shop after the murder and you had to get rid of him to cover up your actions." Realizing that she was probably following my voice, I moved farther along in the swamp.

Another lightning flash. I looked up from my watery refuge to see her standing over me. I grabbed her foot, pulling her into the swamp.

She screamed. "Get me out of here. Help. Help me."

The hysteria in her voice was genuine. Humans didn't scare her, but what she envisioned in the swamp did. The images she conjured of what lurked in the dark waters were more vivid than mine. And more frightening, it seemed. She continued to flail around, her wet hair flying into her eyes, her cries echoing throughout the night.

Her terror was contagious. My body felt drenched in adrenaline. Fear wrapped like a Boa constrictor around me, paralyzing my muscles, dulling my thoughts. If she would just shut up and stop all that yelling, maybe

I could figure out how to extract us from this murky mess. I wanted out as much as she did, but for now I was marginally calmer. My advantage, I hoped.

I dragged myself up the bank and onto drier land.

"Don't leave me." Not her usual commanding tone, but a plea for help.

"Where's the knife? I'll help you if you throw away the knife."

"I don't know. I lost it. Help me. I think something's got my foot." She began to cry—great gulping sobs punctuated with wails of fear.

"It's probably a water plant."

The roar of a bull alligator sounded from somewhere too close by.

Oh, boy. Now we'd done it. We had invaded a bull's mating hole.

I prepared to run, but Constance was still floundering around in the water, too frightened to coordinate her movements.

I couldn't leave her. Or could I? The wind increased and made the palm fronds overhead thrash against one another. A flash of lightning revealed a stirring out in the deeper water. Thunder followed and then another lightning bolt. The object swam toward Constance. She froze, staring in the direction of the approaching reptile.

"Move, Constance. Get the hell out of the water."

She continued to stare, apparently transfixed by the slow, undulating movement of the creature.

Oh, crap. Now I'd have to go back in there and pull her out.

I waded into the pool once more and reached out for her, but she was too far away. I wasn't venturing any farther into the water. I would play hero, but only if I didn't get myself killed in the process. The gliding of the animal continued, unbroken, toward us.

"I need something you can grab. A tree limb or something. You're too far for me to reach. Can't you move a little?"

"Do something. It's getting closer."

"You do something. Like walk out of there."

"I don't want to stir and make him mad."

"He's already mad at us for disturbing his romantic night. Now get your butt out of there."

Flashes of lightning illuminated the area for a moment; then the blackness descended again. Light, dark. Light, dark. Like a strobe signaling disaster.

"Oh, hell. Grab this."

I held my precious sandals toward her. They provided the extra reach we needed. She grabbed onto one of them and I pulled, tugging her toward the shore. Constance fell face down into the water, and I reeled her in like a catch on a twelve-pound test line.

"Now get up and run," I said once we were out of the swamp.

She let go of my shoes and brought up her hand to push her hair back off her face. The other hand held the knife, which she raised toward me. Enough with the aggression; it was really getting old. I whacked her with my shoes.

"You don't want to run, fine, but I do."

She grabbed for my shoes as if to pull me toward her. I let them go and took off for the safety of the ranch.

When I exited the trees, I crashed into something.

Or someone. I realized it was a person when whoever it was shined a flashlight into my face. I slapped it away.

"Eve, are you okay?" asked Frida.

"Oh, you. Thank God."

"Where's Constance? Her father told me she ran off with you in hot pursuit."

"She's back there somewhere, with a knife. I think an alligator's after her."

We started back into the wooded area, toward the swamp, lightning striking around us and thunder roaring in our ears. The wind had increased in velocity and was bending the trees almost in half.

"It's not safe in here. One of these palms could come down on us," Frida said.

"We have to find Constance. She's the killer. She murdered her mother."

"I know. Dwight recounted me the whole story before we loaded him into the ambulance. He saw her run out the back door of your shop, toss the jacket and gloves in the trash and jump into her car, which was parked at the end of the alley. I'd sure like to get her to admit to the killing. I just don't understand her motive."

"That's the very question I'd like to ask her, but we won't have the chance if she ends up in the belly of a gator."

When we got to the swamp, Frida directed her light to the edge of the water. Under a large mossy oak tree sat Constance with her back propped against the trunk and her hair hanging in her face. She was so limp she looked like a wet rag doll. Her eyes were closed, and she was whimpering, muttering to herself, her words indistinct from this distance.

We came nearer.

"Be careful. I think that big gator's around here somewhere," I said.

Constance's words were clearer now. "I just wanted her to stop pawning all the family riches. They were mine. Mine. All that money gone. Then she took the jewels, too. I'm not a bad girl. I just wanted what I had coming to me. Go away. Go away. I'll be good."

I turned toward Frida. "Do you think she's trying to bargain with the gator?"

Frida played her light onto the water in front of the tree.

"What gator? I only see an old rotted log there. Boy, you transplanted northern gals sure are wimps."

"DID SHE FREELY admit her motive for killing her mother? Or was that technically a gator-induced confession, obtained under duress and before you Mirandized her?" I was riding in Frida's cruiser, finally heading home. The rain had stopped and the lights were making rainbow streaks in the oily puddles on the roadway.

"I wasn't trying to question her. Were you?" Frida offered a small smile of satisfaction.

"Nope." I relaxed against my seat. I smelled like swamp, was feeling bone-tired, and dreaded the scolding I was going to get from the gang once they figured out what I had done. When we pulled up in front of my house, it was ablaze with lights. There were cars parked curbside that I could identify as belonging to Alex, Madeleine, Nappi, Rob and—oh boy, I was in trouble now—Grandy and Max.

"Is the early edition of the paper out yet?" I asked.

"No. Why? Do you want to see if the story's in there already?"

"No. I want to find out who put the notice of a party at my house in it."

"I only called Madeleine," said Frida.

I walked into a room filled with silence and accusing eyes.

"I can explain everything."

Tears began to roll down Grandy's bruised face. "We only want to know that you're okay." The others nodded in agreement and soon I was enveloped in a group hug that went on so long I was barely able to breathe.

"Hey. Let go. I was fine until I came in here and somebody decided to crush my ribs."

"Your arm is bleeding," said Alex.

"Constance. She likes knives. The cut's not deep. I washed the gash at the ranch and Frida had a first aid kit in the cruiser."

"She's fine," said Grandy.

I shot her an accusatory look. "What are *you* doing here? Out of the hospital? Out of bed?"

"I came to find out where the locket was."

I looked at her in shock. "That damn locket—"

"Right. It's more trouble than it's worth. I'm giving it back to the family. To Constance."

I turned to Frida. "You didn't tell Madeleine when you called?"

"I did."

"It'll be waiting for Constance when she gets out of prison. Something to remember us by." Grandy seemed pleased with her decision. "I'm so tired of having to defend my ownership. Its significance is long past."

"Aw, shit."

"You don't approve?" asked Grandy.

"No, that's not it. It's just… I left my Jimmy Choos out in the swamp."

A CUP OF hot chocolate in my hand helped me forget about the shoes, at least for the moment. And everyone was eager to hear the truth about Valerie's murder, so storytelling served as another distraction.

"Apparently Dwight saw Constance sneak out of the shop. When he confronted her, she claimed self-defense, saying that her mother had taken a knife from their kitchen, brought it with her to the shop and attacked her in the dressing room. Dwight didn't believe it, but he went along with the story. At least for a while. Then he decided to ask for money in exchange for his silence."

"What did Valerie do with the money she got from pawning the family jewels?" asked Madeleine.

"She bought into Eduardo's drug scheme. Right?" I turned to Frida for confirmation. She nodded.

"Someone, probably Constance, disguised herself in order to sneak back into my shop. She was worried that the cops would search their house, only to find the knife that she had taken from home missing from the set."

Frida jumped in. "She had noticed the set in the store, so she decided to buy them, but when she found the store empty and you in the bathroom, she took a look around and spotted the knife from the set in your shop on the floor. She got lucky and took it, then convinced Dwight to put it in the Sanders' kitchen to make it seem like one wasn't missing. I think that was the night that some of you visited the house." Frida's accusing glance traveled the room, landing on Grandy, Alex, Madeleine, Jerry, and finally coming to rest on Nappi.

"Why would Dwight do that?" asked Madeleine.

"I think Eduardo talked him into it. He can be very persuasive." I flashed back to the scene in the stables when Spelling and Randolph had seemed unable to say no to any of Eduardo's commands.

"Eduardo and Constance were worried that you were coming too close to the truth when you accused Dwight of killing his stepmother," Frida said.

"So both Dwight and I had to go. But I made it out of the swamp alive, Dwight turned the tables on his killer, and Leon had the foresight to protect his son by claiming the body was his."

"Eduardo managed everything but the murder. He sent the hit men after Dwight and your Grandy. He's not against killing but he has others do it for him," said Nappi.

"Yep," said Rob and Antoine together.

"He seemed to be fed up with his wife's behavior earlier tonight when she ran out of the stable," I said.

Frida's cell rang. She answered, listened intently then flipped the phone shut.

"I guess Eduardo was more than a little fed-up. He boarded a plane at Miami International bound for Argentina. He's going home, and not alone."

I tried to imagine who could possibly be going with him. Randolph? Spelling? No. He'd never take those peons. He had told me he was surrounded by idiots. Who then?

All eyes in the room were on Frida. Her face displayed a look of disgust, perhaps because the authorities hadn't been able to take his passport from him, yet her lips twitched as if trying to keep a smile from forming.

"He had his wife with him."

"Constance? She's still in lock-up, pending her hearing," Alex said.

"Well, the passport had her name on it, but the picture was of a tall, dark woman with angular features. I'm told she looked like Eduardo's sister."

"Not his sister," I said. "His personal secretary. I thought there was something funny there."

"Well, regardless. They're halfway to South America by now," said Frida.

"Nonstop flight?" asked Alex.

She nodded.

"Extradition?"

"Maybe. I suspect that the Argentine authorities will be interested in what the U.S. has to say about his drug smuggling. I talked with the DEA and they have heard that he's having some trouble with his drug contacts there. Something about 'not delivering on promises,' meaning he owes them money. So if the police in Argentina don't grab him when he lands, the cartel will." Frida shook her head.

So did Nappi. "It's not smart to play fast and loose with drug kingpins. They understand punishment."

We all got quiet. I would have preferred that the American legal system was handling him and his crimes. I wondered what would happen with the horses, but I knew that, no matter what, they'd have better lives without him and his cronies. He was a cruel man. Cruel to the animals in his care and cruel to his family. A man without feelings, who manipulated the lives of everyone around him. I shuddered when I thought about all of the terrible things he had done. In some ways I had more compassion for Constance, who had acted out of desperation when she saw her inheritance snatched away. Eduardo was all about money, greed, and cruelty.

Alex must have noticed the tension in my body because he put his arm around me. I looked up into his eyes and trembled—not out of fear, but anticipation. For once, my family and friends were tuned into my desires. Max and Grandy fled to the spare bedroom, while the others quickly departed, insisting that I needed sleep.

Alex walked me into the bedroom, his lips hovering close to mine as he laid me on the bed.

"At least this time I won't be in this bed alone," he said.

He might as well have been by himself. I smiled, yawned, and fell into a deep sleep.

THIRTY

As Alex and I were getting ready to leave for our picnic the next afternoon, the doorbell rang.

"I'll get it," said Grandy. "You two lovebirds stay put."

Alex and I were in the kitchen, holding hands across my center island and contemplating the abundance of food Grandy had packed for us.

"We're never going to eat all this," said Alex.

"I don't know. I'm pretty hungry."

"You got up late and had a huge breakfast. You're still hungry?"

I changed the subject. "I think I like this detecting business. Maybe we should join forces and become a PI team."

"You got lucky, that's all."

"Oh, don't worry. I'm only kidding. I think I'll stick with the consignment shop. Of course, I'm going to have to get another job now, seeing as I have to make the payments on this house *and* the payments on my loan to Jerry—or Nappi, or whoever is holding the paper on it."

Grandy entered the room, carrying an envelope. "This arrived for you by special courier. Must be real important. I didn't think there were any special messengers in these parts."

I tore open the envelope. Inside was a letter, signed by Nappi. I scanned it quickly, then began to laugh.

"What's so funny?" asked Alex.

"Well, your number one competitor kept his word. Nappi told me that he had arranged something with Leon Sanders when he returned those papers. Boy, did he! Listen to this. 'So sorry for all of your misfortune. I feel somewhat responsible, seeing as my daughter was the one to have your automobile blown up. She hired one of my more incompetent men to give you a scare. I know how much you loved that car, so I've taken the liberty of buying you a new one. You can take your insurance money and do with it as you like. Perhaps a vacation in the Keys? Of course, I've given her a good talking to and have taken some of her allowance money as reparation.'"

I continued to read aloud, "'Enclosed is the deed to your house in Sabal Bay, and I've forgiven the loan on your business. Jerry will be paying that back to me, seeing as how he was the one foolish enough to sign over all those properties to Mr. Sanders in the first place. As you said, that was your divorce settlement. Now he'll be working for me at very low pay for years. I hope the experience will make him a better man. I'm only sorry that it couldn't have come before the two of you were divorced.' It's signed 'Nappi.' Oh, there's a PS.

"'As for the marriage between him and my daughter, it turns out that Monica isn't pregnant and, having discovered that Jerry is only one of my employees now—and not the owner of a house, condo and boat, as she originally thought—she seems to have fallen out of love with him. She clearly doesn't have the staying power of her father, who continues to be the devoted servant and admirer of your Grandy and you.'"

"Yeah, I kind of got that." Alex rolled his eyes.

"Now isn't he just the most lovely man," said Grandy.

Neither Alex nor Max seemed to agree with Grandy and me. Both wore looks of disdain, prompted—I'm guessing—by an overdose of testosterone. *Men.*

I WAS FEELING pretty damn happy as we drove south on 441. I had my little house in Sabal Bay and my business. I guess that meant I could become more than a "winter visitor" in rural Florida. I could be a resident. Florida would become my adopted home.

I shared my joy with Alex, who still seemed a bit peeved about Nappi's generosity.

"It'll come back around. He'll show up one day demanding a favor."

"I'd be glad to grant it."

"It'll be something outside the law."

"I've done stuff outside the law. Sometimes you have to."

Alex slapped his forehead. "Oh, right. I forgot who I was talking to. The breaking and entering queen."

"Oops. Slow down. This is our turn."

"I still don't see why you want to picnic in the spot where you almost got killed."

"Nostalgia, I guess."

"For what?"

We travelled down the pavement, turned onto the gravel road and then pulled up to the dirt lane that served as the ranch's driveway. Rob's SUV was parked next to Eduardo's old office.

"Don't we ever get to be alone?" asked Alex.

Rob walked out of the building and greeted us.

"What are you doing here?" I asked.

"I could ask you the same."

"We thought we'd picnic. Care to join us?" I asked.

"Nah, I'm here with my lawyer. We're meeting Leon Sanders and his attorney. With Eduardo out of the country and unlikely to return, we're trying to see what it'll take for me to buy this place."

"Really?"

"Yup, and it turns out that the whole thing was registered in Constance's name, with Cory Burnside as a minor partner."

At the sound of her name, Cory emerged from the office.

"Oh, it's you," she said.

"How's Randy today?" I asked her.

"Randolph is at home. I bailed him out yesterday, the same day Eduardo left for Argentina. And, of course, Randy knew nothing about murder or drugs."

"Yeah, right. That's why he was willing to hold a gun on me and my friends and offer to kill us."

"A misunderstanding, my dear."

"What's to not understand about 'bang, bang, you're dead'?"

"Randolph and I are getting divorced, you know." With this comment, Cory turned her bony face away from me and smiled up into Rob's eyes.

"Well, stop by the shop," I said. "I have just the ensemble for divorce court. In a junior size zero. We can take it in for you." I just loved teasing her about her tiny frame.

"THE BUGS HERE are as big as mocking birds," Alex grumped along next to me after we had left Rob and Cory. We were walking out across the paddock toward the woods, retracing the path Constance and I had taken only last night.

"I brought spray." I held up a bottle.

We tramped deeper into the palms until I could see the swamp ahead. In the sunlight it looked cool and inviting, although the mosquitoes were buzzing around our ears. The storm had blown in a cold front, so the day was cool and the wind was at our backs. Alex stopped in a patch of sunlight.

"This is good. The sun will chase away the skeeters, and the breeze will keep us cool, so we won't get over-heated."

Yeah, I saw the ulterior motives behind his 'over-heated' reference.

He spread out a blanket and sat down, then patted the space beside him.

"Just a minute." I walked away from the nest he'd prepared and wandered closer to the water.

"Here they are." Joy bubbled in my throat. I could barely get the words out.

"Here what is?" He got up and came over to me.

"My Jimmy Choos."

"Whose shoes?"

"My favorite strappy stilettos." I gave them an adoring onceover; they were still linked together by the straps. But, oh, the straps! They were so shredded that it looked like strands of linguini were hanging from the shoe. And the heels. No longer three inches high. One was sporting a stubby inch. The other was missing the heel entirely. Something had been chewing on them.

I cradled the mess in my arms and began to cry.

"Eve, honey. I'll buy you a new pair."

"I don't want a new pair. I want *this* pair."

"Well, I'll buy you a better pair. Come sit down with me." He caressed my arm, and I could feel goose bumps travel from my fingers to my shoulder. Maybe I could forget about the shoes.

"Really? A better pair?"

"Sure, sweetie." He took my chin in his hand and turned my face to his. The kiss he delivered made the goose bumps retreat, only to be replaced by Jell-O knees and a gleeful jump of my stomach.

"They cost over three hundred dollars."

He stopped kissing me.

"How much?"

"Three hundred twenty six dollars and fifty five cents. Maybe I can find them at a consignment shop for less."

We resumed our kiss.

* * * * *

ABOUT THE AUTHOR

LESLEY A. DIEHL RETIRED from her life as a professor of psychology and reclaimed her country roots by moving to a small cottage in the Butternut River Valley in upstate New York. In the winter she migrates to old Florida—cowboys, scrub palmetto, and open fields of grazing cattle, a place where spurs still jingle in the post office. Back north, she devotes her afternoons to writing and, when the sun sets, relaxing on the bank of her trout stream, sipping tea or a local microbrew. You can find Lesley online at www.lesleydiehl.com.

Get 4 FREE REWARDS!

We'll send you 2 FREE Books plus 2 FREE Mystery Gifts.

Harlequin® Intrigue books feature heroes and heroines that confront and survive danger while finding themselves irresistibly drawn to one another.

FREE
Value Over
$20

Get 4 FREE REWARDS!

We'll send you 2 FREE Books <u>plus</u> 2 FREE Mystery Gifts.

FREE
Value Over
$20

Both the **Romance** and **Suspense** collections feature compelling novels written by many of today's best-selling authors.

YES! Please send me 2 FREE novels from the Essential Romance or Essential Suspense Collection and my 2 FREE gifts (gifts are worth about $10 retail). After receiving them, if I don't wish to receive any more books, I can return the shipping statement marked "cancel." If I don't cancel, I will receive 4 brand-new novels every month and be billed just $6.74 each in the U.S. or $7.24 each in Canada. That's a savings of at least 16% off the cover price. It's quite a bargain! Shipping and handling is just 50¢ per book in the U.S. and 75¢ per book in Canada*. I understand that accepting the 2 free books and gifts places me under no obligation to buy anything. I can always return a shipment and cancel at any time. The free books and gifts are mine to keep no matter what I decide.

Choose one: ☐ **Essential Romance** ☐ **Essential Suspense**
(194/394 MDN GMY7) (191/391 MDN GMY7)

Name (please print)

Address   Apt. #

City   State/Province   Zip/Postal Code

Mail to the **Reader Service:**
IN U.S.A.: P.O. Box 1341, Buffalo, NY 14240-8531
IN CANADA: P.O. Box 603, Fort Erie, Ontario L2A 5X3

Want to try two free books from another series? Call 1-800-873-8635 or visit www.ReaderService.com.

---

*Terms and prices subject to change without notice. Prices do not include applicable taxes. Sales tax applicable in NY. Canadian residents will be charged applicable taxes. Offer not valid in Quebec. This offer is limited to one order per household. Books received may not be as shown. Not valid for current subscribers to the Essential Romance or Essential Suspense Collection. All orders subject to approval. Credit or debit balances in a customer's account(s) may be offset by any other outstanding balance owed by or to the customer. Please allow 4 to 6 weeks for delivery. Offer available while quantities last.

Your Privacy—The Reader Service is committed to protecting your privacy. Our Privacy Policy is available online at www.ReaderService.com or upon request from the Reader Service. We make a portion of our mailing list available to reputable third parties that offer products we believe may interest you. If you prefer that we not exchange your name with third parties, or if you wish to clarify or modify your communication preferences, please visit us at www.ReaderService.com/consumerschoice or write to us at Reader Service Preference Service, P.O. Box 9062, Buffalo, NY 14240-9062. Include your complete name and address.

STRS18

READERSERVICE.COM

Manage your account online!

- Review your order history
- Manage your payments
- Update your address

> *We've designed the*
> *Reader Service website*
> *just for you.*

Enjoy all the features!

- Discover new series available to you, and read excerpts from any series.
- Respond to mailings and special monthly offers.
- Browse the Bonus Bucks catalog and online-only exclusives.
- Share your feedback.

Visit us at:

ReaderService.com